Lust & Philosophy. A novel

The Exact Unknown and Other Tales of Modern China

Massage and the Writer: Essays on Asian Massage

At the Teahouse Café: Essays on the Middle Kingdom

American Rococo: Essays on the Edge

The Kitchens of Canton. A novel

Confucius and Opium: China Book Reviews

The Mustachioed Woman of Shanghai. A novel

Sexual Fascism: Essays

The Tao of Poison

A novel

Isham Cook

Magic Theater Books

Published in the United States by Magic Theater Books

ISBN-13: 9781732277472
ISBN-10: 1732277478

This is a work of historical fiction. Dates, settings, and background events and some personages are historically factual, while the narrative's main characters, locales, and incidents are either the products of the author's imagination or used in a fictitious manner. Any resemblance to actual persons, living or dead, or actual events is purely coincidental.

Dedicated to the victims of the
White Lotus Rebellion, 1796-1804

Chanakya had personally supervised the creation of an entire army of [poison] maidens. His secret service would identify young and nubile girls whose horoscopes foretold of widowhood. These beautiful damsels would be sequestered at an early age and fed a variety of poisons in graduated doses, making them immune to their ruinous effects. By the time each of Chanakya's *vishakanyas* reached puberty, they were utterly toxic. A simple kiss with an infinitesimal exchange of saliva was lethal enough to kill the strongest bull of a man.

Ashwin Sanghi, *Chanakya's Chant*

Shuliang He and a woman of the Yan clan copulated publicly in the wilds and gave birth to Confucius on a sacrificial mound. He was born with a mound on his head and was thus given the birth name of "Mound."

Sima Qian, *Records of the Grand Historian* (Ch. 47)

Hanzhong
SHAANXI
Wuguan Pass
HENAN
Han River
Hanwangcheng
Xing'an
Baihe
Yunxian
Nanyang
Dengzhou
Ziyang
walled town
Wudangshan
Han River
Gucheng/Guanghua
TONGBAI MOUNTAINS
Taiping
DABA MOUNTAINS
Fangxian
Xiangyang
SICHUAN
HUBEI
Dazhou
Yangzi River
Dangyang
Xiaogan
Han River
Wuchang
Yangzi River
HUNAN

0   50 mi
0   100 km

Central China, Jiaqing Emperor era (1796-1820)

1

The poison maiden

Swinging down her sack, Qiezi dumped out her bloodstained rags and began washing them. She worked with practiced speed, but the current would move many *li* downstream before all were restored to pristine gray, rinsed out and stacked on the old slab of rock beside her. Squatting, she loosened her pants' cotton sash and pulled them down over her hips. In thumb and forefinger, she took from between her legs a protruding stem and extracted a sodden tube tied with a string at the end. Opening the tube, she pressed out a compacted mass of blood and ash into the water. As the little red explosion faded away, she tossed in the remaining shell.

Her ear held a flower, long, white and tubular, which she now took in her fingers. Pressing the splayed petals together, she moistened them in her mouth, twisting them into a point so that the flower held firm as she guided it inside her up to the stem.

Qiezi gathered up the stack of rags and carried them further along the river's edge. She was parting some bushes along the way when she turned and listened: a rustling in the bushes beyond the path, a crunching of the soil beneath departing footsteps. Frowning, she returned to her task and emerged into a sun-filled cavity where more rags hung on a string. She bundled the dried rags into the sack and strung up the wet ones, before bounding up the bank and returning to the village.

Back at the house, Li Er slapped the new daybed. "Whaddya think, Yan Xian? This wood is pretty solid, eh? Genuine *nanmu*."

"Who said it's *nanmu*?" said Yan Xian from the kitchen shed. He returned with a heated flagon of yellow wine.

"The dealer did."

"It has about as much chance of being *nanmu* as this wine of yours is the elixir of immortality. I hate to disappoint you, but it's pine."

"It's not pine!"

"Li Er, how much do you know about wood? Can you identify *nanmu*?"

"Can *you*? Look at the swirls in the grain."

"That's what he told you? All wood has wavy patterns like that. You could never afford *nanmu*. Only rich families can. You were cheated."

"No, I was not. It was stolen from an abandoned house that was flooded. That's why it was so cheap."

"Why are there no water stains?"

"Of course, they restored it."

Yan Xian jabbed his finger at Li Er. "If this were real *nanmu* and word got out, crooks would rob us in our sleep and steal the bed to sell it. You would get us killed! That's why it's not *nanmu*."

Li Er stood up red-faced. "I was not cheated!" he yelled.

"All right, all right, calm down you two," said Lai Xinru. "Sit back down, Li Er."

"In that case I will sell it and buy a new house with the money. And I'll take Li San with me as well."

Yan Xian laughed off this suggestion. He refilled their wine cups and the four of them toasted. "What do you think of that idea, Li San?"

"He'd come running right back, bed or no. He's still afraid to admit he wants to fuck me," said Xinru, holding a bowl of melon seeds. "Now move this *kang* table out of the way so I can sit down. But where do we put these?"

"Put it on the floor," said Li Er. "I'll hold the seeds."

Xinru slipped in between Li Er and Li San and pulled their arms around her shoulders. "C'mon, Li San, don't be shy," she said, pressing his hand down on her chest.

Li San glanced at Yan Xian.

"Go ahead," said Yan Xian, egging them on. "It looks funny, though. Three people sitting on a daybed meant for two."

"Won't your daughter think it strange when she sees us like this?" said Li San.

"Don't worry about her," said Xinru. "She's got a mind of her own. And of course she knows why you're staying with us."

"Why does she have such a silly nickname?" said Li Er. "Qiezi—Eggplant."

"She was always bringing in eggplant flowers as a child, sticking them in her hair. We teased her with the name and it stuck."

"It *is* a stupid nickname. It sounds like I look like an eggplant," said Qiezi, who had entered with her sack. "Ma, eggplant flowers reduce swelling and disperse blood. We made poultices from them, remember? What's that smell?"

"Grab your pipe, Qiezi, and try this 'black smoke' tobacco the Li brothers brought. It's mixed with *yapian*."

"*Yapian*? What do you need that for? That's for dysentery and coughs."

"Helps get you through the long working day. A bit like wine but better," said Li Er.

"How does your daughter know so much about medicines?" said Li San.

"She was very curious as a child. Always hanging out at the apothecary's shop. He had these big books on plants—what do you call them? Botanicals, herbals, or whatever. She copied out tomes of them all by herself. On the shelf over there."

Li San got up to look at the row of sheafs bound in string and flipped through one of them.

"He taught her to read and write," said Yan Xian.

"She can identify any plant?" said Li San.

"Oh, can she ever," said Xinru. "One time, we were at the Daoist temple. There was a scroll painting on the wall. A landscape painting with a tea pavilion. She was staring at it and the priest came up and started explaining it to her, all about the figures in the painting, the men drinking tea. And what does she do, she starts explaining to him all about the trees and foliage in the painting. They were talking right past each other and it was the funniest thing you ever saw. But her knowledge is very useful. She gathers all the medicinal herbs we need. We don't need to rely on quacks."

"How old is she?" asked Li Er.

"Seventeen."

"Why isn't she married off yet? Is it her unbound feet?"

"We're from the hills, you know."

Qiezi returned from the bedroom with a rag and bent down to clean the floor.

Li San had a page open at an illustration, his hand covering up the surrounding text. "What's this plant?"

"Mountain *langdang*," said Qiezi, barely glancing up. "Similar to the *mantuoluo* flower. It's a poison but has calming and sedative properties in small amounts and can put you to sleep."

"That's just what *you* need," Xinru teased Li Er.

"You've memorized everything in these books?" asked Li San.

"The books are just copies, just writing training. The real copies are here," said Qiezi, pointing to her head. "The originals are out there."

"What do you mean?"

"The forests. The trees and plants."

"She really is a beauty, isn't she, Li San?" said Li Er, and turning to Xinru, "She's got your full hips."

"You keep saying that," she replied, sticking her finger in his face. "Don't you start putting ideas into your brother's head."

"There's a market for her type. Connoisseurs of unbound feet. She must attract some attention at the town fair."

"That reminds me, when is the next fair?" said Yan Xian. "The one that all the girls attend—the Seven Sisters Festival. Isn't that coming up soon? You'll see more hips there than at any other time of the year."

"It's the seventh day of this month, Baba."

"That's the day after tomorrow! Are you and Xinru going?"

"We can't," said Xinru. "It's the bad time of the month. For both of us."

"So? What does that have to do with anything?"

"We're unclean. You know the rules."

"Bah! Whoever pays attention to that? Anyway, you don't have to go inside the temple. All the fun is outside."

"It's a woman's festival. It's important to them," said Li Er.

"It's important to the gods," said Xinru.

"Nobody cares about that anymore," said Yan Xian. "You think not a single woman at the festival will be having her unlucky days? They'll be slipping down the temple steps from all the blood leaking out of them."

Li Er's wine cup smashed against the wall behind Yan Xian. "Don't insult the women!"

"Oh, you broke the cup!" said Xinru. "That's it, no more wine for you, Li Er. Control yourself."

"Careful with property that's not yours, Li Er!" said Yan Xian.

"Careful with how you insult your women, Yan Xian!"

The two men were circling each other around the table.

"Don't be like this, both of you! Li Er, now sit back down here. Yan Xian is provoking you," said Xinru.

"He knows that. I can see that grin of yours behind your phony mask of anger, Li Er," taunted Yan Xian.

"Fuck your mother!"

"Show some respect for the man of the house, elder brother," said Li San.

"Yep, there it comes, that big smile of yours. No need to work yourself up about this temple business, Li Er. If the women want to go or not, it's their business. We talk freely in this house. Get used to it."

"And what do you think the temple priest would say if he heard you talk like that?"

"I wouldn't be talking to him like that in the first place. What would he say about a grown man hurling his wine cup across the room? C'mon, let's have another toast."

"You two have to share Li San's cup now," said Xinru.

The brothers resumed their position on the daybed, Xinru entangled between them. Yan Xian filled their two remaining cups. Qiezi squatted before the *kang* table, examining and then loading the *madak* into her pipe. The spectacle of the trio trying to work out whose cup was whose made her giggle.

"I can't believe all the women at the temple fairs are not on their unlucky days," said Yan Xian. "And how would the priests even know? They can't exactly ask them. But I'm sure they'd love to check!" He burst out laughing at this. "Xinru, are you sure anyone cares about that anymore? It's just an old prejudice that died out a long time ago and you women haven't realized it yet. Has anyone ever warned you about it?"

"All of us know of it. It's a tradition."

"Oh, we could ask Old Zhao," said Yan Xian. "He would know. He's a Daoist."

"And if he says it's still followed strictly, as I'm sure he will, then that takes care of that. You three can go to the festival regardless."

"We don't want to be gawkers, with no women accompanying us. And if he says it's not, then all of us can go. I'll go fetch him now. He's only a few minutes away."

"I don't think that's a good idea, with Li Er and Li San here," said Xinru.

"We've known him for years. He'll understand. The two brothers are here because they helped set up our new daybed and we'll tell him they're staying for supper."

"And if he asks how we got it?"

"What's wrong with a daybed? It's a new piece of furniture.

It's for guests. Fix some tea and snacks for him, Xinru."

"I'm in no shape. I've had too much to drink," she said, clasping her cheeks.

"He'll only be staying for a short while. Put the wine away and straighten the place up. I'll be right back."

"All right, you two sit at the table," Xinru said to the brothers. "Qiezi, clean up the broken cup. I'll prepare the snacks. Oh, heavens, I'm flushed."

"Mama, your *naizi* are hanging out. Button up. And fix your hair. They'll be right back."

"How fresh her language is," said Li Er. "You've been corrupting her."

"It's you who's corrupting her. You're the one who took them out," said Xinru. "Qiezi, there aren't any rags drying outside, are there?"

"I take care of that down at the river now. But Rui Mian was spying on me again today."

"You saw him?"

"I heard him."

"Are you certain it was him?"

"I know it's him."

"Who's spying on her?" said Li Er.

"The neighbor here, right across from us."

"With the outhouse facing your door and the bad smell?"

"That's him."

"Why is he spying on her?"

"He's a pervert," said Qiezi. "He hides out hoping I'll be heading down to bathe, so I stopped bathing there."

"What gives him the right to put his outhouse out front?" said Li Er.

"Tell me about it," said Xinru. "It sits right over his latrine pit. Its door used to face inside his house, but he rebuilt it so it faces outward—right in front of our door! And with such a narrow lane, it really gets in the way."

"I was going to ask you about that," said Li San. "The smell is pretty strong."

"We told him and he ignored us. He claimed it's his own property and he can do as he pleases."

"Can't you bring it to the *yamen*'s attention?"

"They won't take any action. They could lash out at us for wasting their time on such petty business. Oh, they're back."

"What's that bad smell outside your door?" Old Zhao asked Yan Xian as they entered.

"Old Zhao, so nice to see you again!" said Xinru, bowing energetically. "Please come in. Come in and sit down."

"Lai Xinru, how are you? And daughter, Yan Zhengzai."

Qiezi bowed to Old Zhao. "Hello, teacher."

"We'd be honored if you could sit here on our new daybed," implored Yan Xian.

"Please don't stand on ceremony with me. I'll just sit at the table."

"These stools are too shabby. Please try the daybed. Here, let me put the *kang* table back on it. Xinru, bring Old Zhao some tea. And some wheat cakes with onion sauce."

Old Zhao remained at the table, and the others standing. Yan Xian proceeded to introduce Li Er and Li San, hired from a distant village, he explained, to do some carpentry work on their house.

"I see. So you built this platform bed?" Old Zhao asked them.

"They're expert carpenters. Even if it is only made of pine," said Yan Xian, sitting down at the table.

"I hope it's not pine, said Old Zhao. "Who makes heavy furniture with pine? Pine is for tables and cabinets. It looks to me like elmwood."

"See, Yan Xian, you didn't believe us."

"You said it was *nanmu*."

"I was only joking! It's elmwood."

"And where are you two staying, may I ask? At the inn?" asked Old Zhao.

"We're putting them up here. The inn is too far away," said Xinru.

"Now you be careful, Yan Xian. You know it's not allowed

for strangers to stay with villagers without registering at the *yamen*."

"People do it all the time, Old Zhao. And it's only for a few days. This is a guest bed, after all. But we wanted to ask you something, about that old proscription against women visiting the temple during their unlucky days. We all want to attend the upcoming Seven Sisters Festival together and show these two handsome chaps around town."

"It's their unlucky days? Of course, they shouldn't go."

"I see. I can't believe that all the women observe it."

"Yan Xian, we don't have to go," said Xinru. "No need to make a fuss about it, now that you have it straight from Old Zhao."

"The festivities are the same every year," said Qiezi. "I don't care if I miss it."

"Old Zhao, can we ask a favor of you?" said Xinru. "You noticed the bad smell outside our door when you arrived. It's Rui Mian's outhouse, which he rebuilt with the door facing outward. It's a real nuisance. Could you have a word with him about it? He ignores us."

"He rebuilt it facing the lane? What gave him the right to do that? Have you been feuding with him?"

"Not at all. He did it without consulting us."

"That's not reasonable. Yan Xian, let's have a word with him now."

Led by Old Zhao the men headed out into the lane, followed by the women. They had to go around the outhouse to reach the entrance to Rui Mian's house. Rui Mian happened to be in the outhouse and at that very moment, the door swung open right into Old Zhao, knocking him down.

"Watch what you're doing, Rui Mian!" said Yan Xian. "Look what you've done! We were just coming to confront you about this."

"I didn't see you coming. I'm sorry but it was an accident."

Yan Xian helped Old Zhao up. "Are you all right, Old Zhao?"

"This outhouse is a hazard for exactly this reason. You need to remove it!" said Li Er, kicking the outhouse.

"Rui Mian, you have the right to your outhouse but not when

it opens onto the lane, and right in front of your neighbor's door!" said Old Zhao.

"It's my property. If Yan Xian wants to build his own outhouse here too, he's welcome to. It's none of my business and mine is none of his business."

"We're decent enough to have our outhouse behind the house."

"Yes, the same place where you dry your women's polluted rags. Is that decent? Do you know how offensive that is? Aren't you aware they can only be dried in the women's chambers?"

"What rags? Show us what rags you're talking about," said Xinru.

"That was until your miss started drying them down by the river."

"How do you know that? Were you spying on her?"

"Everyone has a right to go to the river, and I know where she tries to hide your pollution."

"It's out of the way and nobody would know about it unless you're seeking it out on purpose!" said Xinru.

"You're missing the point," said Rui Mian. "It doesn't matter if no one sees it. It's not only outrageous and disgusting to display women's pollution in public, it offends the heavens! I'm warning you, Lai Xinru and Yan Zhengzai, you will both bring bad luck to us all. And by the way, I also know what goes on in your family inside that house of yours. The whole village knows it."

"Don't change the subject. This outhouse is a danger to people passing by. Kowtow and apologize to Old Zhao for knocking him down before we report you to the *yamen*!" said Li Er.

"Don't push things, stranger. You wouldn't dare do that, for you know what the consequences are of unlawful cohabitation and illicit sex on top of it!"

"What evidence do you have for these unfounded allegations?" said Yan Xian.

"How dare you insult Yan Xian's wife! Let's take care of this matter right now." Li Er threw himself against the outhouse to try to topple it. As Rui Mian pushed Li Er away, Li Er punched him in the face.

"Stop fighting!" said Old Zhao.

With gusto Li San launched a flying kick and dislodged the outhouse, which collapsed in a pile of planks and beams.

"Watch out, Li Er!" shouted Yan Xian as Rui Mian picked up a wooden beam and swung it at him. Li Er caught the beam in his hands and swung it around the other way smack onto Rui Mian's head. He crumpled to the ground. Other neighbors had emerged into the lane.

"Oh, no. It's come to this!" said Old Zhao as he bent over Rui Mian. "Rui Mian, are you all right?"

"You flat knocked him out, Li Er," said Yan Xian. "Let's sit him up."

They slapped him on the face to try to rouse him.

"He's breathing and has a pulse," said Old Zhao.

They carried the stricken man, who lived alone, into his house and laid him on his bed.

"Qiezi, can you tell if he's all right?" said Xinru. "Or do we have to call for help?"

"If he doesn't revive soon, we'll have to get help."

By the time Old Zhao returned with a doctor and several village authorities, Rui Mian was dead.

The Li brothers were held under guard in Rui Mian's house and the witnesses ordered to stay put. Runners were sent to summon the county magistrate from the walled town ten *li* away. He had to be called from home to perform the inquest—it was already early evening—and upon arriving at the crime scene on horseback interviewed the witnesses in turn. The doctor, who also served as the coroner, confirmed the cause of death to be a blow to the crown and right temporal lobe of the forehead. The two brothers were arrested and sent off to the *yamen* along with Rui Mian's corpse.

The next day the witnesses, including the Yan family, were called to the *yamen* for interrogation. Li Er was saved for the last. Bound by his hands and feet, his face glassy from the sweat pouring off, he was pushed down on his knees before the magistrate at his high desk, surrounded by a secretary, a scribe, and cudgel-bearing wardens poised on either side. "If you want to avoid the instruments of torture, testify the whole truth!" said the magistrate, pointing to an array of vises. "Name?"

Li Er identified himself, his home village and occupation, and his purpose in traveling to the present township.

"You have been staying with the Yan family for three days now, but your brother only arrived last night. Why did you come at different times?"

"He had to arrange transport of the daybed we brought. As he must have explained, I arrived several days earlier to acquaint myself with the route to the village and the Yan family home. Then I went back to meet my brother at the furniture market, and we arranged for the daybed to be brought here by mule cart."

"What is the purpose of the daybed?"

"A gift to show our appreciation to the Yan family for hiring us. And also, so that we have a place to sleep while building their new room."

"Was such an expensive and elaborate gift appropriate given your humble circumstances?"

"We got a very good price on it—only 4,000 cash."

"Why did they hire you to build a new room?"

"They don't have a proper inner-outer division in their house. Now that their daughter is of woman's age."

"Did you have any prior acquaintance with the deceased before today?"

"No."

"Yet you attacked him unprovoked, destroying his outhouse and striking him in the face in a drunken rage."

"I lost my temper when he knocked Old Zhao down."

After each response from Li Er the magistrate took his time, fiddling with his fingers on his desk as if absorbed in some imaginary calligraphy, at least until the next question. "What Rui Mian did or did not do is irrelevant. I asked you why you attacked him unprovoked! Is that what a normal person would do?"

"Your lord, I momentarily lost my temper and I regret my actions. I am not a violent person."

"And with that one blow of the wooden post, you hit him exactly on the head's lethal spot. It seems obvious you intended to kill him. How can you explain this?"

"Your lord, it all happened so fast. I was only thinking about protecting myself, as he might have done the same to me! I wasn't trying to kill him. I didn't expect to hit him on the lethal spot. That is the truth."

"Are you aware what the punishment is for intentional homicide?"

"I beg you to be lenient!"

"Li Er," the magistrate announced, "I have found your testimony to be consistent with that of Old Zhao and the other witnesses. Given that you acted in the heat of the moment and in self-defense, you are being spared immediate beheading. But you must suffer the penalty for homicide with mitigating circumstances. I hereby sentence you to strangulation after the autumn assizes. Warden, escort him back to his cell."

Li Er stared ahead dumbfounded as he was led away.

Though there was no evidence of their host's collusion in the murder, the harboring of the two brothers was suspicious, and the magistrate ordered Yan Xian and Lai Xinru to be slapped.

The next day, Qing Da, a *yamen* runner well known to the village, paid the Yan family a visit to apprise them of Li Er's case.

"And what's going to happen to Li San?" they asked him.

"He has been sentenced to 100 blows of the heavy bamboo."

"That's harsh."

"By inciting Rui Mian and destroying his outhouse, he is an accessory to the murder. They are both lucky, however, as they still have a realistic chance of having their sentences commuted by a degree or two after the assizes. This can usually be expected if there is no new incriminating evidence. Remember, though, as this is a homicide case, it will be reviewed by the prefectural court, the provincial court, and finally the imperial court. Now, the prefectural and provincial magistrates almost always agree with the district magistrate's verdict unless any glaring inconsistencies turn up, and there will be no need to launch a higher-level investigation. By the time it reaches the capital, it's only a matter of formality to be signed off on, and time is on your side."

"So what sentences might they receive in the end?"

"Li San, maybe only forty strokes of the heavy bamboo. Li Er, 100 strokes of the heavy bamboo instead of execution, followed by a month in the cangue, and probable exile to a distance of 3,000 *li*. If he survives the heavy bamboo, that is, and some don't."

"How long would the exile last?"

"It's hard to say. It could be for several years. It could be for life."

"Can we do anything to influence the outcome in their favor?" asked Yan Xian.

"No. But I'm afraid it is possible to worsen the outcome—for all of you."

"How do you mean?"

Qing Da set his teacup down on the square table and stood up to examine the daybed. A big, strong man, he lifted the bed's frame off the floor. "Elmwood or walnut?"

"Elmwood."

They followed him into the rear bedroom. It was the same size as the front room and held two beds at either end, separated by a wooden screen.

"Who sleeps in this bed?"

"I do," said Yan Xian.

"And in that bed?"

"My wife and daughter."

"You are aware that a mere screen is insufficient to set off the women's inner chamber?"

"Yes, that's why we hired the Li brothers to build a proper wall. But who cares about that?" said Yan Xian. "Many poor people live in one-room hovels. How can they afford to be so proper?"

"Oh, but you *can* afford to be proper," said Qing Da as he sat back down at the table. "Your family is moving up in the world,

Yan Xian. After all, you hired not one but two skilled carpenters. Many of us are a bit curious, though, as to how a mere farmer like yourself can afford them. On top of putting them up and feeding them, where did you find the money? And even more perplexing, this daybed, which one would suppose you provided for their comfort, turns out to be a gift they provided *you*. How convenient."

"What are you getting at? It's our own affair how we work out our arrangements," said Xinru.

"Exactly. The only explanation I can think of is that these two strapping young boys you hired had more than a financial motive. Guess which household they chose: the one with the two village beauties! Now, Yan Xian, let's stop beating around the bush. We all know about this *zhaofu yangfu* business—supporting one husband by enlisting another. Some families in the area are always rumored to be engaging in it, and we look the other way since it's in no one's interest to stir up trouble where none exists. I would prefer to look the other way."

"What evidence do you have that we are engaging in—"

"Illicit sex? Rumors, gossip. Gossip often has a basis in fact, which can be ascertained under interrogation. As the magistrate is a busy man, I'm sure he would just as soon not want to dirty his hands while the murder is still under review. At least not yet. I don't know. Maybe his suspicions are already aroused. Yesterday he interviewed several witnesses who are your neighbors. Who knows what ideas they put into his head—and what headache they might be creating for him in muddying the case. It would be simple enough for him to extract more information from the brothers about the goings-on in your family. And you do *not* want that to happen. Oh, my heavens, no. You do not want to be called in for further questioning."

"Qing Da," said Yan Xian, "the trial is finished and the verdict is being sent for approval, as you explained. That's the end of the matter. Now would you please state exactly what it is you're getting at or leave us in peace?"

"Please be charitable with me. I am after all on your side. You're quite right, I have very little role to play in all of this.

However, I need to warn you of what might happen if you are investigated for illicit sex at the same time your family is involved in a murder. If this blew up, don't worry about the two brothers—worry about yourselves! Yan Xian, I don't even want to think about the consequences to your family. Lai Xinru, provided you survived the blows of the heavy rod, you would be forcibly divorced from Yan Xian and sent back to your natal family with your daughter."

"There is no evidence we have done anything," said Xinru.

"I'm afraid you don't understand!" yelled Qing Da, slamming the table and splashing his tea. "We are not joking around here. Evidence can be created. Evidence can be extracted. In fact, I'm surprised the authorities' suspicions aren't already aroused. Your fates are perched on a mountain cliff."

"So what do you want us to do?" said Yan Xian.

"Once the process starts, I am, as you can understand, powerless. What I can do is vouch in your favor. If it comes up, I can vouch, at the outset, that I am not aware of any rumors that your family is engaged in *zhaofu yangfu*. And it might be enough to forestall further investigation," said Qing Da, who had been staring at Xinru.

"We have no money that would help settle this," she said.

"Yes. You are—or were—being supported by the two brothers. Well, that source of funding has now been cut off."

"So you want to sleep with me? Is that it?"

With a weary expression, Qing Da reached over and yanked up Xinru's skirt. "Those are some colorful underclothes you have on, Lai Xinru. Red underthings and brightly patterned leggings. Is this how you dress for your husband around the house? Or are they rather for entertaining guests?"

"How dare you treat a woman like that, Qing Da! What is it you are asking for?" said Yan Xian, standing up.

"You don't need to be violent with me, Qing Da. We can take care of this business in a more amiable manner," said Xinru.

"Having seen your frilly underthings, I've seen enough. I've seen exactly what the Li brothers were meant to see—or already saw. If you were to strip naked before me right now, I would be unmoved. All of your desire is wrapped up in the Li brothers, and frankly I can't reconcile myself to that. Especially when a worthier prize is to be had."

"Oh, no. Please, no."

"Qing Da, she's only seventeen and you will ruin her," said Yan Xian. "Please give us an alternative proposal!"

"Qing Da, I'll do anything you ask. Leave my daughter alone. It will spell disaster!"

"How exactly will it spell disaster? The loss of her virginity? But *is* she a virgin? I think I would like to find out. If she isn't, there's no loss. If she is, there's also no loss. You know as well as I do that with her unbound feet, not to mention her dark complexion, she has no marriage prospects. So what 'disaster' are you referring to? Please explain."

"I can't explain but you mustn't," implored Xinru, in tears. She unbuttoned her shirt. "Here, please satisfy yourself with my body. More than one man in this village would trade anything for it—Qiezi, where are you going?"

"I'm stepping outside to the outhouse. I'll be right back."

"Please reconsider, Qing Da," said Yan Xian. "As much as I would protest the violation of my wife, have her if you must, but I beg you not to ruin my daughter. You must trust us that it will bring disaster."

"Why are you both being so intractable? You are in no position to bargain. If your family's honor is on the line, it's not my doing but your own. Once I have satisfied myself with Yan Zhengzai, the matter will be settled. I give you my word you will be safe from further investigation, and you will never see me appear at your house again."

When Qiezi returned, she sat down on the daybed and began taking off her clothes. "Let me take of this."

"Qiezi, dear, don't! Qing Da, you want to see her body? Is that it? Enjoy her that way and then come to me. But don't violate her!"

"Mama, stop!" snapped Qiezi. "Let me handle this."

She was naked now, sitting upright in the middle of the daybed in clear-eyed expectation. Qing Da set his conical hat with its red-tasseled braids down on the square table and pulled off his shoes and pantaloons, while Xinru and Yan Xian stared. He looked up in annoyance. "What are you two doing here! Have you no shame? Go into your bedroom, shut the door and wait."

"You're telling *us* we have no shame?" responded Xinru wide-eyed.

"Don't ruin things now."

Xinru and Yan Xian retreated behind the bedroom door, ajar. Qing Da mounted the daybed. Qiezi adjusted her body to receive him, holding him steady in her gaze: she knew cooperating would get it over with faster than resisting, and though only the most ferocious resistance, followed by her own suicide, would spare her from implicating herself in her rape, it would hardly matter in the end.

"Don't think that bit of blood coming out of you fooled me," said Qing Da as he put his clothes back on. "As I expected, you were not a virgin. You'd better hope I don't catch some disease from you, you little whore."

He slammed their front door upon exiting. Xinru rushed in and burst into tears as she wrapped her arms around Qiezi. "Oh, baby, you have to flee from us, and fast, now!"

"I know," said Qiezi, sobbing. "Don't worry about me, Mama. I can take care of myself."

"We must flee as well, Xinru."

"How much time does he have left?" they asked Qiezi.

"Hours. He will start feeling it soon enough."

"Let's plan to meet up with some relatives of ours in Ba County, across the border in Sichuan Province," said Xinru. "Listen and memorize their names and addresses as if your life depended on it!"

Staggering into the walled town's gate raving and incoherent, Qing Da failed to make it to the district *yamen* of his own accord. By the time he was discovered, he was in a coma.

2

The haunted pagoda

A cleaver and a silver *tael* given her by her father were all that weighed down the sack hanging from her shoulders as Qiezi forded the river at its narrowest crossing. Now on the opposite bank she scarcely halted her pace except that she was hungry, the family meal aborted by the unfortunate events of the past hour. Expressionless yet alert, she stopped and squatted to turn over the undersides of rocks and logs for termites and the larvae of grasshoppers and darkling beetles to place on her tongue. They would do for now and she washed it all down with sweet osmanthus flowers and dandelions, stems and all, and water from cupped hands. The sustenance glowed inside her and she got her energy back. As it grew dark, she slowed her pace and listened. The forest was almost thunderous in its myriad sounds. The way she angled her head suggested they appeared to her as images positioned in a three-dimensional ink painting, with darker strokes in the foreground and lighter strokes in the background. No human figures were in the painting; had there been, and she would have removed them by repositioning the painting.

Her knowledge of the territory quickly brought her to where she wanted to go, a familiar clump of bamboo stalks amidst the matrix of pines, firs, and cypresses. They ranged from her upper arms to her sturdy calves in diameter and she felled the thicker ones, wielding her cleaver like an ax with a few blows on either side. If you're wondering how this mere adolescent was able to impose herself upon the towering stalks, consider that this mountain girl could walk up to a tree and without breaking her stride walk *up* the tree on all four limbs. Hacking the tops away and shaving off the branches, she worked from memory, reconstructing what she had once observed on the river.

She must have felt fortunate to be able to observe anything on the river, for she was the only grown girl in the village allowed to wander alone, the only woman apart from her mother who could wander alone rather than be carried on someone's back or hobble along with a cane. Those villagers who hissed and snickered at her ugly "duck feet" wouldn't last a day out here alone. Had she been blessed with a normal upbringing, we expect her mother had told her, she might have been of some use married off to a man of means. With proper lotus feet, she could have driven him to ecstasy by removing her bindings and letting him smell the odiferous stubs as he washed and caressed them in rose water, or not even wash them before taking them one by one into his mouth, like the male actors in opera troupes are rumored to do with each other's members, and then stick that long big toe of yours into his filthy hole so he could be taken like a woman, a pleasure more delirious than taking a woman and available only to wealthy men. That's the only thing lotus feet are good for and that's how you might have been of some use. As for the other village girls, their lotus feet would find no male orifices to work their way into, no purpose apart from the brutal one everyone understood but never acknowledged: their feet were broken to keep them bound to the spinning wheel and the loom. How lucky you and I are to be mountain women!

Once she had lined up enough poles on the ground to match in length her height with arms extended and half as much in width,

Qiezi lay down exhausted and fell asleep, cleaver in hand.

In the morning, she dragged the poles down to the riverbank and again lined them up flush, the straightest in the middle. From the soil along the eroded bank, she snagged out the long thin roots of a pine tree and used these to tie two short bamboo poles crosswise to the parallel ones, looping them over and through and yoking them together as hard as she could into the semblance of a raft, if only it would work. Hooking it to a thick tree root with more root cord, she pushed the raft into the water. It floated. She tried climbing aboard but it tilted her off. When she managed to board it, her weight submerged the raft below the water. She needed more poles, more tightening, more work, but her hands were numb and bruised. She foraged again for sustenance and rested. The day was already spent. The overcast sky would soon shroud her in pitch darkness, preventing travel down the river in any case. It would have to wait for moonlight.

The next day she cut more lengths of bamboo stalk and added one to each side of the raft, while loosening the cords and readjusting the poles to fit yet closer together. It could not but work this time. That evening the sky was clear and the moon was out. She got on the raft, but what she had not counted on was the extra weight from the steering pole. The raft held—just below the water's surface. She cursed and gazed back toward the bamboo grove. Further widening the raft would mean another lost day. Grimly she stared ahead and pushed off.

The current was strong enough to move her along at a good pace. But it also caused her to turn in circles and get stuck along the banks. She got better at controlling the raft with practice but steering it used a different set of muscles and was even harder than building it! As strong as her arms were as a professional tree climber, the water was a real taskmaster. They were about to give out when she discovered she could zigzag down the river by letting the raft drift until the bank loomed up and then push off again. After several hours, the night-watch tower's drumbeat in the distance signaled the start of the fifth watch. She was approaching the walled town: the danger zone. It's unlikely the nightwatchman and his lantern would notice anything, but that possibility had to be minimized. As she approached the bend of the river and the dock beyond it, she aimed toward the river's far side, placed the steering pole beside her and lay back flat on the raft, half in the water. No frightful voice called out and she coursed past.

In a few hours it would be dawn. She had to keep an eye on the raft. And consider where to ditch it. Traveling in daytime made her visible. On the other hand, the further she went the more anonymous she would be. But she was also in unfamiliar territory. At some point she would have to make her way among strangers. There was general hostility toward the unheard-of phenomenon of a young woman traveling alone. The only recourse was to patch together a robe and shave her head like a Buddhist nun. She must have been wondering about her parents, who were escaping south on foot and would soon be in Sichuan. They knew people there and would manage. She would manage. But as prepared as she was for surviving alone, she was still in shock, a stunned creature drifting on a raft.

The dawn brought mist and shrouded the river. She heard voices but couldn't see them and they were looming up. A man screamed. "Look, it's floating on the water. A ghost, gliding on the water!"

"That's not a ghost, you idiot," said another. "It's a girl, pushing a raft. See, it's right under the water. She's sitting on a raft."

Their sampan came into view. "Who are you?" they said.

"Who are *you*?" said Qiezi.

"Your raft isn't holding up. You need help. Here, we'll help you."

"No, I can manage."

"You made this raft yourself? It won't last another hour."

"I've been on it since yesterday."

"It won't last, I'm telling you," said the first man. He was young and stared at her open-mouthed.

The other man looked a couple decades older and was

bearded and his hair had a Daoist topknot. "Where are you going?" he said.

"Xing'an."

"Xing'an, in *that*? You'll never make it! The river widens up ahead and you'll flounder and drown."

"You know the area?"

"Of course. We live here."

"I need to find a place to stop off and rest."

"Come on our boat and join us. Let the raft go. It's useless."

"No, it's my raft."

"Let her hitch it to the boat," said the elder. "Come in the boat and dry off. You'll get sick in the water like that. Are you hungry?"

"Yeah."

"Give her some fish cakes."

"Thanks. I need to get to Xing'an."

"We can take you halfway. To Flowing Water. From there you can keep going downriver or go by land."

"How far to Flowing Water?"

"About a day."

"Overnight?"

"Yes. You can sleep with us," said the younger.

"Don't frighten her. He means you can use our mat. We'll leave you alone. You can rest now if you want. We're busy fishing."

"I don't want to get off in the town. Can you drop me off at another place?"

The elder laughed. "Of course, such a beautiful girl alone in public isn't safe. But how can you survive all by yourself?"

"I'm from the mountains," she said between bites of fish cake.

"A mountain girl. What's your name?" said the younger.

"Mantuoluo."

"*Mantuoluo*. What kind of name is that? A tribal name?"

"Yes."

"I thought so. Your dark complexion. And your unbound feet. Are you a Miao? From Sichuan?"

"Yeah."

"What are you doing alone?"

"That's my business."

"Family trouble, I bet," said the elder.

"We can take her to the pagoda."

"What pagoda?"

"An old abandoned pagoda on the way to Flowing Water. You can shelter there."

"That sounds good."

"You look exhausted. Lie down under the awning and rest. We should reach the pagoda by the first watch," said the elder.

"You're sure I'm not taking you out of your way?"

"No. We cover this whole area."

Qiezi curled up on the dirty straw mat, her sack hooked through her arm, and fell asleep.

She had been out for who knows how long when singing startled her from her slumber. She looked around in confusion. The sun was on the other side of the sky. The younger was humming a tune.

"Oh, she's awake," said the elder.

The younger turned to her and sang:

When the beauty was here, flowers filled the hall.
Now that the woman's gone, the bed lies empty;
Only the rolled-up embroidered quilt sleeps there.
It's now three years and I can still smell her scent:
A scent departed yet still lingering,
A woman departed yet not returning.
Yearning yellows the falling leaf,
White dew beads the green moss.

"What are you singing?"

"A poem, called 'Long Yearning.' Haven't you heard of it? It's by Li Bai, the famous poet from the Tang Dynasty."

"How would I know that?"

"You don't know any poetry?"

"Of course, she doesn't know any poetry," said the elder.

"What mountain girl can read?"

"I *can* read."

"How can you read? I can't even read," said the younger.

"How do you know poetry then?"

He tapped his head. "It's all in here. Memorized. I hear poems and remember them."

"Where did you learn to read?" the elder asked Qiezi.

"The apothecary taught me. But he didn't teach me poetry."

"Really."

"You must be very smart," she told the younger.

"Yes, I can't read and even I know poetry," said the younger. "But you can read and you don't know poetry. I can teach you. Here's another poem. It was written by the Huizong Emperor in the Song Dynasty for his concubine:

Drinking wine together in the glow of the nephrite lamp,
I think back on our embrace, it felt so good. But it hurt, oh it hurt.
I gently pushed him away.

The younger grew more animated as he spoke, mimicking the lines with bodily gestures:

Now I hear him tremble and I blush with shock.
We thrust up against each other.
We become crazy, together as one, arms clasping, lips meeting, tongues entwining.

"I don't understand," said Qiezi.

"That isn't poetry," chuckled the elder.

"Fuck your mother. It's a famous poem! Now here, let me demonstrate it. Stand up. I'll recite it again and show you." The younger embraced her. "Now push me away when I say, 'I gently pushed him away.'"

Qiezi pushed him away. The younger pretended to tremble and shudder, rubbing and grabbing his groin. He threw his arms around her again and tried to kiss her. Qiezi repelled him. He grabbed her shirt and her breasts slipped out. "What are you doing!" she gasped, yanking her shirt down.

"You're not playing your part! You have to continue. You need to kiss me with your tongue," he said.

"Who says I want to play your part?"

"He's playing with you," said the elder. "Relax."

"Yeah, don't worry," the younger said with a laugh, sitting down. "I'm only joking with you."

"You've both been drinking."

"Here, have some spirits," said the elder, handing Qiezi his bowl.

Squatting with them, she took a sip. "That was very rude of you," she said to the younger. "Don't do that again."

"What? Now, hold on. You're telling *us* what to do? After rescuing and feeding you?" yelled the younger, standing up.

"That's not the way to behave toward a young lady, raising your voice like that," said the elder. "Use gentle words." He went back to gutting the fish they had snagged. "Play along with him. Though of course, he does have a point. You should show some appreciation for our generosity," he continued, running the blade of his cleaver along her shirt, splitting the seam and opening it along the side. "These rags of yours are barely holding up. You need new clothes."

"They're all I have," she said, holding her shirt in place.

"What did we tell you about showing some appreciation? Take your hand away!" said the younger, ripping Qiezi's shirt open. He also had a cleaver—hers, she realized, taken from her sack.

"We'll find you a new shirt back in town if you stay with us. And these pants too," said the elder as he hooked the edge of the cleaver under her sash.

"Please don't cut my sash. I'll take it off."

"Let us help you." The elder proceeded to sever her sash and pull her pants down off her hips, before tossing her clothes in the water, along with her sandals. "You won't be needing these anymore. Now that's more like it. A wild mountain girl in her natural state."

The younger was already leaning back under the awning with his own pants down. Qiezi removed a bloody object from between her legs and tossed it in the water, before squatting over him and the elder in turn. When they were finished, they told her to stay put under the awning.

"When will we reach the pagoda?" she asked.

"Who said you're going to the pagoda?" said the elder. "Don't you want your new set of clothes?"

"Can't you let me off at the pagoda?"

"Can't you shut up?"

"You said you would. I've been cooperating with you."

"She's starting to annoy me," said the younger. "You'll be lucky if you make it as far as the pagoda. Should we tell her?"

"Tell her what?" said the elder.

"That we have to kill her."

"That's hardly been decided. We may have some use for her. At least until tomorrow."

"I want to be of use to you. I can cook for you. I can gather all kinds of vegetables and herbs."

"Who asked your opinion?" said the younger, slapping Qiezi in the face. "She's already a nuisance—a dangerous one. We'd better kill her now."

"I'll scream."

"So what? No one will hear you."

"Someone surely will. It's only early evening. My body will be discovered downstream, and you'll be prime suspects when you dock."

"She can't be seen with us on the river," said the younger.

"That's only a problem in the daytime," said the elder. "I'd like to have another go at her tonight. Such a precious creature. We're not going to find the likes of her again."

"Why don't you take me to the pagoda and leave me there? You can tie me up so I won't escape. You can do anything you want with me."

"I told you to shut up!" said the younger.

"Keep your voice down. People may hear us," the elder admonished him. "Let's keep her for a few hours while I think about what to do. No more word from you," he warned Qiezi, pointing the cleaver at her, while the younger guarded the other side of the awning. "Or we'll send you and your raft adrift after slitting your throat."

"I'm not going to cause any trouble—"

"Didn't we tell you to shut up?"

"Yes, you did. But I'm not afraid of you. Let me join you. As a fisherwoman. I want to learn about that. I can teach you about foraging."

"Hold it!" said the elder. The younger was about to strike Qiezi with the cleaver. "Not one more word out of both of you! Take the pole and steer for a while," he told him.

The sampan hovered on the water as darkness gathered.

"Here, you take the pole. I'm feeling tired." As the younger reached over to hand the elder his pole, he tripped and fell.

"What's the matter with you?"

"I feel dizzy."

"I don't feel very good myself. Was that a bad batch of fish cakes?"

"They've been fine until now."

"I don't have any more strength either. Let's lie low and tie up the boat at that bank over there."

The two men stayed where they were, immobilized.

"Let me help you," said Qiezi, taking the pole herself and stepping onto her raft.

"Stay under the awning, if you don't want us to kill you."

"I think it's the other way around."

"Whadd'ya mean?" said the younger, lifting his head from the floor of the boat, his speech slurred.

"You should be grateful you have someone to bury you."

"What are you talking about? Who *are* you?"

"You wouldn't understand."

"What's happening to us?"

"You were right, she's a ghost," said the elder. "Where are you taking us?"

"To the pagoda."

"No! It's haunted! Take us to the Buddhist temple."

"Where is that?" said Qiezi.

"Another few *li* beyond the pagoda. This side of the river. You can see it through the trees. Help us!"

"You won't make it that far," she said to him.

The elder's eyes widened in shock. "You're a spirit from the haunted pagoda!"

He crawled after her with his cleaver. Qiezi knocked it out of his hand with the steering pole, sending it into the river. He flopped onto the raft and drowned, his face in the water. This forced her off the raft and into the water as well. She climbed onto the sampan, smacking the younger on the head with the pole until he released his grip on her leg.

He continued to moan as the naked girl pushed down the river looking for the pagoda. By the time she spotted it, he was silent.

Qiezi lashed the raft and the sampan to a tree by the riverbank and gathered the remaining fish cakes and her own cleaver. The elder's body was the heaviest and it took all her effort to drag him up the footpath and into the pagoda. The younger's body was lighter, but as she pulled him over the sampan's edge she slipped and cut her foot on a sharp rock in the water. Bleeding profusely, she dragged the second body up to the pagoda by her heels. She returned to the water to clean her foot, grabbed two more items, the steering pole and the elder's flask of spirits, and returned to the pagoda, careful not to soil her gash. She then stripped the corpses of their clothes. The younger's she wore. The elder's she spread out on the stone floor to lay on, while tearing off a strip to tighten around her injury to staunch the bleeding. Her back to the wall, she poured the strong spirits on the wound and waited for the bleeding to stop, gobbled down the remaining fish cakes, and sobbed herself to sleep after the long day.

In the morning, she hunted for medicines. She was looking

for the three-to-seven-years plant, so named for the time it took to mature, shavings from whose ginseng-like root placed on the wound would heal it fastest. This was not at hand, so she scraped the resin from a pine tree to disinfect her wound, though it tarred her fingers black. Since poison in non-fatal doses could cure, as an extra precaution she applied the purple-hooded petal of the crow's head, which resembled the prepuce over her own Yin button, on her gash, the pine sap on her fingers shielding them from its toxic touch. As there was no time to weave a new pair of sandals, she grabbed several taro leaves as big as lotus leaves, wrapped them around her foot and secured them with root string. Now a bit more ambulatory and using her bamboo pole as support, she looked around for more essentials, one in particular, her loadstone the golden ocean flower, needed to keep her mind clear; the last of her supply had been tossed off the sampan. If she could find the yellow celestial seeds flower with its eerie blood-red veins, the very flower Li San had randomly opened her copy of Li Shizhen's *Compendium of Materia Medica* to only the day before yesterday, it would also serve, but none did she see.

Back at the river, Qiezi got in the sampan after detaching it from the raft and headed downstream. Soon she ran into another pair of fishermen, haggard types who drew up alongside her, dispensed with niceties and reached over to drag her into their sampan. The strength she had in reserve for a moment like this, the coiled sinews of a creature accustomed to bearing sacks of grain as hefty as herself up vertical terrain, sliced cleanly through the man's fingers but deep into the boat's rim and lodged in the seam. She extracted the cleaver in time to swing her steering pole around and smack the other man on the groin. Bones cracked and the severed fingers shrieked. She pushed off against their boat without a backward look. Fired by adrenaline, she sped through the water. Their sampan stayed away—not sure it managed to stay afloat. She spotted the temple. Securing her boat at the bank, she limped up the path.

She entered the temple courtyard. No one was about. Perhaps the monks were out begging for alms, or in lunching or napping.

It was early afternoon. She peered into the nearest hall. A tall young monk with strong eyebrows was sweeping. He waved her away. Then squinting his eyes, he came up and stared at the strange waif with a bamboo pole, horrid rags drooping from her and foot wrapped in leaves. "What do you want?"

"Something to eat," said Qiezi.

"You can't eat here. Go to the women's monastery."

"I'm in a bad situation. Please give me something to eat and I'll leave. And I need a robe."

"What happened to you?"

"I was attacked by fishermen down there."

"Whose clothes are these?"

"Never mind."

"You're so young. I thought you were an old beggar woman. I'll get you a bowl of rice gruel, but you can't stay here."

"Don't tell anyone I'm here."

"I have reason enough not to tell anyone. Go wait outside the gate."

Her filthy hands were still shaking from the encounter on the river as she downed the gruel.

"What's the matter with your fingers?"

"I need some oil to clean off the pine sap."

"How bad is your foot?"

"I can take care of it. Please, I need a robe."

"There are no robes here for women."

"Any robe is fine. You can see these clothes won't do."

"Go to the nunnery."

"I have something to tell you. This has to be a secret. There are two dead men up the river. I can show you where they are."

"Oh, heavens. I'll go summon the *yamen* runners and you can lead us there."

"No. Only you."

"Why? What—did you kill them?"

"No. I found them dead. Would I be telling you about them if I had killed them?"

"This is a matter for the *yamen* runners."

"Come with me now or I'll run away and you won't find the bodies."

"Are you crazy? They will be found without you and you'll be the prime suspect. You'll be caught before you know it, assumed guilty and tortured until you spill the truth."

"Come with me now. I'll show you where they are and I'll be gone. We can take the sampan upriver."

"Whose sampan?"

"Get me a robe and come."

"Are you dangerous?"

"Do I look dangerous?"

He considered with a sigh before deciding to cooperate. He went back into the temple to fetch her a robe, and they went down to the river. The two of them pushed upstream and tied the sampan at the bank by the pagoda.

"The haunted pagoda!" exclaimed the monk.

"You believe that? Go up into the pagoda and wait for me. I need to wash my foot. Give me the robe. I want to change into it."

"Don't change here. You might be seen."

Qiezi glanced toward the river. "Go up and wait for me."

He stayed where he was and watched as she waded into the water and submerged herself, scrubbing her hair. What then emerged was no longer the grubby vagrant but something yet more distressing and unfamiliar to his eyes. Her rustic features and dark complexion, who might have been taken for a female coal miner, were transformed by water and sunlight. The baggy fisherman's clothes now clung to her like seaweed, and he saw her round hips and bulging bust, and with her disheveled hair now slicked back and out of the way, the fine cheekbones, a face of classical perfection, a woman of exceptional beauty. As she lifted her arms to squeeze the excess water from her hair, black flames of armpit hair as obscene as anything between her legs shot out of her sleeves. And as she bent down to look at her foot, he glimpsed a hanging breast and its big brown nipple through the gap in her shirt.

"Let me see the wound," he said.

"It's not getting any worse. I'll tear more strips from these rags to bind it. Now give me the robe."

"You'd better change in the pagoda. It's safer there. I'll stand outside."

They entered the pagoda. The monk went up to the naked corpses laid out side by side in the center of the floor. They were intact and without signs of mischief.

"This is where you found them?" said the monk.

"I found them in the sampan and brought them here."

"I wonder if they were poisoned. But arsenic blackens the flesh. Their flesh has yellowed a bit, that's all. How did you discover them?"

"You saw that raft down there? That's what I was on. I found them drifting in their boat yesterday, already dead."

"I thought you said you were attacked."

"I was, this morning on the way to your temple. Another boat of fishermen. I severed the fingers of one of them when they tried to rape me. I'm afraid they're going to come back looking for me. If you ever see a fisherman with missing fingers, it's him. Let me change into the robe."

"What kind of creature are you to attract so much trouble? A fox spirit? A witch? Are you real? Change here and let me confirm you are human!"

"Give me the robe."

He was holding it to his chest and breathing sharply. He extended it to her then pulled it back before she could take it.

"Give me the robe."

Now snorting hoarsely and losing the power of speech, he blurted out "No!", more to himself than to her. Shifting his gaze from her to the floor and back to her, he flung the robe down and spread it out, tears dropping from his eyes.

"No, you'll die!" she said. "I'll tell you the truth. I am poisonous!"

"How can you be poisonous?"

"I poisoned those two men. That's how they died!"

"How can you poison me? You can't poison me. I won't let you!"

A stronger power had taken over his limbs. He tore open her shirt, stripped her of her pants, and dragged her onto the robe.

"I am telling you, you will die!"

Had you been a witness to this scene, looking through one of the pagoda's windows, you would have seen a streak of sunlight illuminating the ripped deltoids of a man as he folded back female legs and dug his face between them like a tiger feasting on its prey, silent but for his grunting. He mounted her and worked up to his final spasm before collapsing upon her. She kept him inside her.

When he awoke, the sun was still out but dusk was gathering. "I must go. You be out of here soon, before any *yamen* runners show up."

"How are you feeling?"

"Tired. Drained."

"No, don't leave me."

Her legs were clamped around him, preventing him from getting up.

"Let me go. What we've done is shameful, terrible. I must return to the temple."

"Stay with me a while."

"What's your name?"

"Mantuoluo."

"Mantuoluo? The ocean flower?"

"Yes, the golden ocean flower."

"That's not your real name. Why did you name yourself that?"

"I need it. The ocean flower. Have you seen any around?"

"I recall seeing some purple ones, but I can't remember where. Why do you want it? It's poisonous."

"Purple ones, yellow ones, white ones, they'll all do. I need it. My body is saturated with it."

"I don't understand."

"I've eaten the flower all my life, since I was old enough to go out and wander as a child. I almost died the first time I ate it. But it opened my eyes and I've never been without it. I can't stop eating it."

"How can that be? How can you eat a poison?"

"It's not a poison in small amounts. It's a medicine, and it's magical. But I've eaten so much of it over the years that I need more and more. I can't die from it. I will die without it."

"What's magical about it?"

"The plant spirits come to life. They talk to you."

"Let me go. I have to get back."

Her contracting Yin muscles kept him fastened to her. "You won't make it. It's too late."

"What do you mean?"

"Let me comfort you in your last hour."

He looked at the corpses and back at her, only now comprehending, his eyes widening in horror. "You only slept with them, and they died?"

"Stay with me. Love me. Can't you feel my desire? Can't you feel how wet I am? This is now the apex of your life, with me. Your life's work is now complete. Appreciate it! Appreciate me!"

"Why are you doing this to me!"

"You forced me. I told you, you would die. You didn't listen."

"You seduced me."

"You wanted me."

"You're a witch!" She was still attached to him when he stood up. "Get off me!"

"I am not a witch. But you're going to die. Come to terms with it! You can't run away. You'll soon collapse. I'm sorry! Let me attend to your body here in the pagoda."

He managed to peel off the frightful creature and they both fell on the floor. "No!" he shouted, breaking down in tears. "I don't want to die."

"I'm sorry but it's your fate." She wiped the streaming perspiration off his face.

"I must return to the temple. I can't be abandoned here!"

He got up. Grabbing his robe, he staggered down to the river, fell into the sampan naked and tried to push off. She went after him and watched as he got nowhere. "You have to untie the boat."

"I'm losing strength. Take me back to the temple."

"It's too late. If you flee in the boat, you will only drift in circles. No one will see you. Come back to the pagoda."

At the water's edge, Qiezi sat down with knees pulled up to watch him die. As he slipped into unconsciousness, she donned his gray robe. Grabbing the cleaver from the sampan and using the water's surface as a mirror, she shaved off as much of her hair as she could. She had to make another trip to the pagoda to clean, dress and bandage her foot. She wrapped his body in the robe he had spread out on the floor, after washing out its dirt and dust and semen stains. Grabbing the robe's corners, she cinched him up the path and into the pagoda. She placed his body next to the other two. His penis was still erect—a death erection.

Now she was a Buddhist nun, if only in appearance. She couldn't tell you much about the creed aside from cursory visits to temple fairs with her parents. But she knew that even bad people tended to leave nuns alone. The river was a different matter. The sight of a solitary nun in a sampan would have been so odd and outrageous that word would travel fast; and she had had enough dealings with fishermen. She would have to make do on injured foot; reed sandals could be made later. She still had her silver *tael*, cleaver, and a tin bowl filched from the sampan in her sack, soon to fill up with edibles and medicinals gathered in the woods along the way.

3

The bath

The official notice at the temple entrance warned fairgoers to be on the lookout for unsavory elements taking advantage of the pushing and shoving to pick pockets or fights. Already Yan Xian was struggling to detach a child beggar that had latched himself to his leg. Lai Xinru grabbed the urchin by the ears and when that didn't work resorted to kicking him off her husband. No less aggressive were the limbless on their wheeled boards blocking your path, the deaf, dumb and blind, and people with eyes melted shut from burns or smashed noses and cauliflower-like growths protruding from facial orifices, jabbing their begging cups into you and it took all your self-control not to lash out at them. But as you worked your way through the crowd the brutish became more civilized: peasant families squatting and munching watermelons and seeds or sipping tea, farmers with a mule or donkey hitched behind them shouting out prices for their Indian corn, beans, and wheat, and others with trinkets laid out on strips of felt—hair ornaments and headbands, pearls and jewelry, copper waterpipes—and on one straw mat, for the occasion, a three-string fiddle, lute, flute, panpine, and clappers.

"Courtesans," remarked Yan Xian, as they passed by an alcove where women in embroidered jackets and skirts were placing plaster models of frolicking children at the feet of Guanyin, the goddess of mercy.

"You wish. No, concubines," retorted Xinru with a whiff of contempt, overly conscious of her own shapeless trousers and plain tunic buttoned up the side. "They're praying to get pregnant. I can't fathom how they put up with the heat in all those layers. Look, a performance is going on."

"Where?"

"Can't you hear the drums? Let's go see."

Xinru tugged Yan Xian through the labyrinth of steaming food stalls and the crush of thousands of fairgoers. The pattering of sticks and gongs grew louder and flashes of color came into view: brightly costumed figures running around on a raised stage with a high roof.

"Acrobats?"

"I think it's an opera."

"Is that a man or a woman? The one wearing the mask."

"Of course, it's not a woman. Women aren't allowed to perform in public like that," said Yan Xian.

"Are you sure? I've seen women in the traveling troupes passing through our town."

"They're the wives of the actors."

"No, they perform too."

"Most have criminal backgrounds, the actors in those troupes. That's why they're travelling all the time. Staying one step ahead of the law. But no one would dare call them out while they're performing," said Yan Xian. "Hmm, that gives me an idea."

"Wait—did you see that mask? It changed color. It was red, wasn't it? Now it's blue."

"I wasn't paying attention."

"No, I must have been imagining it. Look, it changed again! Now it's yellow. He didn't do anything and it changed."

"He must have switched it when he turned around."

"He's turning around again. It's the same."

"No, it changed again. He did it right in front of us, just now. See, it's white."

"Yeah, he only passed his hand over his face."

"Let's try to get closer to see how he does it. It's so fast."

"You're not from here, are you?" said a lady standing next to Xinru. "I guess you've never seen *bianlian*, the face-changing opera before?"

"We've never seen a show this big before," said Yan Xian.

Xinru was engrossed in the spectacle and ignored the woman.

"You're from Hubei? Shaanxi? I noticed your comely unbound feet," said the woman.

Xinru gave her a quick looking over and saw the tips of her lotus slippers poking out. "Mind your own business."

"I'm complimenting you. I really am. I envy you. If you knew how much I hate these broken stubs of mine."

Xinru and Yan Xian stared ahead, transfixed by the opera.

"Have you seen the 'Sunning the Feet' contest?" said the woman.

"What's that?" said Yan Xian.

"It's over there." Pointing to the right of the stage, she covered her mouth and giggled. "You won't believe it. You'll throw up."

"Why would we want to throw up?" said Xinru.

"Oh, it's one of the highlights of the fair. You have to see it to believe it. Come on, I'll show you."

The couple stood there warily.

"C'mon!"

"*Aiyo!*" yelled Xinru. For a confusing moment she couldn't figure out why she was rooted to her spot. A one-eyed man with a scar across a misshapen face had crawled up and in one swift motion grabbed her lower leg, tore her slipper off and held his exposed erection in an iron grasp against the sole of her foot.

"Get off her, you freak!" said Yan Xian as he punched him and tried to pull him away. The lady jumped to the rescue as well, kicking the man in the head. "Get away, you pervert!" she shouted.

The humanoid spider locked itself on Xinru, who had fallen on the ground, and they couldn't dislodge him. With a contorted face he yelped, heaved, and ejaculated. Xinru was digging her nails into his vise grip as semen splattered her face. Then with the same force with which he had grabbed her foot the gnome tore through the crowd, which inadvertently helped him escape by getting out of the way. Most of the onlookers had no idea what was happening, including a few who had been in the gnome's way and found themselves knocked down. "A thief?" some were asking.

"Catch the pervert!" yelled the lady.

Yan Xian had already disappeared in pursuit.

"Oh, god, how disgusting!" exclaimed Xinru.

"Are you all right? I'm so sorry this happened to you," said the lady as she wiped off Xinru's face with a handkerchief. "Oh, poor thing, you're crying. Here, let me take you to the tea pavilion and you can sit down and recover yourself."

Yan Xian returned. "I couldn't catch him. I grabbed his queue, but he had greased it and it slipped right through my hand! What kind of monster was that? Unbelievable!"

"I've heard rumors about this pervert. Shall we find some runners to track him down?"

"No, no, no. We don't need to turn this into a big matter. Xinru, are you all right?"

"I'm fine. Did he steal anything?"

"Let's go over to the tea pavilion and clean you up," said the woman, her arms wrapped around Xinru as they pushed their way through the crowd.

They sat Xinru down in the pavilion. The lady ordered a hot towel to be brought over at once.

"*Xiasi wole!* I have never been treated like that in all my life. Oh, heavens. Oh!" gasped Xinru, collecting herself.

"It's your unbound feet, dear," said the lady. "Perverts go crazy over them. Seeing as your slipper—oh no, where is it? We forgot to retrieve it."

"I'll go back to find it," said Yan Xian.

"He was so strong. Like a wild animal. I couldn't get him off me. How was he able to do that?"

"Those skimpy slippers of yours show off your feet. Did he hurt your foot?"

"I think it's fine. I'm very grateful for your help."

"Call me Sai'er. Kang Sai'er."

"Lai Xinru."

Xinru draped the steaming towel over her face before wiping it clean. "Did I miss anything?"

"There's more here." Sai'er applied the towel to a stain on Xinru's bosom. "Your foot's dirty and soiled as well. Let me clean it up for you."

Sai'er called for another towel as Xinru stared ahead, still livid.

"So, tell me, what brought you here to Taiping? You're from the mountains somewhere?"

"We crossed over from Shaanxi to visit some relatives up in the hills nearby. But they're no longer there. In fact, the whole village was abandoned! We have no idea what happened to them."

"Bandits have been infesting the hills. Where are you staying?"

"We thought we'd see if this temple allowed visitors and chanced upon this fair."

"Oh, I see. You don't have a place to stay. Stay with me. I have space."

"You don't have to do that."

"I insist. Where else are you going to go? Let's be friends, dear."

"How can we ever pay you back?"

"You don't need to pay me back! Have you eaten? Waiter!— no, let me take you both to dinner. There's a proper restaurant in town."

"The slipper's lost," said Yan Xian, arriving back.

"Don't worry about the slipper," said Sai'er, who was caressing Xinru's foot in both hands. "We can take care of that nearby. You can go barefoot until we find a shop. Throw this slipper away."

"This adorable woman is inviting us to dinner."

"That's too kind of you. You shouldn't."

"Don't stand on ceremony. I don't suppose you're still up for seeing the 'Sunning the Feet' contest? It's on the way out the back of the temple."

"I'm fine. Let's go have a look," said Xinru. "Nothing can faze me after that horrible experience."

Lai Xinru and Yan Xian had heard inklings of these contests but only now got to see one with their own eyes, the temple fairs back home being skimpier affairs. They squeezed through the crowd and approached the wall behind the stage. There they were, a whole row of them lined up on a long bench, faces made up so artfully they all looked the same age, gesturing and giggling, dressed as resplendently as peacocks in their satiny tunics and skirts and trouser-clad legs protruding from their skirts, and poking out of their trousers, the tiniest lotus feet in town encased in shoes of finely embroidered silk, little strategic bells tinkling from the heels or silk butterflies affixed to the toe whose wings flapped at the slightest motion. The contestants were competing for the attention of the male connoisseurs kneeling before them in rapt worship, oohing and aahing in ecstatic agony as their hands sought to rape a foot but could only shape the air around it, as if a ravishing woman allowed you to pass your hands over her body as long as you didn't touch it; others strained their nostrils to try to catch a whiff of the foot's natural scent.

"If one of their fingers so much as grazes a foot, the contestant master will smash their hands with that bamboo rod," said Sai'er.

"I've never seen a bare bound foot," said Yan Xian. "I don't suppose they ever take their shoes off?"

"No respectable woman would ever expose her feet to anyone but her husband…except when money is to be made. Come, there's more."

If Xinru was impressed she didn't show it; presumably she felt uneasy enough, being barefoot herself. "This is not quite what I expected when you said it would make us throw up."

They followed Sai'er out of the temple grounds to a narrow lane across the street and into a dark corridor off the lane. She handed a few coins to a man blocking the way and they were let through. Some were sitting on stools with bare stubs extended, others behind curtains strung from a wire.

"What's behind that?" asked Yan Xian.

A woman who poked her face out from behind a curtain. "You can do anything you want with mine."

"It smells bad here," said Xinru.

"They don't wash their feet. The men don't want them to," said Sai'er.

"Look at this, Xinru," said Yan Xian, who was standing before another specimen. "I thought she was giving me a handful of chestnuts but it's her foot she's holding in her hand. It's all red."

"Indeed, dyed with chestnuts. Haha!" chuckled the foot's owner, a toothless woman of indeterminate age whose face was caked in white makeup.

Xinru took one look at the woman and ran out of the corridor holding her mouth. They found her squatting in the lane and gagging. "What a horrible face! Like a ghost. And when she started laughing, I felt sick."

"She used arsenic to whiten that makeup," said Sai'er. "Well, enough of this. I've caused nothing but trouble for you today. Let's go have a nice meal."

"If I had any food in my stomach, I would have brought it up now."

"Don't tell me you two haven't eaten anything? Oh, you poor things. Let's go. I'm hungry too."

"We've been too busy traveling to think of eating."

"It's a shabby little restaurant, but it has private rooms."

"We couldn't care less where we eat."

With mincing steps, hooked on Xinru's arm—her lotus feet could proceed at a normal pace if she latched on to someone for support—Sai'er led them down several streets to the restaurant, after stopping off at a cobbler to fix Xinru up with a new pair of slippers.

The private rooms were on the restaurant's second floor. The rice paper windows set in the latticework frames that faced the street were intact and untorn, suggesting the food as well might be acceptable. The array of items Sai'er ordered came in one at a time but soon filled up the big round table—young bamboo shoots, leafy cabbages, pickled purple radishes, boiled soybeans, edible black fungus, water chestnuts, fried beets and garlic bolts, giblets and feet of the goose, sweetened goose-fat dumplings, squash and eggplant soup, chrysanthemum cakes, and a pot of steaming rice.

"I hope you don't mind mostly vegetables. It's what I'm used to."

Yan Xian and Xinru were too busy eating to respond, and Sai'er soon had to replenish the table with more dishes.

"It's not because I'm a Buddhist. Adapting to a vegetarian diet helps you survive in famine times. But I'm sure you know about that if you live in the hills."

"Why practice being hungry? If there's food, it's to be eaten," said Xinru.

"We used to live in the hills. Then we moved to a village near a walled city," said Yan Xian.

"Hanzhong? Xing'an?"

"In that general area. There was too much competition in the hills for arable land. More and more migrants keep on coming from the east."

"We have the same problem here. I'm from the east myself. Shandong."

"You came all the way from Shandong?" said Yan Xian. "That must be why your Chinese is so proper, like they speak in the capital."

"I came with my family as a young woman. I've been here now for over twenty years. We were from a walled city on the Grand Canal called Linqing. The city was taken over by rebels for almost a month until Banner troops rescued us. Many people were killed. We had to flee because the troops suspected those of us who survived the siege of being rebels, even though we weren't."

"You seem to have built up a nice life for yourself here, what with your white silks and kingfisher blue jacket."

"You can too."

"What do you mean?"

"Have you heard of the black wind?"

"What's that?"

"The wind that's going to come and plunge the earth into darkness. Have you heard of the Maitreya Buddha?"

"No."

"I belong to a society that worships the Eternal Venerable Mother. She's preparing to send the Maitreya Buddha down to earth at the turn of the next *kalpa* to exact vengeance for mankind's sins."

"Why?" Xinru asked.

"The black wind's going to cause widespread destruction in preparation for the new era of the Maitreya."

"What is that, some strange mixture of Buddhism and Daoism?" said Yan Xian.

"When is this going to happen?" said Xinru.

"There are signs it will happen soon. Any time now."

"So how can your group live a luxurious life if the whole world is destroyed?"

"Society, not group. We support each other and share everything. Many members are people of means and they donate nice clothes."

"That's where you got your clothes?" asked Yan Xian.

Sai'er smiled.

"I mean, aren't you going to be destroyed too?" asked Xinru.

"Of course not. The Eternal Venerable Mother will protect us. You'll be protected too if you join our society."

Xinru slapped her chopsticks down. "I've heard about these groups. They're usually started by a man with a beard—like my husband's beard though his isn't long enough—who has a great love of himself, and he's good at charming and bewitching women. So he spouts a ridiculous mishmash of Buddhist and Daoist sayings he picked out from a scroll stolen at random from a neighborhood temple, and once he's got these women under his

spell he gives them private training, which involves sleeping with
him in exchange for getting to see his scroll, which he claims was
dictated to him by the Buddha himself though he can't even read
but got a boy monk he sexually abused to recite it to him aloud
until he memorized it, and each of the female devotees imagines
she's the only one with a special relationship to him and he
persuades them to gather their own followers, the more beautiful
the better, to join the group but only after donating all their
money, but they too are only allowed into his presence if they
sleep with him. But he keeps gaining more and more followers
since the more followers he has the more 'proof' there is of the
truth of his claims. And the next step is to start frightening them
with absurd nonsense about the end of the world and then
threaten to expel them if they blab about it, including the women
he gets pregnant who have to hide their belly under the loose
robes he makes them wear in order to hide their belly and then
bury their fetuses in a ditch—"

"Keep your voice down, dear," said Yan Xian, patting Xinru
on the shoulder. "The waiters in the corridor can hear you."

Sai'er covered her mouth and laughed. "Oh, how I
underestimated you two." As if letting them in on a secret, she
added, "To be perfectly honest, I don't believe any of it either."

"Then why did you dump it all on us?"

"The only way to get the attention of simple folk is to frighten
them with news of the coming of the *kalpa* and the Maitreya. I
was testing you and you passed the test. But anyway, Xinru, may
I call you Xinru? As I said, we are a society, not a group. And it's
not like what you describe. We don't cheat people. And we don't
have a master with concubine disciples!" She lowered her voice
again. "We have a *female* master. A Mistress."

"What's the point of such groups if it's not to bamboozle and
scam people?" asked Yan Xian.

"No, you don't understand. We are made up of people like
you and me. Most people are good. Actually, it's loneliness.
People are lonely. That's why they join. That's why I joined."

"Why should we have to pay to join a group only because we

are lonely? That's what friends are for," said Xinru.

"We don't any have money," said Yan Xian.

"I know you don't have money. You don't have to pay anything."

"But we have to donate things."

"Let me explain. How do monks live? They're supported by their monastery, which is supported by their temple, which is supported by their community and the wealthy people in the community. But everyone must work, right? Some monks beg for alms, others are paid to officiate at funerals, and so on. Everyone contributes what they can. We have important people in our group—several ranked title holders and proprietors of successful businesses. We also have people who live from hand to mouth—restaurant cooks and waiters, peddlers, vegetable and bean curd sellers, weavers, cart drivers, stone masons, household servants, and even a few *yamen* clerks and runners. All these people have skills and trades and knowledge, and each helps out in their own way."

"We're just poor farmers."

"Then you can work the land! We have land and we need you. When people pool everything instead of scraping by in isolation, there's bounty to share in. Now, besides your knowledge of the land, tell me what you're good at."

The couple didn't have an answer.

"You must have some cooking skills, at least."

"Basic."

"How about carpentry skills?"

"Not much."

"Can you read?"

"No."

"Any knowledge of medicine? Plants and herbs?"

"Our daughter has."

"Where is she?"

"Back home staying with relatives."

"Why don't you bring her here?"

"It's not convenient now."

"It will be very convenient once you realize your family's turn of good fortune. Healers are promoted fast."

"Promoted to what?"

"Look at me—how I'm dressed."

"You're a healer?"

"Yes. We always need healers. I do *tuina.*"

"Massage?"

"And moxibustion. And cupping and scraping. Can you massage?"

"No."

"Well, that's a good place to start. I'll train you two. You can't go on looks alone."

"What do you mean?"

"How can such an attractive couple be without a livelihood? Xinru, may I compliment your husband's looks without your taking offense?"

"What looks? Maybe twenty years ago," said Yan Xian.

"That's for women to decide. Some men become more handsome as they age. As for yourself, Xinru, how many women would die for your gorgeous sad round eyes on that fine neck of yours? And with your full chest, narrow waist and big rump, you're so wholesome, a real rustic beauty. Once I've dressed you both up in some nice silks and embroideries, you'll command a greater following than any of us!"

It was not so much the force of Sai'er's logic, nor the authority of her firm chin, which began to seduce and hypnotize them as her lullaby-like lilt, for they had never heard Mandarin spoken so exquisitely.

"You're an attractive woman yourself," said Xinru. "I've never seen such pale brown eyes, so clear and light, the color of fresh wood. And your natural brown hair. Are you a ghost or an alien from across the sea? Are you truly a Chinese?"

"Entirely Chinese, as is my willowy figure, which I disguise in all these layers of clothes. I'm as skinny as winter tree branches underneath," she laughed.

"You have such nice hands."

"You mentioned men of many trades in the group. How can they accept being bossed around by a female leader and losing face like that?" asked Yan Xian.

Sai'er grabbed both their hands in hers. "Women make better leaders than men. We're smarter. We lead by example. *I* am a leader."

"Isn't it illegal for women and men to mix in groups?" asked Xinru.

"We meet several times a month at night in different members' homes. We often meet in my house, and I'm hosting the next session, in fact. We're discreet and have good relations with the *yamen* people, some of whom are members themselves. We are growing in size and influence. The main thing is, we treat men and women equally. Where else are you going to find that?"

"It's unheard of," said Xinru. "But I'll be looked down upon with my unbound feet."

"Not in our society you won't. You'll have to see for yourselves. Let's head to my place now."

"Will your family accept us? Do you have space?" said Yan Xian.

"I have no children and live alone. I've lived alone for years. I used to be a nun, after my husband abandoned me when he discovered I was barren."

"A nun!"

"I've lived in various Buddhist and Daoist nunneries."

"Sorry to hear about that."

"Who cares about that ancient history now? You are my new family."

Sai'er's house was reached through a labyrinth of lanes and squeezed between several family-run shops occupying the same two-story structure. The lower floor contained a kitchen alcove at front and a single spacious room of threadbare elegance. Large stone slabs lined the floor and wooden latticework the walls; the furniture was spare but select, a square redwood table and stools and a matching console table with a small shrine set along the wall between a pair of vertical calligraphy scrolls. The scrolls formed a couplet from Tang Dynasty poet Bai Juyi: "In the spring chill she was led into the steaming hot spring / Whose silky waters washed away her skin's lustrous layer of fragrance."

"Hey, help her with that," said Xinru, jabbing her husband and pointing to the heavy bucket of steaming water Sai'er was hauling up the stairs to the second floor.

"You stay right where you are," Sai'er insisted. "I can carry this up perfectly well myself."

Over cups of yellow wine, Sai'er explained what the first session would entail. The mistress would be presiding and more than happy to meet them. The only thing they needed to learn was an eight-character mantra: *zhen kong jia xiang wu sheng lao mu.*

"Eternal and Venerable Mother in our original home in the world of true emptiness," Yan Xian and Lai Xinru repeated back each in turn. "What does it mean?"

"Exactly what it says. Keep reciting it so that it rolls off the tongue and you'll be regarded by everyone as old friends. It's a relaxed and informal affair. We recite and sing lines from our scriptures. We meditate in lotus position and massage each other's backs. Some people stay later for more advanced massage treatments. And we all wear white robes, so we'll need to get you outfitted with that as well."

"The meeting takes place in this room?"

"Yes. Everyone brings their own cushion to sit on, along with a vegetarian dish, and once the meditation is over, we lay out all the food on the floor for a feast."

"Males and females massage each other's backs?"

"Yes."

"Xinru will love that—if it's a couple of handsome young lads massaging her at the same time," said Yan Xian, the wine already loosening him up.

"The Mistress matches up different people in each meeting."

"You'd better get used to my husband. He says anything that comes to mind. Anything."

"And she *does* anything that comes to mind. You won't find two more daring people in all of Shaanxi, and probably Sichuan as well. Here's to *our* new disciple! I think we're going to have some fun with you," he laughed, extending his wine cup to Sai'er.

"I need to pop open a new flask."

"Your home is so luxurious," said Xinru, "but where do we sleep?"

"Upstairs. Let me show you now. I'll bring the wine."

Carrying the flask and the cups on a tray, Sai'er led them up a staircase to the second floor. Besides a finely carved rosewood canopy bed, the room's centerpiece was a *nanmu*-slatted bathtub planted in the middle of the room, with accompanying shallow bathing basin, pans, and washstand. While they were getting tipsy on the wine below, Sai'er had made more trips upstairs with hot water for the tub. She affixed the wine tray to the edge of the tub.

"I've never seen such a big basin before," said Yan Xian.

"It's a tub for soaking. We're bathing and soaking before we…." Sai'er gestured toward the bed.

The couple looked confused.

"Oh, but we can't. The mistress of the house can't be allowed to sleep on the floor," protested Xinru.

"Who said I'm sleeping on the floor?"

"But where…you're…?"

Sai'er nodded.

"I'm shocked."

"Good."

"This is the women's chamber! Yan Xian must sleep downstairs," Xinru pointed.

"Yes, you two sleep here. I'll sleep downstairs," said Yan Xian.

"The downstairs is not for sleeping. You're sleeping with me, right here in my bed. It's big enough for three people."

They were utterly at a loss.

"You should be thrilled at having the privilege of my bed. And now it's bathing time. How often do you bumpkins bathe, once a month? Never? You stink after so many days on the road."

"We're not that grubby. We bathe in the river a lot in summer. In winter, once a month or so. You're right, we haven't had a bath in a while. We just squat in a shallow basin like that one there and douse ourselves with water."

"That's what I'm going to have you do now. Xinru, you wash up first. I'll go next, and your husband last. Then we'll use the tub. Hurry up now and get undressed. We need to wash those clothes of yours as well. They smell like they haven't ever been washed."

"Right in front of each other? No."

"I'll go downstairs while you two bathe," said Yan Xian.

"You stay where you are. I thought you called yourselves daring. Now listen to me, you two. Free thinking requires hard work. You need to be pushed to the next level and challenged with new ways of doing things. We're going to start with obedience."

"We could be arrested for mixing this way," said Yan Xian.

"Not in my house you won't. Come on, off with the clothes, both of you! Hot water is in the pans for washing."

They did as they were told. Sai'er slathered Xinru with pig pancreas soap and scrubbed her all over, groin included, with a loofah sponge while Xinru rinsed herself with a pan of water. Xinru repeated the procedure with Sai'er and after that her husband. A red-faced Yan Xian tried to hide his erection. Sai'er carried on calmly before stepping into the steaming jasmine-scented tub.

"This tub is meant for one person but two can squeeze in. Come into the tub with me, Xinru. Yan Xian, you use it after we're finished. Get in the bed and wait for us," she told him. She handed him a cup of wine and they downed another toast.

The women soaked in silence. Sai'er smiled at the normally garrulous Xinru, who stared back at a loss for words.

"Here's to *yuanfen*!" announced Sai'er, offering Yan Xian more wine.

"Yes, to our happy fate in meeting you! But I never thought I'd meet anyone more provocative than myself," he quipped. "And a woman at that!"

"Why provocative?"

"You've created an unheard-of situation in this room," he said with worried amusement. "We're only poor farmers but we would never dream of putting strangers up in the same room, let alone the same bed!"

"Where would you put them then?"

"We have a daybed in our outer room for guests, and two inner rooms, one for us and one for our daughter who's already grown into a woman."

"And where do the millions of poor families whose house consists of only a single room put up guests?"

"They must have curtains or dividers. I mean, it's unimaginable what would happen were the village head to make an unannounced visit to inspect the house."

"You're frightened over nothing."

"We were just visited by a *yamen* runner who inspected our house."

Xinru glared at Yan Xian, trying to get his attention.

"Runners don't just barge into homes unannounced," said Sai'er, who was getting louder. "There's always a reason. There must have been a reason. Was someone on your street hiding brigands and they were doing a house-to-house search?"

"No, nothing like that."

"Are you really afraid your house will be inspected when no one else is the least bit concerned about it?"

"But no one would ever do *this*."

"Do what?"

"Males and females from different families bathing together in the same room and sleeping in the same bed."

Sai'er stood up in the tub and stared at Yan Xian. It had grown dark outside. Her figure glistened in the light of an oil lamp mounted on a sconce with a reflector, small-breasted with delicate hips and a patch of brown pubic hair that streamed black above the water's surface. "I have no idea what you're talking about. Everyone does it."

"Everyone?"

"You didn't know that?"

"I don't believe it."

Sai'er stepped out of the tub. While toweling herself dry, she jabbed her finger at Yan Xian and yelled: "When normal people mingle with friends in the privacy of their home, they do things together because they have no choice but to live in close quarters. They grab what time remains to them in this life because it can be taken from us at any time. How old are you both now, forty? How many people in your village live past forty? I can't believe I've made it this far, already an old auntie at forty-five, without expiring or being killed. You should consider yourselves lucky. I'll confess something I didn't want to reveal earlier, but our family were in fact rebels back in Shandong. My mother and I became nuns because there was a bounty on us. Now, either you see ghosts in daytime or you're too dense to understand, but isn't it rather odd to be the only ones cowering in fear over imaginary specters? I'm stunned to hear this. Those prohibitions are only for show!"

"You yourself had to come all the way to Sichuan to escape the law."

"Our situation was different. We were rebels. That's the only thing that will land you in trouble—becoming a rebel. But you are ordinary people."

"Being caught having illicit sex is one hundred strokes of the heavy bamboo. That's a fact. We would be forcibly divorced and Xinru and our daughter sent back to her natal village, never to see each other again!"

"Do you know anyone this has happened to? You're the first I've heard who takes those prohibitions seriously. We joke about how silly they are. If you only knew how runners spend their time, *wode tian*! How many runners do you know? The best of them—those not in our society anyway—run prostitution dens out of people's homes. They laugh about the work they do, regard it with contempt, since they are paid almost nothing. They're actors, pretending to march the delinquent around from time to time before everyone goes back to their business. Now come into the tub so I can have you smelling nice and sweet. The water is still warm."

Sai'er went over to the far corner of the room to urinate in a chamber pot.

"I think she's a little crazy," Yan Xian whispered to Xinru.

"Do you think she's bluffing? She's trying to soften us up for some purpose."

"Should we make a run for it?"

"I don't want to cause a scene. And we don't have a choice. I hope she's not dangerous. Let's play along and see what happens. Humor her. Just don't spill anything about our situation."

"Did you hear me, Yan Xian?" Sai'er commanded from across the room. "It's your turn in the tub."

Yan Xian got in the tub and watched as Sai'er sauntered up and positioned herself behind Xinru on the bed.

"I'm going to show you two how to do a sitting massage. You'll be wearing robes during the session. You can do it over the robe but can get a better grip by reaching under the robe. You start off by pinching and squeezing the skin in your fingers like this. As the flesh warms and becomes more pliant, you gather larger handfuls, whole folds in your hands like this. Work all the way up along either side of the spine and go all the way down between the crack of the buttocks since that's where the spine begins. Knead everywhere, the neck and the shoulders and the armpits as well. With practice you can even wedge your fingers under the shoulder blades. And you also need to dig into the acupressure points, but I'll teach you that later."

"What if a man grabs my jade gate while massaging me?" asked Xinru.

Sai'er reached between Xinru's legs and clamped her fingers on her vulva. "Like this? Don't resist. Let the Qi flow. Nothing is unseemlier than a complaining woman. You're receiving the healing arts."

"They really do that?"

Sai'er pulled Xinru close by the neck and plugged her mouth on hers. Xinru burst out laughing. "I've never done this with a woman before. Slow down, please."

"Maybe they will. We're all naked under our robes."

"Ah? Why?"

"To humble your pride and make everyone equal. You can wear your period bib during your unlucky days, and then you don't have to bathe before the session. Now let's switch and you do my back. My skin is quite thin and loose and easy to grab. Grab me hard."

Xinru attacked Sai'er's backside as instructed.

"Harder. I need it *hard*. Harder! Bruise me!"

Sai'er told Yan Xian to join them on the bed and massage her front at the same time.

"Harder, I said. Both of you! Squeeze my breasts, my nipples, hard! Harder! No, do it harder! Like this." She turned Xinru around, squeezed and mauled her chest and breasts before slapping her on the face. "I told you to squeeze harder!"

"What are you doing!"

"Waking you up!"

She slapped Xinru again. Xinru touched her mouth and drew blood on her fingers. "This is the second time today my face has been defiled and disgraced."

Sai'er glued her mouth on Xinru's again and held it before releasing her with the words, "I love you."

Squatting over Yan Xian, Sai'er proceeded to "lower the Yin to join the Yang" and impale herself upon him. She rode him hard, squealed and convulsed in climax, and collapsed next to him, pulling Xinru to her other side.

With eyes closed she said, "Now both of you, recite for me the mantra I taught you."

4

The nunnery

iezi's corn cake crumbled apart in her fingers and onto her robe. "What the hell is this stuff made of?" she said.

"You have to mix it into the porridge," said Ye Yuejiang. "We hate his cooking."

"*His* cooking? What's a man doing in the nunnery?"

"We used to all have cooking duty until the abbess let her tenant take over."

"Why?"

One of the nuns sitting across from them pointed to the door with her eyes, but it was too late to prevent the loud rap on the table. The senior nun glared at them before stepping back out.

"Don't raise your voice since we all get punished if Dequan tells the abbess," said Zhilu. "Remember you're on probation for a year. Don't spoil things for the rest of us."

They ate in silence.

Yuejiang got up to peek into the corridor. "She's gone."

"Why is probation so long?" said Qiezi.

"To make sure prostitutes aren't pregnant," said Zhilu.

"Who says I'm a prostitute?"

"You look like one."

"Don't listen to her. It's common for abandoned women to flee to nunneries and we all go through this probation because of some bad women," said Yuejiang

"And she thought that hatchet job she did on her hair would pass for a nun?" said Zhilu.

"After a year you can apply for ordination in Xi'an."

"What's ordination?"

"Where you take the robe and receive tonsure. Until then we do mutual head-shaving."

"You become a nun," said another.

"With the ridiculous name of *Mantuoluo*?" scoffed Zhilu. "What kind of name is that? It's a made-up name, isn't it? I bet you're hiding something. What did *you* do to make you flee to a nunnery?"

Qiezi ignored her. "I can cook better than this. Can I see the kitchen?"

"Be careful with Mou Yushun, the cook. He'll make a pass at you."

"Yep, she's a prostitute," said Zhilu. A couple other nuns giggled.

Qiezi got up and headed for the kitchen. Mou Yushun was alone at his lunch. The stinging haze of chili peppers hung in the air and mingled with the dizzying fragrance of onions and garlic seared in lard. Qiezi pursed her lips in a pout and glowered.

"So you're the new one," he said.

"Did you make the corn cakes? You overcooked them."

"It's not your role here to complain."

"I'm trying to help. You should take them out of the stove a little before they're ready. And the corn meal was only ground once. It needs to be ground twice. At least twice."

"Grind it yourself, then."

"You should mix it with soybean flour. And we should have millet porridge too, not only rice porridge."

"There's no millet around here."

"That's not true. There are millet fields and the harvest is over.

Why do you get to eat onions and garlic?"

"I'm not a monk. I can eat anything."

"Why can't we have onions and garlic?"

"Smelly foods aren't permitted to nuns. They distract from meditating."

"How can we meditate if we're hungry? We can't live on only corn and rice."

"What did you expect when you entered a nunnery?" he exclaimed, meeting Qiezi's eyes for the first time before his gaze returned to the swell of her breasts under her robe. "Perhaps you've heard of transferable merit?"

"What's that?"

"You've a lot to learn." Jabbing his finger he said, "Your job as a Buddhist is to help others through good deeds. Your suffering earns merit for others. That's why you have simple food, so others can have more. The nuns can explain it to you. Or shall I tell the abbess what a pest you're being and let her explain? Now leave me alone and return to your duties."

"Why are *you* doing the cooking? The nuns told me they used to do it."

"It's none of your business."

"Can you let me make the corn cakes?"

"I told you to leave."

"Please. I'll make them for everyone."

Mou's gaze remained locked on her torso. "Hmm. It might save me a lot of trouble, come to think of it. I'll have to ask the abbess."

Qiezi returned to the table, her head held high.

After the afternoon silent meditation, the nuns resumed their daily chores. As her assigned sister, Yuejiang showed Qiezi how to sweep the floor to the abbess's exacting requirements.

"Why is Zhilu so mean to me?"

"She's still upset because the abbess expelled her lover Qingtao after she caught them having sex."

"Her lover?"

"Another nun."

"Why wasn't Zhilu also expelled? And what does it have to do with me?"

"I think she's afraid Zhilu will go crazy if she's kicked out. Her family is from a nearby village, and they might also cause trouble because they donate to the temple. She hasn't been right in the head since that happened. Don't take it personally. Ignore her. It's been a problem, as she's gotten lazy and refuses to work. She even steals from the temple and the abbess found out she sold some stolen things to Mou Yushun's brother."

"The cook?"

"Don't talk about this to anyone."

"What happened to the other girl?"

"We don't know."

"How long have you been here?"

"Two years."

"How old are you?"

"Twenty."

"Why are you here?"

"I don't want to get married."

"Do you like it?"

"No. I want to leave but have nowhere to go. How did you hear about our temple?"

"From a vegetarian hall," said Qiezi.

"Where?"

"I was in several. The last place was horrible. They tried to force me to have sex."

Yuejiang stared. "In a vegetarian hall?"

"There are different kinds. It was a *caitang*."

"No, you have to go to a *zhaitang*, a proper vegetarian hall, not a *caitang*."

"*Now* I know. But I didn't know the difference at the time. The first place I went to was a *zhaitang*, They didn't need any helpers and only let me stay one night. They referred me to another vegetarian hall, a *caitang*. It was very poor and the guests were all old or sick. The food was worse than here. Though it was divided into male and female sections, they said I was too young and pretty and word would get out and they didn't want trouble. They mentioned another place where they said I would better fit in. This *caitang* was Daoist. Monks and nuns were working there together, a mixed-sex hall. They took me on as a cook and gave me a bed. The food was better. The porridge contained fish and you could get full. But the male guests started giving me dirty looks. I ignored them. One day the head monk started yelling at me for not cooperating. That's when I found out that the girls who weren't virgins were expected to sleep with the guests! That's what we had to do just for room and board. It was how the hall gets a steady supply of patrons."

"How did they know you weren't a virgin?"

"I never told anyone I was a virgin because I didn't know anything. Somehow they assumed I wasn't. So I quit. Another girl told me she was also quitting and knew of a Daoist nunnery in Hubei Province that was safe and invited me to go with her. I thought about it but was reluctant to travel that far. Then the head monk sarcastically said I'd be better off at the 'good girls' nunnery up the hill. I took his advice and here I am."

Qiezi set her broom against the wall and wiped the sweat and dust from her face. Even under the courtyard eaves there was little relief from the sweltering sun.

"Today is bath day," said Yuejiang. "The sweeping is scheduled on bath days because it's the dirtiest job. I'll show you how to use the bath."

"It's been over a week since I've bathed. That last *caitang* didn't even let me use a bathing pan unless I cooperated with them. I tried finding a sheltered spot on the river but too many fishermen were always around."

"We can bathe twice a week in hot weather. But don't enter the bathing room when the abbess is bathing."

"Why not?"

"Oh, it's strictly forbidden. One girl got expelled when she opened the door while Deming was bathing at a different time from her normal time. After Deming, it's Dequan's turn, and then the nuns one after the other according to seniority. Don't worry, just follow us. The others should be returning from their bath soon."

"So we're last?"

"Yes, Zhilu, me, and you. Zhilu used to have seniority but got demoted after her scandal."

The bathing room contained a wooden tub large enough to accommodate several people and smaller basins for individual use. Zhilu was already in the room and squatting in one, naked but for a rag wrapped around her hips."

"What's this?" said Qiezi, pointing to the tub.

"You've never seen a bathing tub before?"

"No. We use a squatting basin at home like she's using. And there's a secluded spot by our river." Qiezi stared at the tub. "I'm not getting in that water. Look at all the scum floating on the surface."

"You don't have to. We're lucky because we're last. We don't have to keep the tub full for the next group. Scoop up the water from under the surface and pour it over you in one of the basins."

"You mean the water is never changed?"

"The abbess says water is too precious to waste so much. One full tub is for all of us."

"The whole nunnery?"

"The whole nunnery. It's miserable bathing in winter because the water's not only dirty but cold by the time we get to it."

They removed their robes.

"What are you doing!" gasped Yuejiang. "Where's your underwear?"

"What underwear?" said Qiezi.

"Like mine, and Zhilu's. Don't you have underwear?"

"No."

"You know, any old pants you used to wear? You cut off the legs and that's how you make underwear."

Qiezi stared dumbfounded at the shreds of cloth hanging from Yuejiang's waist. "Of course, I had pants. But I never wore underwear. I usually wore crotchless pants."

"What?" exclaimed Zhilu. "Like those crotchless training

pants little children wear? You can't hold your stool and urine?"

"No! All of us women wore them. For convenience when out working in the fields the whole day."

"What are you, a mountain savage? Where are you from?"

"How can you clean yourself there if you're wearing something?" said Qiezi

"Clean yourself there? You *don't* clean yourself there. That's disgusting!"

Qiezi was again at a loss. "You can soak in that dirty water, but you can't wash your privates?"

Yuejiang and Zhilu were equally shocked and said nothing. After drying herself with a towel, Zhilu departed. Yuejiang used the same towel to dry herself and handed it to Qiezi.

"You all use the same towel? I may come from the mountains, but we at least use our own towels," she said.

"You're not ashamed to show your privates?" said Yuejiang.

"Why should I be?"

"They're unclean."

"I never heard that before. They're only unclean during your unlucky days."

"That's not what I mean. They're spiritually unclean."

"No, they're not."

"In that case, you can't be a Buddhist."

"I don't want to be a Buddhist, then. I would rather be a savage," said Qiezi, her arms folded across her chest.

Yuejiang laughed. "I know what you mean. But you're the first person I've met who isn't ashamed."

"You'll catch a disease from soaking in that water. Let's go find a creek or brook where we can wash."

"We're not allowed out of the temple unless accompanied to the market."

"What? What do you mean?"

"They say it's not safe. The temple is responsible for us."

"You don't even have a farm where we can work outside? Don't you grow your own vegetables?"

"There's a small patch of land in back but it's gone fallow. We buy rice and corn from the market."

"That's crazy. Why can't they have us tend to it? I know how to farm. And there are forests nearby. We can gather herbs and mushrooms. I can show you how to forage."

Yuejiang thought Qiezi was joking. But that evening Qiezi was given permission to try her hand at the next day's corn cakes. First thing after morning meditation she led Yuejiang out of the courtyard for a foraging expedition.

"I can't leave," said Yuejiang, halting at the temple gate.

Qiezi stepped across the stone threshold and pointed. "Walk over it."

When Yuejiang hesitated, Qiezi pulled her across. "Now you're free. See how easy it is? Let's go."

Qiezi paused at the top of the hillside and breathed in the air. "I smell water down there."

Bounding down the hill, Qiezi found the creek; Yuejiang straggled behind, limping with her bound feet. Qiezi dropped her robe and started scrubbing it in the water. When she pulled off Yuejiang's tattered underwear, Yuejiang lost her balance and fell laughing into the water. They sat down in the creek, letting the water course over them.

"Squeeze the water out of your robe and it'll be mostly dry by the time we're back," said Qiezi.

Yuejiang unwrapped her feet. "I'm so glad I can clean my smelly feet."

"Why do you bind them, now that there is no need to?"

"You can't let them out all at once. The skin will crack and bleed and it's extremely painful. I want to grow them back out if possible but it's going to take years. I still need to bind them tightly when I go out walking or it's unbearable."

"I've never seen an exposed bound foot," said Qiezi, inspecting Yuejiang's foot in her hands. "My mother's feet also aren't bound."

"You're so lucky."

Yuejiang held her legs together and turned glum.

"What's the matter?"

"I have a problem there. It's inflamed."

Qiezi parted Yuejiang's legs and examined her. "Yes, it's infected. That white stuff coming out of you is caused by the same thing as those black stains in the bathing tub. I know what can cure it, the bark of the cork tree, but I'm not sure we can find that around here. We may have to visit an apothecary. In the meantime, let's keep our eye out for honeysuckle or foxglove flowers. They can help too."

"You're not going to confess this to a male apothecary, are you? I will die of shame."

"I'll buy the medicine for you. I don't have to say what it's for. Let me take care of it."

"How do you know so much about this?"

"Plants are my life. I need to ask you, are you a virgin?"

"Yes, of course."

"That infection of yours, it's usually caused by sex. So you must have gotten infected from the water in that tub. How many other nuns are infected? Don't they boil the water before filling the tub? I'm not sure how much longer I can last here. I've never lived in such filthy conditions before."

"Where will you go?"

"Hubei. I should have gone with Gu Jingjing."

"Who is she?"

"The girl who quit the *caitang* when I did."

"Can you go there now? Do you know where it is?"

"More or less. I can find it."

Yuejiang grabbed Qiezi's hand and said, "If you leave, I'm going with you."

"Are you sure? You should think about it carefully. Can you walk all day with those feet?"

"I will force myself to."

"It's very dangerous for women traveling alone. If you go with me, you're so brave."

Yuejiang tried to plunge her mouth on Qiezi's but she turned away. "Oh, no. We can't kiss."

"Why not?"

"I can't."

"You don't like women?"

"It's not that. There's another reason. I can't tell you now."

"You have a disease?"

"No. Be patient and I'll explain another time. I like you. I really do. And your name is so beautiful—Moon River. Leaf Moon River." Qiezi caressed Yuejiang on the face. "Your parents knew how to name you since you have a moon-shaped face. Many moon-faced girls look fat but yours is just right, with your wide-set eyes. They're so exotic."

Yuejiang tried to kiss Qiezi again. "No, don't. I can't. I promise you can kiss me in the future."

Yuejiang wrapped her arms around Qiezi and buried her head in her breasts. "Yours are so big."

"Big and floppy. I envy yours which stick straight out like peaches."

"It feels so good to hold someone."

Qiezi got up. "Let's get to work. We need to gather things, go back and grind more corn and bake the corn cakes in time for lunch."

They wrung out their robes, which they dried themselves with, and wrung them out again before putting them on. Qiezi pointed out various edible herbs and fungi and picked out flowers to nibble on. While Yuejiang was busy filling up her basket, Qiezi dug mysterious things out of the soil and from under dead logs and rocks and stuffed them in a small sack.

The corn cakes proved acceptable. At least none of the nuns complained about them. It was also the first time they had eaten corn cakes spiced with chili peppers. Some asked Qiezi what else she had mixed into the cornmeal that made them feel fuller than usual. "A secret recipe," she said.

Only Zhilu was sour. "You're in trouble! You and Yuejiang left the temple this morning without permission and the abbess is very angry."

Qiezi's baking was thenceforth not allowed to conflict with morning assembly and meditation. This meant she could only prepare each day's batch the day before in the afternoon. As she didn't want Mou Yushun around when she was in the kitchen, she asked Yuejiang to keep watch.

"Don't worry, now that he only cooks in the morning, he won't bother you. He always takes an afternoon nap at that time anyway."

The next afternoon, a suspicious Zhilu stole into the kitchen to observe from behind the newly appointed cook at her task. "What the hell are you mixing into the cornmeal? Oh, god, it's insects! And worms!"

Zhilu ran out of the kitchen hollering, "She's poisoning us!"

"Who is? What's going on?" said the others.

"The savage. She's poisoning the corn cakes!"

Zhilu ran down the corridor, yanked open the door to the bathing room and yelled, "Abbess, that witch is poisoning us! I just saw her—"

Now, before describing what happened next, and why Zhilu halted petrified in mid-sentence, we might pause to consider how the occupants of the bathing tub would in retrospect have wished they had reacted with the benefit of more mental preparation. Surely they would not have budged a whit, not even turned their heads, as if what they were engaged in couldn't be more boring, while Zhilu would have found herself at the receiving end of the following sort of judgment: "If you *ever* open this door again during our private bathing, you will be cast out of the temple naked like a whore! Do I make myself clear?"

Yet even the most collected of us will be caught off guard in an emergency, or the mere announcement of such. Startled, they scrambled out of the tub. The tub was made of vertical cedar planks reinforced with wrap-around iron bands. After years of use the bands had rusted, and the planks now collapsed under the combined weight of Deming, Dequan, and Mou Yushun (and his erection) climbing over the rim at the same time. The tub's contents, bodies and all, poured onto the floor.

"Is somebody dying?" said Dequan, once the senior nun had gathered herself. She was answered by an empty doorway: Zhilu and the others drawn to the commotion had already fled in mortification.

The enraged abbess, once she learned that no one in fact had been poisoned, had Zhilu expelled from the temple. But Zhilu was not so easily cowed. She was confident the abbess would take her back after calming down and realizing her protegee only acted to protect the nunnery from the deranged and dangerous mountain vagrant who had been taken in in error, one who moreover might even be a criminal on the loose.

Late that night Zhilu snuck back into the temple and slipped under the abbess's bed, who awoke at the rustling and sprung out of the bed shouting, "Thief!"

This was all too much. Zhilu was stripped and bound naked to a column in the meditation hall. Encountering the abbess's redoubled wrath instead of gratitude, she grew distraught and defiant. She cursed the abbess, something no one had ever done. The abbess told Mou Yushun to wrap the rope across Zhilu's mouth to shut her up. They went back to bed, leaving the matter till morning. It wasn't long, however, before Zhilu gnawed through the hempen strand and resumed her cursing.

"You cunt! You fucking cunt! The *yamen* is going to hear about this—all about you and your vicious treatment of me and your shameless activities in the bathing room. And you side with that savage? You're a disgrace. You don't deserve to run a nunnery," she ranted, spitting on the abbess when she reappeared with Dequan, Mou, and all the nuns.

"Remove her from the post. Lock her up in the storage house for a few days. Maybe that will bring her back to her senses," said the abbess.

Zhilu now grew hysterical and the three of them struggled to hold her down as she kicked and screamed.

"Don't just stand there, help us!" said the abbess.

Some nuns, including Yuejiang, assisted Mou and Dequan in tying her up and bundling her off to the storage house. Qiezi looked on in sad silence.

Agitated and confused, the abbess seemed at a loss until

remembering something. "Well, Mantuoluo, what's this I hear about you poisoning the corn cakes?"

"Abbess, I didn't poison them. I only added some insects to the batter. I am very sorry for this misunderstanding."

"Insects! Why?"

"The food is all Yin. We need more Yang in the food, more sustenance. We're weak and we have no energy."

"Insects! Are you crazy?"

"I know how to forage for plants and herbs and insects. The insects are harmless and provide energy. You can't taste them once the corn cakes are cooked."

"That is unacceptable. We don't eat insects in a Buddhist temple. We don't even kill insects! I am taking you off cooking duty. And throw your revolting batter away. Now all of you go to bed. Due to tonight's disturbance, you may rise an hour later tomorrow morning."

Lest Zhilu's ranting be heard from the storage house and disturb everyone's sleep, the abbess grabbed a hoe and went to give her a sound beating to shut her up.

In the morning, Qiezi brought porridge and water to Zhilu, along with her robe. She was lying on her side, her hands tied behind her back and feet tied together.

"Zhilu, don't be angry with me. I'm not your enemy. You can hate me if you want, but I don't hate you. I wasn't poisoning the corn cakes. Really, I wasn't. I added the insects to give them Yang. I know a lot about food and medicine. We shouldn't have to eat insects but it's free sustenance. The food isn't right. I only wanted to make it better."

Zhilu stared vacantly.

"Here, have some porridge." Qiezi put the bowl to Zhilu's lips but she wouldn't open her mouth. "You must eat. If I untie your hands, do you promise you won't do anything to upset the abbess? Then you can eat by yourself. The abbess is going to forgive you. I will make sure she forgives you. I saw her this morning and she's already calmer. She let me bring you this food."

A tear streamed down Zhilu's face as Qiezi untied her hands.

Qiezi wiped off Zhilu's tears and sighed. She laid Zhilu's robe over her. At the doorway she said, "I have to lock the door or I'll be in as much trouble as you. I'll bring you more food tonight."

That afternoon a crashing sound was heard in the storage house. The abbess went in to investigate. She returned with the hoe in hand. Later Qiezi visited the storage house. Upon returning, she said to Yuejiang, "I have no idea what happened, but the abbess beat her again, badly. She hasn't touched any food or water. She's in a very poor state."

Qiezi and Yuejiang went to see Zhilu the next morning. She was lying in the same position, naked again, hands bound and dark bruises on her body. Her lips were parted and encrusted, face ashen. Her eyes opened with no recognition of the girls. They tried to make her drink water but it rolled out of her mouth.

"Zhilu, what happened! What did you do? I can get you medicine, but you *must* cooperate. You must drink. You have to live. We can make this right."

Back at the temple a short while later, Qiezi pulled Yuejiang into the kitchen and said, "Tonight or tomorrow, she's going to die. You said her family has connections here? They will find out. That means the abbess wouldn't dare try to hide her death, right?"

"No. I know her. No matter how cruelly she treated Zhilu, she would never do that. She'll make up some story."

"The story will be she was beaten to death—by me—in revenge for being accused of poisoning her. The magistrate will come as soon as he hears of it. The abbess doesn't have to say anything. The nuns will come out with it. They will support her as they don't want any trouble, and the matter will be over and done with. We will still all be hauled off to the *yamen* for interrogation, but it's a foregone conclusion. The motive is too clear. So, I must leave."

"But even more suspicion will fall on you if you leave. You'll be the prime suspect!"

"I'm aware of that. But I'll be sentenced to death either way. I'd rather not be in custody when that happens. I'll be gone, and they won't find me."

"No. You might not be sentenced to death, given mitigating circumstances."

"I can't afford to be in custody."

"When will you leave?"

"Now."

"Now!" Yuejiang dropped her head in her hand. She looked around and up in thought, and said, "All right. I've decided. Let's go. I am going with you."

"Are you sure you understand what you're getting into? You will also be implicated if you flee with me."

"Yes. But they might see us."

"I already told the abbess I'm going into town to fetch medicine for Zhilu. Grab any money you have and meet me outside the gate. Don't bring anything else. I have the essentials we need. Walk normally and if anyone confronts you, say you're going to the apothecary with me. Keep walking and don't look back. Come right away. Don't take anything with you except money."

They both made it out of the temple safely and headed down the hill and out of the village.

"We must get as far from the temple today as possible. How long can you walk?" said Qiezi.

"I'm not sure. I'm not used to walking far."

"We'll sleep in the woods. I hope you can adapt to strange food and no bed for a while."

"No problem."

Yuejiang was struggling under the weight of something.

"What are you carrying?"

"I have two strings of cash in my robe."

"That's too heavy! I had no idea you had so much money. Let me carry one of them. We'll need to find a place to convert them to *taels*. I also have a *tael*. For the time being, we don't have to spend any money."

They found a shadowed spot to relieve one of the loops of cash from Yuejiang's robe: a thousand copper coins strung together through a hole in the middle. Qiezi slipped it under her robe over her shoulder. She opened her sack. In it were two cleavers and two tin bowls. "One cleaver is mine. The other is for you; I took it from the kitchen. You can't survive without one. I'll carry both for now. We can take over a kitchen somewhere and cook."

"Who would let you do that?"

Qiezi held a cleaver to Yuejiang's neck. "Who says anything about getting permission?"

Yuejiang stared.

Qiezi kissed her ear and whispered, "I'm joking."

"You scared me!"

After an hour of walking supported on Qiezi's arm, Yuejiang was limping.

"Your feet are already in bad shape? Hop on my back and let me carry you."

"I'm so embarrassed I can't keep up with you," she said as she wiped away a tear.

"I was waiting for you to come out with it. I wouldn't have let you go with me if I had problems with your feet. I used to run women around our village and up mountainsides like this for small change. You haven't built up your legs and ankles enough."

"How can you handle my weight plus two strings of cash?"

"I've carried heavier than you. I'll go as far as I can. You can try walking again after you've rested a bit. I want to keep going till dark. We can find a place in the woods for the night."

As they were passing through a village, Qiezi noticed an itinerant doctor who had set up a street stall, with a foldout table and a chest full of pharmaceuticals. She went over to have a look. Yuejiang had fallen asleep atop Qiezi but now got back on her feet.

"What's wrong with her?" said the doctor. "Cramping? She can't walk?"

"Do you have the *mantuoluo* flower?"

"What's that?"

"How about the celestial seeds flower?"

"What do you mean, the celestial seeds *flower*? Do you want the seeds or the flower?"

"The 'celestial seeds' is the name of the plant, *tianxianzi*, not the seeds. It's also called *langdang*. Don't you know it?"

"What do you need that for?"

"Never mind what it's for. Let me see what you have."

"What does a young girl like you know? Let me take care of her. I'm a doctor. Let me see her legs. I may have something better."

"Do you want my business or not?"

Annoyed, he rummaged around his cabinet and pulled out some tiny brown seeds. "Here are your 'celestial seeds.'"

Qiezi examined the seeds and smelled them. "Do you have *sanqi* root?"

"No."

"How about *huangbo* bark?"

"No. You don't want the seeds?"

"What kind of medicine is this? These are radish seeds."

"Are you questioning my judgment?"

"Let's go," Qiezi said to Yuejiang.

"You should at least buy the seeds, after all this fuss," said the doctor.

"I don't buy from quacks."

"You called me *what*? You dare to question my authority?" He struck Qiezi's arm with a small knife he had produced out of nowhere. "Now beat it, before I do worse to you," he said in a low voice.

Several male onlookers had approached, and one said, "Well, well, what do we have here? A couple of nuns with the nerve to be out and about by themselves? Got kicked out of your nunnery, did you?"

"They look to me more like prostitutes disguised as nuns," said another. "Doctor, are you letting them go without giving them a proper examination? That's why they came to see you, isn't it?"

"We can help you," snorted the first. "I bet they've got nothing on under those robes."

"I can get them to remove their robes without setting a finger on them," said a third, who grabbed a bucket off a night-soil cart a farmer was hauling by and hurled its contents onto Qiezi and Yuejiang as they were walking away. The crowd howled in laughter.

"Don't run," said Qiezi. "Keep walking and don't look back."

The crowd got distracted by the altercation that broke out between the ruffian and the farmer whose bucket of night soil he had stolen, enabling the girls, splattered with human excrement, to slip away. They backtracked across a field toward a creek they had passed and hid themselves in some bushes.

"When it gets dark, we can wash ourselves and the robes in the water. I have something to eat," said Qiezi, pulling out an onion and a bulb of garlic cloves. "It's not much but I'll forage for something later."

"How can we eat anything with this horrible smell?"

"The garlic and onion will ward it off. It's all my fault. I lost my temper at that quack. But I got so angry at his cheating. I shouldn't even have inquired. We hadn't prepared any cash. If I had bought something, how could I have removed the coins from the string without revealing how much money we had? And those were dangerous men. No telling what they might have done to us. I'm such an idiot!" She looked at the blood on her arm.

"He stabbed you?"

"It's only a nick."

"Now I see why you can't survive without a knife. We could have threatened them to make them back off."

"No. The cleavers are a last resort. Try to escape first. Flash knives around and they'll have the whole village after us. That's another problem caused by my idiocy. Now the village will know of us when the *yamen* runners come by inquiring about two fugitive nuns."

"We can't make clear decisions in this state," said Yuejiang.

Qiezi laid her head on Yuejiang's shoulder. Before they knew it, they had fallen asleep.

It was dark when they awoke. They soaked themselves and

their robes in the creek and sat back down to dry off. In the moonlight Qiezi scavenged for fungi, flowers, and edible larvae. "Yes, it's horrible to eat insects but put that out of your mind and eat. Trust me, they're safe and nourishing. We'll need all the strength we can get for the Hubei journey."

"How long is the journey?"

"We're close to the border—I asked on the road while you were asleep—but we have much further to go in Hubei itself. There's a direct route with fewer mountains, but people coming from there said all the towns and villages are burnt down and it's too dangerous."

"What's going on?"

"No idea. They said we could be killed if we're caught. So we have to go the long way along the river. It could take a week. At least."

"What medicine were you trying to buy from the quack?"

"That's what I wanted to talk to you about."

"Why we can't—"

"But I just thought of something. I have an idea. I don't why I didn't think of it before."

"Tell me."

"I'm poisonous."

"Ah?"

Qiezi explained how lifelong ingestion of the *mantuoluo*, the golden ocean flower, had addicted her to it. While she no longer experienced its visionary effects as before, she couldn't do without it and grew miserable and ill when deprived. Yet despite her body's thirsty need for more and more of the poison—in amounts that would fell a throng of ordinary mortals—she remained ever saturated with it, as her unfortunate rapists understood at death's door.

"That's also why I acted so stupidly today. I haven't been able to find any *mantuoluo* flowers, and it's making me muddled. I need to find some soon or I'll become even stupider. You can help me look for them. They're trumpet-shaped like a *suona* horn and white, yellow or purple. About this long. They look somewhat like morning glories."

"What were those 'celestial seeds' you were asking the quack about?"

"They're the same medicine but not as potent. The *langdang* flower is shorter and yellow with creepy-looking purple veins. It's even less common around here, but if we spot any I can use it. So that's why I can't kiss you. But maybe I can. I think my saliva contains less of the poison, and I wanted to be cautious with you the other day. The garlic we're eating will take care of that, though. It cleans the mouth. And how could I have forgotten, but garlic might cure your infection down there! And you know what else? I think the *mantuoluo* in my Yin lubrication can cure it as well, if we apply a tiny bit. Let's try the *mantuoluo* first. Here, kiss me and make me excited. If you don't mind my garlic breath."

"Mine too," said Yuejiang.

After embracing, Qiezi applied a dab of her secretions on her finger to Yuejiang's inflamed labia. "That's all we can do down there tonight, dear, until we're certain it works."

5

Purple Cloud Palace

When the path along the riverbank was level, they walked. Often the hillside's steep incline went right down to the river's edge and only by grabbing onto things could they proceed. Often there was no path at all and Yuejiang had to be born on her back. At some point—she had only been given rough directions—Qiezi had to decide it was time to break away from the river and head south straight into the mountains, and now it was time. From a distance one saw only the furry texture of pines and cypresses, which giants were rumored to recline on to take a nap. Qiezi wasn't considering giants but the mountains' positions in relationship to the stars, more reliable as a navigational tool than the sun's course across the sky.

Climbing wasn't the problem. Wherever she was, familiar territory or not, the mountains were her home, and the trees her friends. They greeted Qiezi with the most lavish apparel the season would allow; once in their midst they unspooled an intimate world of motley hues and smells. Under the hothouse canopy, the cotton rosemallow's virgin flowers were already blushing rouge over the course of the day, embarrassed by the lascivious scents spat out by the rutting caramel tree. It was not just for their shameless sensuality that Qiezi "collected" these trees in her encyclopedic mind but the real gifts they offered, their profusion of fruit and nuts, berries and bark. What she didn't eat or give to Yuejiang she added to her little pharmacopoeia. The nuts of the silver apricot tree whose leaves turned gold eased urination. The autumn blizzard of white flowers on the scholartree cleansed the blood and cured piles. The gall of the nutgall countered coughing, diarrhea and excessive bleeding of the womb. Oh, and there it was, just what she had her eye out for, the cork-tree bark whose tea would purify her companion of the foul nunnery water she had stewed in. It contained black soap, as did the seven-leaf tree also caught in the corner of her eye. Black soap aided against deadly diseases of the lung, liver, and stomach, and the afflictions of the vagina, but it had to be prepared with care because soap when ingested is toxic. The tallow tree produced by contrast a white soap, lamp oil, honey, and treated boils. The bright red leaves and bark of the sweet gum tree treated boils, carbuncles, arthritis, lumbago, oedema, oliguria, and lactation deficiency. And the majestic cinnamon tree softened the blood and the unlucky-day cramps, and seasoned meat.

The problem was determining the fastest route, as time was running out. A direct approach wouldn't necessarily save time, up and down and up and down when going round might cover the same ground faster. However, circumambulating mountains was pointless when the clefts and cleavages between them were relentlessly high. Without level land, one still had to climb, horizontally rather than vertically. Climbing Qiezi could do well enough. She preferred to leave the rice terraces behind and make a beeline for the steepest routes where there was scant human habitation and she could go naked, stark naked but for her indestructible sandals woven of kudzu vine, as naked and free as when she had been a little girl in the trees. Some of her neighbors back then were so poor a whole family shared a single shirt and pants and worked the fields without so much as a stitch on. She had to go naked now since Yuejiang couldn't hold on when Qiezi was climbing on territory so steep her hands had to take over, hauling twice her weight in flesh and copper up by roots and branches, advancing from vine to tree and tree to vine without setting foot on rock. And as her robe only got in the way, she fashioned it into a sling for Yuejiang, tying it under her arm and over her shoulder.

Certainly, a stray farmer poking around was liable to chance upon strange movement in the trees. A monkey? A big cat? No, it can't be: the gleaming amber flesh, the swinging tits of a naked female! But he'd better think twice about calling the men of the hamlet to come and capture the astonishing creature. By the time they had gathered, she would have left them far behind. And if by some ingenuity they had outpaced her and were waiting for her at the mountaintop, the first to try to grab her would witness his hand tumbling down through the trees, severed at the wrist by her cleaver.

"I'm thirsty," said Yuejiang.

"A waterfall is up ahead."

Yuejiang looked hard. "All the way over there on the next hill? How long will it take us to reach it?"

"Not until dark."

"How will you be able to find it?"

"I can find it."

Yuejiang was sobbing.

"Stop blubbering. I need water more than you do. Be patient."

Whether due to tiredness or the distraction of Yuejiang's complaint, as Qiezi jumped to the next tree she misjudged the thickness of the receiving branch. It bent low, snapped and they both dropped to the ground. Luckily the ground was close and Qiezi broke their fall.

"I can't go on! I can't keep on eating leaves and insects. You keep saying be patient but I'm just a big burden on you. I'm slowing you down and we'll never get anywhere like this. You go find the nunnery and leave me here to die!" cried Yuejiang through a flurry of tears.

"Shut up!" yelled Qiezi, slapping Yuejiang in the face. "I'm in charge here. You're going to the nunnery with me."

"How can you stand such a useless girl? Let me die, please!" sobbed Yuejiang.

"Don't you understand this is the best thing that could ever happen to you? You're learning how to survive. Nothing is more valuable than that. You need a lot more surviving to do, in fact. I've been too nice to you."

"Indeed, you have!"

Qiezi stood over her pointing. "Fine. You stay here and wallow in your tears. I'm going to find some water. I'll give you one day to catch up with me at the mouth of the waterfall. If you don't make it, tough luck!"

Yuejiang continued wailing.

"No, I have a better idea," said Qiezi, plopping herself down in front of Yuejiang and spreading her legs. "Lick me. Lick me here!" She grabbed Yuejiang by the hair and yanked her face into her groin. "Lick me! You always say you want to. Well now, do it! Lick me harder!"

Qiezi held Yuejiang's reddened face against her for several long minutes. Yuejiang stopped crying and Qiezi began rolling her hips.

"Still thirsty?"

"It's not dangerous?"

"It's dangerous, all right. You'll start feeling it soon. The only antidote is the star fruit, and I haven't seen any of that around here. Let's hope the gods are favorably inclined toward you!"

Collecting herself, Yuejiang sat up and kissed Qiezi on the mouth. But the new arrangement forced an abrupt change in their itinerary.

"We're going down to the waterfall's plunge pool. We can get there faster, in a couple hours, I think, though we'll lose time going back up the mountain tomorrow. You will need water before delirium sets in. We can sleep there tonight."

"Delirium!"

"You will know soon enough."

Before dark they reached the plunge pool. They drank, washing down nutritious white-skirt fungi made palatable by the tangy pulp of loquats Qiezi had snagged along the way. They hadn't been there for more than a few minutes when sleep began to sweep over them like a gust of wind. Qiezi caught herself and lifted her head. "Drink more water."

"I'm too exhausted," said Yuejiang.

"So am I."

"I'm dizzy and I think I'm going to throw up."

"Drink."

"Oh, I'm so dizzy. That high cliff is tilting over. It's going to fall on us."

"No, it's not. Now sleep, dear."

What she didn't tell her was that they would be climbing up the same mountain face in the morning.

Hours later, Qiezi awoke. She slapped Yuejiang on the cheek to rouse her and checked her pulse. Speedy heartbeat, dry mouth, feverish, and fast asleep.

Then Qiezi heard Yuejiang moaning. It was morning. Qiezi packed her limp figure in the sling and set off. Things did not get off to a good start. The dead weight on her back soon came to life, struggling to break out of the sling and knocking Qiezi off the tree she was perched on. The tree caught the sling and they were slung together, Qiezi hanging on one side of the branch and Yuejiang on the other. Yuejiang began attacking Qiezi on the face and chest.

"What are you doing? Stop it!"

"Oh, god, there's blood everywhere! Look, it's streaming out of me! I'm going to die. If you come at me with that disgusting thing of yours again, Mou Yushun, I will slice it off with the cleaver!" Yuejiang's nails renewed their assault.

Qiezi's head was caught between the branch and the sling. As she was being scratched and mauled, it took supreme effort to ease the sling away so that she could turn herself around and arrest Yuejiang by the arms. Once they were facing each other they both screamed: Yuejiang at Qiezi's blood-smeared face and

Qiezi at Yuejiang's chalk-white face, eyes dilated black, and her unrecognizable expression. It was a man's expression and voice.

"Calm down, Yuejiang, calm down! I am not Mou Yushun! Did he rape you?"

As suddenly as she had sprung to life, Yuejiang fell back into slumber. Qiezi sighed with relief. As she suspected, Yuejiang would live; the critical period had passed and her burst of frenzy was proof of that. She would live because Qiezi was losing her own deadliness. Unless she chanced upon the flower soon her life would drain away. She got right to work, methodically shifting the sling down the branch one node at a time until it rested against the trunk. With root strings severed from the tree above she bound Yuejiang in the sling and kept another string ready to gag her should she start shrieking again.

With Yuejiang secured to the trunk, Qiezi climbed back down to the plunge pool to wash the blood off her face and chest. She saw in the pool's mirror a web of cuts and bruises but no gushing gashes. Now tidied up, the naked mountain girl resumed carrying the swaddled lotus-feet girl up the vertical mountainside tree by tree.

For three long days Qiezi bore the insensate lady on her back, her occasional outbursts growing more muted. Through the trees she espied her first pilgrims wending their way along trails on the facing mountain. The girls were on the right track. Also in the distance, the telltale cluster of Wudangshan's five peaks— confirming the mountain temples to be in reach. They were still high up and out of the way enough to keep their journey secret. It would be unthinkable for Qiezi to appear before pilgrims or peasants, not to mention brigands, in her present state. However, she needed directions to the Nanyan temple complex halfway up the mountain. If only Yuejiang would wake up and get her strength back so they could walk together. Well, that settled it. Getting her out of the sling and into her own robe, Qiezi hiked Yuejiang on her back, tying her arms together under her breasts and holding her by the thighs. With her head drooping on her shoulder, the girl appeared to be asleep rather than unconscious.

It was time to descend and join the pilgrimage.

Once she had made it onto the busy route, Qiezi queried an approaching pair of middle-aged women. "Elder sisters, is this the way to Nanyan Palace?"

"*Nimen zenmele?*" said one, worriedly looking down at Qiezi's feet where a pool was forming.

Qiezi could now feel Yuejiang's hot urine flowing over her buttocks and legs. "Oh, no! Oh, heavens. She's been feeling a bit sick. It looks like she lost control of her bladder."

"It's about two hours to Nanyan if you're fast," said the other. "Yes, you'd better get the girl there as soon as you can. They have doctors. What happened to your face?"

"We'll be all right," said an exasperated Qiezi as she sped off with her ill companion, trailing a stream of golden liquid behind them and drawing looks from other pilgrims. The elder sisters too continued to stare. Yet Qiezi was joyous. After three days of holding it in—a symptom of *mantuoluo* poisoning—Yuejiang would soon be coming to. And a short while later she mumbled, "Where are we?"

"If you had any idea what you put me through, you bad girl."

"I don't understand."

"You have no memory of what happened?"

"No."

Qiezi kissed her. "I'll explain later. Keep resting. I need to move fast so we can reach Nanyan before dark."

"What's Nan—what happened to your face?"

"I'll tell you later. The nunnery."

"We're already there?"

"Well, no. In fact, I don't know where Gu Jingjing's nunnery is. There are thirty-six nunneries on the mountain."

"Thirty-six!"

"She didn't know either. Her sect isn't formally recognized, and it's only being temporarily hosted at one of the nunneries."

"How could she find it, then?"

"She told me they would ask around with a code phrase that could only be used once, so it's of no use to us. They'll find it—

she and another girl she went with; I forget her name. They know someone there."

"How in the world will *we* ever find it?"

"She said once she found it, she would leave a message for me with the keeper of the Golden Pavilion on the mountain summit. But they're only a few days ahead of us and may not have even arrived there yet. I'm assuming they took the direct and dangerous route. I hope they made it."

"She can read and write?"

"Yes, she's from a good family."

"Why is she not still with her family?"

"She didn't say. She begged me to come with her. She grabbed me and had tears in her eyes when I refused. She said she would forever keep up hope I would change my mind."

"Is she…"

"Yeah."

"Have you two…"

"No. I only knew her for a couple days."

"She knows about your flower problem?"

"No. I fear she's going to be jealous and upset when she sees you with me."

"Is she pretty?"

Qiezi nodded.

Upon reaching Nanyan Palace, a gatekeeper took one look at them and refused entrance. "Go ask some beggar women back in the village if you're new to begging here."

"We are not beggars. We only want a little water and food after the long journey before we head for the Golden Pavilion."

"You'll never make it today. It's 20,000 steps to the summit and very steep! What business do you have there?"

"Please tell us where water is available and we can rest for a bit."

"Go further along that path and you'll find a small cave called the God of Thunder Cave. That's where a Daoist hermit lives and maybe he can help you."

"How do we reach the summit?"

"You have to go the opposite way, down the hill that way."

"That goes to the top?"

"Yes. You descend first before the climb begins. You'd better wait till tomorrow."

They found the cave. Sitting at a table by the entrance in his blue robe and cap and long wispy beard, the hermit was writing calligraphy with such stillness and composure they thought he was a life-size plaster model.

"*Daozhang*, may we come in?" said Qiezi.

He nodded once, without turning his head.

"We've been traveling for days. My companion is recovering from an illness. We need some food and water. I promise you we are not beggars. Tomorrow we will ascend to the summit and later go to a nunnery."

"What's wrong with her?"

"She ate something bad along the way and got poisoned. She's fine now and only needs a little rest." Qiezi eased Yuejiang down on a stone ledge in the cave.

"*Daozhang*, we're very grateful to you for your kindness," said Yuejiang in a weak voice.

"Oh, you have a well in here?"

"It's spring water and you can drink right from it with the ladle. What happened to your face?"

"I fell. We've had a tough journey. We're hungry."

"Where are you coming from?"

"South Shaanxi."

"You walked all the way here?"

"Yes."

"Are you educated? Can you read and write?"

"I can," said Qiezi.

"Write your name down here."

She applied brush to paper.

"You write acceptably. Mantuoluo. That's not your real name."

"I'm looking for the flower."

"You can sleep on that ledge tonight. I'll be back with some food. Let me have a closer look at you," the hermit said to

Yuejiang. "Do you need medicine? A priest in the shrine close by makes medicine. He may have something."

"Can I go with you then?" said Qiezi. "I have medical knowledge. I want to see what he has. Her body has cleared the poison, but her feet are in bad shape. Her ankles haven't built up strength yet and are very sore."

Up at the shrine, a cauldron in an adjoining room simmered with a noxious black soup being boiled down to a paste to be pressed into disks for adhering to various parts of the body.

"I see you're making medicated plasters. Can I ask what herbs you're using?" Qiezi asked the priest.

"It depends on what part of the body you need it for."

"Pain relief in the calves and feet."

He showed her a shelf filled with variously labeled plasters and picked out one. "This is for swelling in the muscles, relaxing the tendons, and activating the collaterals. And this one is for repairing tendons damaged from injury or trauma."

"What are you making in the cauldron now? What's in it?"

"A lot of things. Angelica, atractylodes, safflower, rhubarb, myrrh...frankincense...lovage rhizome...calomel...."

"Those herbs form the base of most medicated plasters," said Qiezi.

"Of course, different medicines suit different symptoms. But I know what you're thinking. The plasters aren't all from the same batch."

"You have nothing better for healing? Such as the three-seven root? Or for pain? The celestial seeds? The golden ocean flower?"

"Angelica and corydalis for pain. Poppy seeds and hemp seeds when they're available. How do you know so much about this? And what happened to your face?"

"How much does one plaster cost?"

"For the cheapest, that would be fifty cash."

"I have no money."

"I can't give them away, you know."

"I fell. I need something for my chest as well." Qiezi opened her robe.

"In all my years of preparing medicine for women," said the priest, "you are the very first to expose yourself. No woman would ever allow me to touch any part of her body *over* her clothes, much less under her clothes." He pulled out a little ivory statuette of a nude female reclining on her side. "We use this medical doll to point to where your symptoms are."

"I don't think she's revealing herself for your pleasure," said the hermit.

"We haven't bathed in days. I don't want it to become infected. Do you have salves?"

"I have a salve. I can give you a little. It's made of white wax and has pine oil, ginger, musk, camphor, borneol, and dragon's blood. But you shouldn't apply it on fresh wounds."

"They're already scabs. You do it. My hands are dirty."

"How in the world did you get these cuts from a fall?" said the priest as he spread the salve on Qiezi's breasts.

Back in the cave, the girls feasted on rice porridge and freshly picked shiny black plums.

"Are you going up to the summit in those soiled rags of yours? They smell bad. The whole cave smells," said the hermit.

"We don't have anything else. Can we use your well water to wash them?"

"What will you cover yourselves with while they're hanging out to dry? They should be burned, not washed. I'll inquire with the priest if he can dig out something else for you to wear."

"Oh, we would be so happy. We can't thank you enough," said Yuejiang.

"I see you have a bathing basin. Do you mind if we bathe?" said Qiezi.

"What? Here? In front of me? Oh, heavens."

"We'll be fast. You don't have to look at us."

The hermit went back to his calligraphy. As Yuejiang was squatting in the basin, the priest entered.

"I brought you several plasters. You don't have to pay for them—oh, I'm sorry. I didn't realize. I'll come back later."

"It doesn't matter," said Qiezi.

"They insisted on bathing," said the hermit. "Can you find them anything to wear? Their robes are filthy and soiled and not fit to be worn anymore."

"I'm not sure. I'll go see. I'll be back shortly."

Qiezi removed her robe and the two strings of cash.

"What's that? Cash?" asked the hermit. "Two intact strings of cash? You carried that over the mountains? I thought you said you had no money."

"I don't want to open the string just to buy a small item. We had planned to exchange the cash for *taels* but couldn't find a place to do it."

"You thought you could find a money shop in the mountains?"

"The money might come in handy where we're going. I can't explain now."

"You carried that girl *and* two strings of cash over the mountains all the way from Shaanxi? Are you out of your mind?"

"I'm stubborn," said Qiezi. "I'll open one of the strings now and pay you and the priest for the medicine and clothes and your hospitality. You're the first person we've encountered who's been...kind to us." She started crying.

"She's from the mountains and is very strong and capable," said Yuejiang. "She could carry you."

"I can see you're both exhausted," said the hermit. "I don't need your money. I don't know about the priest."

"Come on, baby, let's get cleaned up before he returns," said Yuejiang, leading Qiezi over to the bathing pan.

When the priest returned, the hermit told him they could pay him from one of their strings of cash.

"All I could find were these small-sized men's cotton pants and tunics," he said. "But it shouldn't matter for the time being. No one will bother you going up the mountain. Try them on and give me the robes to dispose of. I don't need any money."

Though the clothes hung a bit capaciously on their frames, they were very pleased and proud and wore them to bed. They fell instantly asleep.

In the morning more porridge was waiting for them, but the

girls remained asleep for most of the day. Even after awakening in the late afternoon, they were still too tired to get back on their feet. Not until the day after did they depart, after many thanks to the hermit.

Built by the Yongle Emperor 372 years earlier, the 20,000 rugged stone steps to the top would normally have been a snap for Qiezi, even with two strings of cash and Yuejiang on her back. The higher and steeper ascents also had stone railings. But she had become a great deal weaker, the grinding weeks having caught up with her. And there was another, graver reason: the dearth of the golden ocean flower and her body's rebellion against this outrage. She could no longer carry Yuejiang. They climbed laboriously, stopping off at each landing to rest and taking a day to scale an extent manageable by a healthy individual in a few hours.

The Golden Pavilion was no larger than a bedroom, and the faithful could only prostrate themselves at the entrance before the bronze god, Zhen Wu. Constructed from twenty tons of copper, the elegant structure was carried all the way to the mountaintop from Beijing. But to Qiezi, blazing more brightly than the two-tiered flared roof gilded in 300 kilograms of sun-kissed gold was a mundane bamboo slat of the sort hung on restaurant walls listing the dishes on offer, which the keeper produced for her after rummaging around his booth. On it were eight characters written in golden ink:

曼陀羅紫霄宮晶晶

"I found it! They're here, they made it!" she exclaimed. "They're at the Purple Cloud Palace. Where is that?"

They were told they had to go all the way back down past Nanyan to reach the palace. Since it was already evening, they descended only as far as Taihe palace, where a *zhaitang* provided tofu soup with cabbage and rice and they found space to sleep on a temple floor.

Getting an early start, they reached Purple Cloud Palace by noon. They were confused to discover it wasn't a nunnery but a monastery, until a priest pointed to a nuns' quarters through a side door in the courtyard. Appearing with a senior nun, Gu Jingjing was overjoyed to see them. She had intense, close-set eyes on a long narrow face, and her hair was cut short, like a boy's, rather than shaved like a Buddhist nun. Introducing Yuejiang, Qiezi explained they had fled the awful nunnery almost as soon as she had arrived. She asked Jingjing about her own journey.

"Oh, it was terrifying. All the cities and towns along the way were abandoned or burnt down. We had to scavenge for food and found almost nothing. We were all skin and bones and only now beginning to recover. From what we could piece together from people fleeing, there was rebel activity last spring. Local troops and their hired thugs are still combing through the area killing people at random as suspected rebel sympathizers. White Lotus rebels."

"What are White Lotus rebels?"

"No idea. We couldn't go back and thankfully made it here alive last week. We were running and hiding in forests. Our clothes got torn and we had to tie them together with twigs. We're now properly attired again, as you can see! But you two look exhausted. Come on in, let's find you something to eat."

"You should have seen the state of *our* clothes. A priest donated these men's clothes to us only yesterday. Oh, and there you are—I'm so embarrassed I forgot your name!" said Qiezi to a calm-faced girl who had stepped up, with a braid draped over her chest. How could this same girl have survived such a journey and look so composed? she thought.

"Qiu Lu'er. I remember you, Mantuoluo."

Over lunch they were joined by Ren An, the senior nun, and a woman whose clear face and close-cropped hair belied her age.

"You've met Ren *daozhang*. And this is Xie Yinhe," said Jingjing. "She is our leader."

Qiezi and Yuejiang seemed unsure who to defer to first and bowed to both at once.

"Call me Mistress Xie. Ren *daozhang* belongs to the temple and manages the nuns. She has kindly agreed to host us."

Ren had a topknot and was enrobed in the usual dark blue, while Xie, Jingjing, and Lu'er wore immaculate lotus-purple tunics over apricot-colored pants of matching thin cotton. If Jingjing was disconcerted to see Mantuoluo with so beautiful a travel mate, she didn't show it. Lu'er was quiet and observant. Where Ren was placid and gracefully inscrutable, Xie was lively and endearing.

"Why haven't you all shaved your heads?" said Qiezi.

They looked confused for a moment. Yuejiang giggled.

"This isn't a Buddhist temple!" said Xie. "It's Daoist. Daoist nuns don't shave their heads. Except for Ren *daozhang*, we are not nuns. We're healers. Jingjing has told me about you, Mantuoluo. She says you're very knowledgeable about herbs and medicines and you're literate," she said.

"I studied with a local apothecary."

"He had time for you?"

"I supplied most of his medicines."

"How?"

"Foraging."

"I see. How did you survive the passage here? Where did you stay and what did you eat?"

"Foraging."

"Heavens," said Ren. "How did *you* manage with your lotus feet?"

"I was carried most of the time," said Yuejiang.

"She *carried* you?"

"I want to give you both something. It's now time to part with this burden. Forgive me for exposing myself," said Qiezi as she removed her tunic.

Ren and Xie appeared too stunned at the particulars of their journey to take in at first what she was removing from her torso.

"What happened to your breasts?" said Jingjing.

"Two strings of cash? Where did you get this money?" asked Xie. "Don't tell me you brought it all the way from Shaanxi!"

Qiezi handed one string of cash to Ren and the other to Xie.

"Oh, goodness," said Ren. "This is a fine donation but it's not required."

"I'll be back in a few minutes," said Xie. "I want to show you something, Mantuoluo."

While Xie was gone, the four girls recounted more of their respective travails. Xie returned with a polished wooden box containing several rows of drawers. She pulled out one drawer and handed it to Qiezi. It contained slices of something translucent, wafer-thin and dark red in the middle. "Can you identify this?"

"That's velvet antler. It tonifies the kidney and bone marrow. It promotes Yang and men's virility but women can benefit too from Yang replenishment. We could use some of that now."

"How about this?" The second drawer contained shriveled chunks of grayish yellow roots.

"Oh, the three-seven root! I've been looking for that. It's the best medicine for stopping bleeding."

"It's from Yunnan."

"But it's not that fresh."

"And this?" The third drawer held what looked like shiny dark stones as big as mushroom caps.

"That's the Yin-Yang fruit of the Chinaberry tree. It's for blood circulation and nourishes woman's Yin and Qi, but it's toxic if too much is taken."

In the fourth drawer were coiled yellow-green spirals of some kind of twig or leaf. Qiezi picked out a few buds with her fingers and smelled them. "*Shihu*. It's for people fond of wine, as long as their liver isn't in too bad shape. It grows in this region; I saw it."

"We grow it here, out back in the herb garden."

"That must be why it's curled. The wild version is more potent, because it absorbs more nutrients from other plants. It clears heat and nourishes Yin."

In the fifth drawer were pale yellow dried bulbs.

"*Tianma* tubers. Also good for Yin. They reduce swelling in the lower limbs for those with the 'thirsty' disease. It treats headaches and dizziness."

The sixth drawer revealed a mess of leaves and shriveled gray stems.

"Horny goat weed. Makes men's jade stem stand and one of the best medicines for women's Yang deficiency. Also dispels wind and dampness and cures cloudy-eye disease."

In the seventh drawer were shriveled brownish yellow tubers.

"Sealwort. Good for swelling and inflammation of the joints. Another good medicine for the thirsty disease."

"All right, that's enough. You've convinced me. We could use someone like you to help tend our herb garden," said Xie.

"You could make better use of me by letting me out into the forests to forage. Look what I picked up on the way here."

Qiezi spread out on the table an array of dried flowers, seeds and bark from her cloth kit, explaining each of them in turn.

"Let us think about that."

Qiezi looked through the rest of the medicine cabinet and said, "Are these all the medicines you have?"

"No, I have a lot more."

"Mistress Xie is renowned throughout the mountain for her medicinal knowledge," said Ren.

"Do you have atractylodes? It's for Yuejiang. Her *yindao* got infected. I've picked up some cork-tree and scholartree bark but haven't been able to prepare them without proper implements and boiled water. Mixing in atractylodes will boost the effects."

"And the berries of the five-flavor vine," Xie added. "Let me have a look at her."

"It's a lot better than it was when I was at the nunnery. I got it from the dirty water we were forced to bathe in," said Yuejiang.

"Yes, diseases of the *yindao* are often hard to treat, since one symptom gives rise to another. You need to defeat them together once and for all. It looks fine on the outside but it's swollen on the inside. We'll try applying some golden larch," said Xie.

"What's golden larch?" asked Qiezi.

"Hah! Caught you on that one. A plant you don't know about. Naturally, since you won't find it around here. It's from Zhejiang Province."

"How did you acquire it from so far away?"

"You can get anything if you pay for it."

"What I'm looking for most of all is the golden ocean flower. The *mantuoluo* flower. It grows back home but I haven't seen it anywhere the whole way here."

"The same as your name. Why?"

"It's a powerful medicine with many properties. It kills pain and induces sleep. I need it. You don't know of it?"

"Of course, I know it. A temple gardener has been keeping a supply of it, I think. I don't use it as medicine since it's very dangerous if not prepared right. It's poisonous."

"I have long experience in preparing it. Take me to him this evening."

"You two need to rest after your long journey. You both don't look so good. I'll inquire about it tomorrow and let you know."

"*Please.* I need it. It's very important to me. I'll explain later. I won't be able to sleep tonight unless I see it."

"But why do you need it? Are you in pain? And why this evening?"

"The flowers exhale in the evening."

"I'm not acquainted with the gardener that well, and I'm afraid he'll have retired to his quarters by then."

"If he's growing the flower, he'll be eager to show it off."

Jingjing and Lu'er led Qiezi and Yuejiang to the sleeping quarters and got them settled in. They napped, were shown around the nuns' quarters and dined with the nuns. Xie then escorted Qiezi to a distant part of the temple and the garden in question.

It took the gardener, an old monk, a moment to recollect Xie. He seemed to regard their intrusion with suspicion but agreed to show them around.

"I can already smell them. Oh, my dear ones, it's been so long!" gasped Qiezi upon spotting a row of dozens of the erect white trumpets-within-trumpets tinged with violet. "They're double-nested! You have double-nested *mantuoluo*! Where did you find them?"

"That's a secret."

"Can I have one?"

"What are you going to do with it?" said the gardener.

She responded by plucking one of the flowers and popping it in her mouth.

"What are you doing? You can't do that! It's poisonous! Spit it out now!"

Qiezi grabbed another five flowers and began stuffing them in her mouth.

"You fool! You idiot!" yelled the gardener. "Get the flowers out of her mouth," he yelled at Xie. "She will die!"

"Spit them out, Mantuoluo!" said Xie.

Qiezi backed away from them as she chomped on and swallowed the flowers. Xie and the monk reached for her, but she shot away as fast as a bird and was gone.

"I'm sorry. I had no idea she would do that!" said Xie, at a loss.

"Who is she? Is she trying to end her life? We have a problem on our hands. And I'll be blamed for it! We must find her and purge her stomach."

"She's new and only arrived today. She told me she was experienced with this plant and desperate to see it."

"I don't care how much she knows about it. Nobody can consume so much and survive!"

Xie knew that even with the nuns fanning out through the multiple levels and labyrinthine passageways of the vast temple, it would take all the priests and workers they could mobilize to locate Mantuoluo in time to save her life. However, Yuejiang promptly filled her in, and she relaxed. Not only would she not die, she'd be illuminated by the flower. You might even see her Qi spouting out of her.

"This must be kept quiet from Ren *daozhang*," Xie told them. "Where's Jingjing?" she asked Qiu Lu'er.

"I have no idea."

Still, they had to find Mantuoluo. It was the distant melody of a bamboo flute that drew Yuejiang to the Hall of the Sixty, across from the grand Hall of the Father and Mother. In it stood the gilt star goddess with her three eyes, four heads, and eight arms, surrounded by sixty life-size painted human-gods arrayed in yellow robes and perched on pedestals, each offering a desired destiny. Behind one row of pedestals and out of view of the flautist priest they found Jingjing and Mantuoluo embracing and kissing. Mantuoluo turned to them with a triumphant look. They escorted the young couple out.

Back at the nuns' quarters, Yuejiang pulled Qiezi aside. "Isn't kissing her on the mouth reckless and irresponsible?"

"I kept my mouth closed. I told her why."

"Will you abandon me now?"

"No, why should I?"

"You love her, don't you?"

"Why should that mean I want to abandon you? I have both of you. Your task now is to love each other."

Later, as Xie started off to visit the old gardener to tell him the good news, he himself came running up in an agitated state. "They're all gone! My flowers are all gone! She's a witch!"

"What flowers?" said Xie.

"My *mantuoluo* flowers. All of them, gone! We need to find the witch and kill her!"

"Why do you call her a witch?"

"No person could survive what she ate and live. She came back to life and stole them. She must be a witch, a fox spirit, and she returned to steal my flowers. I'm going to the temple authorities now to tell them so we can hunt her down, and you're going to help us. They will not be too pleased to have a witch in their midst!"

The gardener dashed off toward the temple interior. Ren *daozhang* had appeared and saw the gardener's fury. "What's going on? Who was he talking about? The new girl?"

"It's all a misunderstanding!" said Xie. "She ate the gardener's poisonous *mantuoluo* flowers to satisfy some addiction she has. He thinks that because she didn't die, she must be a witch. She's right here with us. She can't be a witch."

Jingjing and Lu'er came running up. "But she's not here. She's gone."

"She must be aware she will be apprehended. Maybe she *is* a witch," said Ren. "If she returns, we'll tie her up. I know how to tell if she's a witch or not. If she is indeed a witch, we'll turn her over to the authorities. If she's not, we'll hide her until this all blows over."

They were assembled on a veranda outside the temple wall at the back entrance of the nuns' quarters. Yuejiang had joined them. She was standing below a pomelo tree when she noticed some wood shavings falling upon her. She caught herself, resisting the urge to glance up into the branches.

"And if she doesn't return?" said Xie.

Turning to Yuejiang, they asked, "Do you know where she is? Is she a witch?"

"She is not a witch. She is not a fox. She'll return when she's ready. I really had no idea things would turn out like this. But she is not a witch."

Just then the gardener appeared with three men bearing hoes. "We want to search your quarters for the witch."

"That's not allowed," said Ren. "No men are allowed inside. No men have ever been allowed inside."

"I have it on the authorities' instructions to search your quarters."

"I don't believe you. Not until they appear to me here in person could I ever permit this."

One of the men now spotted Qiezi up in the tree. She was whittling a severed branch with a cleaver. Next to her lay a stack of chiseled branches.

"There she is, the witch! Come down here at once so we can kill you. Or we will have to climb up and do it," said the gardener.

"Mantuoluo, what are you doing?" said Xie.

Qiezi wiped the sharpened point of the branch with a leaf before speaking. Casually she said, "These spears are for hunting wild boars. They can pierce right through a boar's body with ease. And if I so much as prick the boar, it will quickly die from the juice of the crow's head flower I'm coating it with."

Ren turned to the gardener. "It's clear to me you haven't told the authorities. For your own safety," she added with a nod toward Qiezi, "you'd better leave now and not mention this affair to anyone, which will cause you more trouble than us."

6

The obscene temple

s the clear sun, the soft breeze, and the bright moon complement each other, so do the five spirits of intelligence, intention, temperament, energy, and soul.

The Hymn to the Five Spirits sung and the Eternal Venerable Mother prayed to on bamboo mats around a long low table in Sai'er's house, they set to a communal repast of spiced stewed tofu, legumes steamed in rice, boiled greens and sweet potato seedlings, bamboo shoots and taro root, and other surprises the guests all had a hand in. Even fish was on offer, not forbidden by this congregation, silver carp from the river broiled in noodles and peppers. The lavish hostess (at least in such a devotional context) topped it off, of course, with Shaoxing wine. She sat at the kitchen end of the table, while at the head sat the Mistress, Zou Run, and twenty predominantly female congregants. Except for Yan Xian and Lai Xinru, all wore flowing white gowns.

"Today is auspicious," announced Sai'er, "because we have a new couple to initiate. Our first initiation in this the Year of the Dragon!"

"Here's to the dragon qualities of power, strength and good luck," chimed in Zou Run. Hair bound in a jadestone cap, the stocky, deep-voiced Mistress was handsome and could toast like a man. "*Ganbei*!"

"*Ganbei*!" cheered all in unison, pointing their tiny ceramic cups at the blessed couple.

"We're very grateful for your hospitality, and we're eager to learn the healing rites," said Xinru. "Eternal and Venerable Mother in our original home in the world of true emptiness!"

Everyone echoed the mantra.

"We'll be starting as soon as we've cleaned up," said Zou Run. "Sai'er dear, should we go upstairs for the initiation or perform it here?"

"Right here. Last time were different circumstances and not needed this evening," said Yin Yan.

"Oh, yes. I forgot. I presume that's the only thing on the agenda tonight?" said Zou Run.

Though a few years younger than Sai'er, Yin Yan's supple movements indicated she had been around long enough to attain a privileged status. Her hairstyle and face were striking: hair bound in a bun but for bangs cut high across her forehead and three braids dangling from each temple; and the kind of slanted eyebrows that inadvertently made her look angry, which she countered with an honest gaze and a ready smile. She could control people with her eyes.

The dishes cleared and tablecloths bundled up, the table was revealed to consist merely of two sturdy wooden cots of woven bamboo padding placed end to end. Already Yin Yan and Sai'er were helping Xinru and Yan Xian out of their clothes. "You two lie down on the cots face up," said Sai'er.

"Everything off?" blushed Xinru.

"Everything off," said Zou Run. "Doff that pride of yours with your clothes. By turning your body over to us we can heal you. It's only hard the first time. As soon as you realize your body is not your own but belongs to everyone, it will all make sense. You're in good hands."

"Shouldn't a proper woman commit suicide to preserve her honor if a strange man so much as sees her naked? There are five other men in this room besides my husband!"

The congregants laughed. This shocked Xinru more than her nakedness.

"Don't believe those old fables. Of course, in public we must play-act and affect female modesty. But you're safe here."

Half the congregants sat before the cots cross-legged on mats. The other half circled around until a signal from Zou Run to halt; each then sat behind the person in front of them and began to massage them beneath their garments. Sai'er spread a thin layer of oil over Yan Xian, and Yin Yan likewise over Xinru. They unveiled a cabinet filled with blue-and-white porcelain jars in a variety of shapes and sizes. Each took one of the jars and affixed something inside—moxa wool—which they lit over the bare flame of an oil lamp. They then slid and pushed the open end of the jars over the couple's torsos in a circular motion, digging into their flesh. Smoke leaked out of small holes in the jars.

"Do you see how thin the jar's rim is?" said Sai'er, getting Yan Xian to run his finger over it. "It's the same thickness as a *guasha* plate used for scraping."

"I've heard of scraping. Does this have the same effect?"

"This *is* scraping." Turning to everyone she said, "What does scraping do?"

"Opens the meridians, dredges the collaterals, purges blood stasis, loosens the muscles, and reduces swelling," they chanted in unison.

"Notice that we can press harder when the edge is circular," Sai'er continued. "A straight edge might injure or cut the skin using the same pressure. The extra pressure massages the muscles as we're scraping. See here where your skin is turning red? It will stay purplish for a couple days. It's not painful, right?"

"A little uncomfortable but not so bad."

"What's the heat and the smoke for?" said Xinru.

"That's *aicao* from the mugwort plant—moxibustion. What does moxibustion do, everyone?"

"Dispels cold and dampness, warms Yang, tonifies Qi, nourishes the blood, and soothes the muscles," said all on cue.

"Usually we start with massage, followed by traditional scraping and moxibustion. But this three-in-one *qiankun* jar—the heaven-and-earth jar—saves time for our purposes this evening."

The initiates' marks and blotches proliferated under the curious porcelain device.

"Can't medicinal herbs have the same curative effects?" said Yan Xian.

"Yes, of course," said Zou Run. "We combine medicine and body work, though medicines must be matched with specific maladies. Alas, nobody here has that pharmaceutical expertise, except for a few basics, such as Sai'er's medicinal wine," she said, pointing to a large ceramic jug.

"It contains deer antler, deer blood, bear and snake bile, black wolfberries, mulberries, and ginseng steeped in aged maize spirits," Sai'er confirmed.

"What's it for?"

"To make you and your wife more *se*." Everyone giggled at this. "But I only prepared it in summer and it won't be ready until winter. It contains too much heat when the weather is warm." Turning to Zou Run, she added, "They tell me their daughter is versed in medicines, but she's up in Shaanxi staying with relatives."

Yin Yan paused her scraping. "How did she learn?"

"She studied with an apothecary from when she was little," said Xinru. "And ended up knowing more than him."

"How old is she?"

"Seventeen."

"Only seventeen?"

"She foraged all his medicines and can read medical books."

Yin Yan looked intrigued. "Bring her here."

"It's not possible now. We hope to eventually."

"Now for the fun part," said Sai'er. They pulled out more porcelain jars and placed them atop the cabinet. Two of these looked like large bowls or globes that narrowed at the top. "What does *baguan*—cupping—do, everyone?"

"Opens the meridians, tonifies the blood, dredges toxins, reduces inflammation, and counters pain."

"Very good. Look again at how thin and delicate the jars and cups are," Sai'er pointed out to Xinru. "They were made in Jingdezhen. Typically glazed ceramics or bamboo cups are used but these are better."

Yin Yan held one of the big jars over the flame for a few moments and shifted it to Xinru's chest. It sucked up an entire breast. She repeated the same with the other breast.

"Like magic, eh?" she said to a baffled Xinru. "Don't worry, they won't fall off. They're held in place by suction and, look, I can't even pull them off. Also, see the translucent dimples in the jar? They're turning red. That's the color of your breasts now."

In the meantime, Sai'er brandished a tube-shaped porcelain jar in one hand, while oiling up Yan Xian's manhood in the other. When he was tumescent and half erect, she applied the cylinder to the flame and transferred it to his penis, guiding it though the open end. His shaft expanded and bulged against the rim to form a tight fit. Sai'er slid the cylinder up and down the lower portion of his shaft. "That's your blood being pulled to the surface of your jade stem. We'd better call it a ruby stem! Don't release yourself. You need to hold it in. This is training in male longevity. Every time you expel your *jing*—your essence—you shave days, weeks off your life. If you feel you can't control it, I'll stop."

"You'd better stop now," said Yan Xian, as red-faced as his ruby stem.

Sai'er squeezed his shaft at its base but it was too late and he shuddered. His guilty essence poured out as she removed the jar. She gave him a playful slap on the face. "*Wa sai!* So much! That's a whole year off your life, naughty boy!"

More laughter.

As Sai'er cleaned him up, Yin Yan pried the jars off Xinru's breasts with her fingers under the rims. Sai'er took one of these jars and firing it up again, placed it over Yan Xian's entire groin, penis and scrotum.

Yin Yan fired up another tubular jar. She told Xinru to open her legs and fastened the tube over her clitoris. "You don't have any *jing* to lose, but you do have your precious pearl and an endless supply of Yin. Inside your jade gate is a spongy spot on the front surface, your milk fruit." She slid her fingers into Xinru's vagina and stroked upwards. "Do you feel it?"

Too embarrassed to yell out in pleasure, Xinru gasped and jerked her hips as Yin Yan brought her to high tide.

"Now it's time to do your backs. Xinru, we'll start with you since I want Yan Xian to watch," said Sai'er.

Zou Run directed the congregants to switch partners with those sitting in front of them. As Sai'er rubbed tea-tree oil over Xinru's back and legs to disinfect and ease the flesh, Yin Yan assembled enough porcelain jars for two people, seventy-two cups in all, the size and shape of apples. She handed Sai'er a heated cup, who glided it over Xinru's flesh as with the moxa jar but faster, crisscrossing the back and pulling the cup off with a pop. This was repeated with several more cups. Sai'er then pricked Xinru's skin with a lancet in five places along both sides of her spine, and Yin Yan plugged heated cups over each spot. As these "wet" cups filled with blood from the incisions, more rows of "dry" cups (minus incisions) were affixed to the rest of her back, buttocks and legs. Soon she was covered with thirty-six cups.

"Look, Yan Xian. The dimples on the dry cups are turning red, but those on the wet cups are turning black, with black blood."

"I have to undergo this too?" he asked.

"What is she doing to me?" said Xinru.

"See, she didn't feel a thing," said Sai'er.

"She's dredging you of stagnant blood filled with toxins and waste," said Zou Run.

"How do you feel?" said Yin Yan.

"No problem, I guess. Relaxed."

After a few minutes, Yin Yan lifted the wet cups off one by one, revealing a jellied layer of spent blood under each, which Sai'er scraped off with a *guasha* plate. The dry cups by contrast revealed round puffs of reddened flesh like mushroom caps that collapsed back as soon as the cups were dislodged. When all the cups were removed, thirty-six circles remained. Sai'er wiped Xinru down with a cloth soaked in strong spirits. Her ten cuts had stopped bleeding.

"How long will those circles remain?" said Yan Xian.

"A couple days, a week. The darker the circles, the more toxins were dredged. Now, sit up Xinru and let me look at your breasts. Oh, yes, here we are. See the brown spots along the undersides? More toxins." She turned to Yan Xian. "Your turn."

When Yan Xian's cupping was finished, he and Xinru were presented with their own fresh white gowns, capping off their initiation. Everyone cheered and clapped and downed another toast.

"For our next meeting—should we hold it here, Sai'er, or at my place?" said Zou Run.

"Your place next time. I'm sure our new members will be eager to see it. It's bigger and more comfortable than mine."

"What's going to happen?" said Xinru.

"Well, we haven't performed the 'deep valley' exercises for some time," said Zou Run. She lowered her voice to a mock whisper: "Or the 'uniting Yin and Yang' exercises."

The male congregants cheered. The females covered their smiles and blushed.

"Nothing more challenging than what you went through today, except all of us women participate," added Sai'er. "We'll keep it a secret for now, but you'll be quite ready for it."

"That's child's play," said Yin Yan. "Wait till you see what Master Pu has in store for us, whenever he returns."

"*If* he returns. Puqing is old colleague," Zou Run explained to Yan Xian and Lai Xinru. "He went back to Henan Province a year ago to attend to a grave family matter and no word has been heard from him since."

"What does he have in store for us?" said Xinru.

"Ancient Daoist longevity practices involving the arts of the bedchamber which only he understands. Some of these practices are still known today but they're only for men. But he possesses secret manuscripts that require the participation of both sexes. He won't show them even to me, although I can read."

"He will have to show you if he wants to pass them on to you, won't he?" said Yin Yan. "I'm sometimes suspicious he made it all up to enhance his mystique and collect more adherents."

"I'm confident they're genuine," said Zou Run.

"What made him come all the way to Sichuan?" said Yan Xian.

"We're both from Henan and have known each other for years," said Zou Run. "But Sichuan is very large. We have more space to work out here."

There was a knocking at the door.

"Everyone be quiet!" said Sai'er. She peeked through a crack in her window. "No, it can't be!"

She opened the door and standing in the entrance was a tall man of indeterminate age with a braided beard and dressed in a brown Daoist tunic and pants.

"Master Pu!" exclaimed Sai'er.

"That's impossible," said one of the congregants.

"Oh, what a dramatic effect, Mistress, setting us up for this wonderful surprise!" said Yin Yan.

"No, I really didn't," said Zou Run, also stunned.

"It can't be," said Sai'er. "This is too auspicious."

"Eternal and Venerable Mother in our original home in the world of true emptiness!" said the man.

Everyone repeated the mantra and ushered Puqing inside.

"I reckoned you were at Kang's house, since I didn't find you at yours," he said to Zou Run.

"We're shocked, because we were just now, right now, talking about you, and you happened to show up."

"It is indeed a coincidence! But the coincidence is not that *I* happened to show up when you were talking about me. It's that I showed up when *you* happened to be talking about me. Were you consulting the *I Ching* beforehand?"

"No. We were inducting a new couple," Zou Run said, introducing Yan Xian and Lai Xinru.

"Master Pu, you look tired," said Sai'er.

"A bit. I've walked a good sixty *li* today."

"Let's fix you up with a nice meal. We have leftovers from our dinner earlier. Yin Yan, dear, heat up some wine for him."

"Where have you come from, Puqing?" said Zou Run.

"Dazhou. What were you talking about regarding me just now?"

"The secret rites you had wanted to perform with us before your untimely departure. We've been waiting in expectation for a year. In fact, I must confess our recent members were recruited on the promise you would return."

"Well, then, I have the good fortune of arriving while the congregation is assembled, and we can perform them forthwith."

"No, Puqing. It's too sudden. You're exhausted and this must be delayed for another night."

"I insist. A little food will restore me. Please introduce me to your new members. Many of you I don't recognize."

"All right. I hope you can all stay longer than usual on this most auspicious day!" Zou Run said to the congregation. "But is Sai'er's space acceptably outfitted, Puqing?"

"These mats will do. We need to create a calm room."

"What is a 'calm room'?"

"A pure chamber. With an altar and a large censer. And no windows with holes or cracks. The air must be sealed tight inside."

"Is this censer big enough?" said Sai'er, holding an incense burner in both hands.

"Not nearly big enough."

"Why do you need such a large censer?"

"We're not burning incense but the hemp plant."

"The hemp plant? That's only used for fiber and weaving."

"It's the finest medicine for promoting *se*. And it needs to be breathed in."

"Promoting *se*! I've never heard of this medicine before. Did you recently discover it? Does it work better than velvet antler or horny goat weed?" said Sai'er.

"It's mentioned in the Daoist writings. It works much better than any other medicine for promoting *se*."

"And does it work as well for women as it does for men?"

"It's for both women and men. And it works without delay, though it may not work for everyone the first time. But since we don't have a large censer, we'll have to use a brazier."

"A brazier? A brazier in a sealed room will cause fire poison," said Sai'er.

"We only need to keep the room sealed for a few minutes. And you have good charcoal, hard-wood charcoal?"

"Of course."

"After we've ingested the smoke and the medicine is working, the windows can be opened. Start the brazier going now and keep the windows open until we begin."

"Master Pu, where did you acquire these teachings?" said Yin Yan.

"I cannot reveal my source. They originate from the Sui Dynasty, probably even centuries earlier."

"That's over a thousand years ago," said Zou Run. "You have them memorized?"

"Hundreds of rites survive. In printed copies. I have the essential ones memorized, such as the *Initiation Rite of the Yellow Book*, which we will perform now."

Sai'er and Yin Yan served Master Pu food and drink and introduced the unfamiliar congregants, who bowed to the floor. He nodded to each and ate quietly. Zou Run kept him company while the others grabbed their mats and went upstairs to get the brazier going. On the way up, Yin Yan turned and asked, "Master Pu, will we be removing our clothes?"

"Some of you will."

Once everyone had gathered upstairs, Puqing arranged a group of mats in the middle of the room, which he surrounded with more mats. The bathtub was moved to the window end of the room where it would be out of the way during the rite. The Master and Mistress sat cross-legged on Sai'er's canopy bed and addressed the members sitting before them.

"Listen up everyone," said Puqing. "The instructions are complicated and I will only go over them once. Once commenced, the rite can only be enacted, and I cannot repeat the instructions to those who forget. Your role as congregants is to learn fast, without needless repetition. If anyone forgets something, someone else will remember and will step in to show you what to do.

"When the hemp is burning, circle around the brazier and breathe the fumes all the way into your lungs. Keep doing this. After a few minutes, you will start to feel peculiar, as from several cups of wine. That means it's working. You will also feel a bit *se*. The medicine doesn't work on your jade stem or jade gate through the blood. Instead, it penetrates your spirit and your awareness. The mere idea of *se* will become fascinating and take over your thoughts. It's this that will make you ready and willing.

"If some of you don't feel anything, you will next time, so be patient and concentrate on the rite. But only some of you will be performing the rite tonight, and the rest of you will watch. We need all five of you men. How many of you women here are now having your unlucky days?"

Four raised their hands, including Xinru.

"I'm not right now but expect to in a day or two," said a fifth.

"I'm about finished with mine today," Yin Yan added.

"Let's not use you tonight, Sister Yin. We'll need you to help guide the others. Do you all feel prepared?" Puqing asked the ten women and men.

"Master Pu, we still don't know what you will have us do," said He Le, one of the menstruating women.

"Why are you choosing those of us on our unlucky days?" said Yin Yan. "Is it so that we won't get pregnant?"

Puqing acknowledged this with a nod and a smile. "The rest of you will all have your chance on different nights."

"But men are not supposed to release themselves during the clouds and the rain, are they?"

"That is correct. But we don't want to take chances, do we?"

The congregation had long been disabused of the prevailing prejudice that the menses, and by association the woman herself, was dirty and taboo. On the contrary, the monthly blood was sacramental—and packed with Yin. But Yin Yan still had to ask, "What about the mess? I mean, the mats can be cleaned easily enough, but...."

He Le lifted her gown and pointed to the cloth sling around her hips. "My bib is full."

"Do you have any objections?" said Puqing.

"Well, no, but how will we be partnered up?"

"You will see."

As he proceeded with the instructions, mild disbelief gripped the congregants. The chosen ten looked fearful, not so much at what they were about to undertake as at the prospect of fumbling and making a mistake.

Thereupon Puqing bowed to an altar table set up for the occasion and invoked the hemp goddess Magu and the sex goddess Sunü. He grabbed a handful of dried hemp leaves, flowers, and seeds, and dropped them on the brazier's grill. There was much coughing as the congregants circled the crucible. He bade them keep inhaling, and soon the entire room was shrouded in smoke.

"Master Pu and Mistress Zou, won't you partake of the medicine?" said Yin Yan.

"We need to keep our minds clear to observe and direct."

"How long must we keep the windows closed? It's unbearably hot," said Sai'er.

"A few minutes more."

One woman not among the chosen sat down, wiped her brow and pulled off her robe. She was glistening with sweat. A few others thought this was a signal to begin and removed their robes as well. "What are we supposed to do?"

"We haven't begun yet!" snapped Puqing.

Some started gasping. Sai'er opened the shutters. Xinru began breathing rapidly and was crying. "I can't breathe," she said.

"You *can* breathe. Slow your breathing down, dear," said Yin Yan, wrapping her arm around her.

"The room is closing around me. It's crushing me. I feel a pressure on my heart!"

"Relax. Relax. Breathe with me."

Yan Xian, Sai'er, and Zou Run came up. "She's panicking," said Zou Run.

"She'll be all right. Sit her down," said Puqing.

Everyone was standing around, confused.

"All sit down now," said Sai'er. "Let's turn this into a calm room as Master Pu intended." She sang the Hymn to the Five Spirits and everyone sang along.

Xinru felt better after a few minutes and was excused from the rite. One of the chosen males said he wasn't up for it. He was seconded by another, who feared he wouldn't be able to rise to the occasion.

One of the chosen females blurted out, "What is this crazy medicine? I can't remember a single thing about what we're supposed to do. My head is so mixed up now. Can I just watch?"

That left three couples, two of which were married. They were switched, on the assumption their Yin and their Yang would leap out with a fresh partner. Puqing designated the youngest couple—He Le and a young man named Shen Wei—the lead pair. The six disrobed and arranged themselves on three mats. He Le wouldn't be described as beautiful, but she had a fetching face with slanted almond eyes peeking out under low-cut bangs, and a big smile; not yet twenty and slim, her small breasts, consisting solely of nipples atop protruding areolae, some found most enticing. She was regarded by the congregation as smart and dedicated. Shen Wei was also well liked. Fair complexioned, quiet, and dreamy, he was one of the few literate ones and composed poetry. He also had an outsized jade stalk, long, thick, and reliable, and this fact had been slyly communicated to Puqing, who assigned him to the lead pair.

"*Aiyo*," exclaimed He Le, as her dripping blood unexpectedly executed a fine calligraphy on the mat. "What do I do now?"

"He Le, dear, let me take over for you," said Yin Yan, pulling Shen Wei onto a fresh mat. "I guess it's about time, eh?" she whispered to him, pinching his stalk. "Let's see if this thing of yours works."

In a steady, stentorian voice Puqing began to recite:

Water flows to the east and clouds drift to the west.
Yin nourishes Yang with a Qi so subtle.
The mysterious jing rises to the tutorial gate.

Shen Wei remembered to sit facing Yin Yan, with her knees hooked over his. He remembered to massage her below the navel with three circular strokes, before moving his hand down to open her outer labia. He remembered to pull her hips close and place his stalk against her jade gate without entering, while cradling her head with his left hand and reaching around to massage her lower back with his right. As for the rest, his mind went blank.

Puqing was staring and waiting.

"Sorry, Master Pu, the medicine is working, as you can see, but it muddles the mind and I've forgotten what I'm supposed to do," said Shen Wei.

Puqing incanted the instructions:

The divine gentleman holds the gate.
The jade lady opens the door.
As our Qi is united, may Yin bestow her Qi upon me.
Yin and Yang bestow and transform.

He then stared at Yin Yan.

"I can't remember anything either," she said.

He spoke for her:

The 10,000 creatures are nourished and born.
Heaven covers and earth supports.
May Qi be bestowed upon the bodies of these humble supplicants.

Meanwhile, Shen Wei's stalk had vanished.

"You are not to enter her yet!" yelled Puqing. "Remove it." Turning to the two other pairs, he said, "Can you repeat everything exactly as they have performed it now?"

Both couples frowned at their respective jade staffs, now mere turtle heads retracted into their shell.

"Let me see if I can coax them back to life," said Sai'er, "Sometimes it requires a special touch. And gesturing to Zou Run and the other couple, "Mistress? Can you help?"

One of the observers said, "I have no idea what's going on."

"Neither do I," said another. "The medicine is making me silly."

As the women assisted the two hapless men, Puqing gave up waiting for the lead pair to continue and carried on reciting the instructions in the hope they would follow along. To Shen Wei he said, "Raise your head and inhale living Qi through your nose. Swallow Yang according to the numbers three, five, seven, and nine and recite: 'May the Dao of heaven be set in motion.' To Yin Yan he said, "Recite: 'May the Dao of earth be set in motion.'"

The pair repeated their lines.

"No! You need to swallow Yang according to the breathing pattern first. Three, five, seven, and nine."

This done, Puqing continued: "You may now enter her to a depth of half of your jade stem while reciting: 'O, celestial immortals, I would shake heaven and move earth that—'"

The goddesses Magu and Sunü are wont to get along splendidly but it's a delicate operation, and Shen Wei and Yin Yan burst out laughing.

Puqing stood up. "You two have defiled the rite! Remove yourselves from the chamber so that we may continue!" he thundered.

The room went silent.

"Master Pu, it's too hard to do this without more practice," said Sai'er. "Really. Please don't be upset."

"This isn't like you, Puqing," said Zou Run. "You're exhausted from your journey and you need to rest. We can do this another time."

"Master Pu, we weren't making fun of the rite. We would never defile it on purpose," said Yin Yan. "The hemp medicine is very strange. It's making us nervous."

Puqing sat back down. "You're right. I shouldn't have attempted the rite tonight. The fact is there is something on my mind and I've been out of sorts. I wanted to do it tonight because it may be the only chance we'll have."

"What do you mean?"

"I have bad news. Dazhou is engulfed in rebellion, which has already spread to Dongxiang, Bazhou, and Tongjiang. Taiping is next."

"What rebels?" said Zou Run. "White Lotus?"

He nodded. "Imperial troops are arriving. Thousands of local militias have been dragooned into the military. Fighting is going on. I don't know the outcome yet. But the rebels will not be able to hold out except by retreating and regrouping in the mountains. The highest mountains in the region are here. They will be coming here. And the army will follow."

Though none except Sai'er and Puqing had likely experienced a siege, all knew what it would entail. Everyone gasped. Some of the women started crying.

"What will happen when the rebels arrive?" said Shen Wei.

"They will burn down this town. Every house and structure. If you aren't burned to death inside your home and manage to escape into the street, you will be ushered directly into their ranks. They'll probably brand you on the face with the 'white lotus' characters to prevent you from deserting. Or kill you if you resist. That's how the rebels recruit people to their ranks."

"And if government troops arrive first?"

"The same. They will arrest you if they find any evidence you are sympathizers. That includes dressing in white, blue, or black. Particularly if you're all dressed the same way. Those are the three colors the different rebel factions have adopted here in Sichuan. It also includes any suspicions of the three prohibitions against sect activity: 'gathering in people's homes at night until dawn,' 'mixing freely with men and women,' and 'being vegetarian and consorting with devils.' Anyone who turns out to be a leader, any kind of leader—that includes you, Zou Run, and you, Sister Sai'er, if they find you have hosted a congregation—will be tortured and executed by slicing."

"Are they looking for paper men?" asked Sai'er.

"They don't need to find paper men. Blank paper will be enough evidence against you."

"What are paper men?" said Xinru.

"Some rebels claim they can enlarge their ranks with magical spells. The cut human figures out of paper. Then they cut off a man's queue and mix it in a bucket with human urine and excrement, and the paper figures are said to come to life."

"Who believes that?"

"Of course, it's nonsense. But ignorant folks believe it. That's why I have nothing to do with them, though many congregations have gotten mixed up with them and tragically became implicated. Or their neighbors accuse them of harboring paper men to shift suspicion onto them. The worst are the militias. They don't need any evidence. They will concoct and plant evidence against you. They not only do the government troops' dirty work; they slay whole families at will to plunder their homes."

"What are we going to do?" said Yan Xian.

"Flee! Any day now you will see smoke on the horizon—a sign that fighting is on the way."

"Where can we flee to?"

"We can't go to the south or the west, which are crawling with troops and militia. We can only go east or north. Hubei is too dangerous due to all the rebel activity there last spring. It all started in the south and west of Hubei. That leaves only the north, and I am not very familiar with the territory."

"Yan Xian and Lai Xinru are," said Sai'er. "That's where they are from. South Shaanxi."

"How did you make it here?" Puqing asked.

"We were looking for relatives who lived in the area, but they were gone. We followed the rivers. The Ren River and the Back River. And we had to do a lot of climbing in hilly terrain," said Xinru.

"Could you guide us there and provide temporary refuge?"

Xinru looked at Yan Xian, who said, "We could show you the way. But we have a problem."

"What problem?" said Zou Run.

Yan Xian and Xinru exchanged glances again. "Should we tell them?" he said.

"Please confess everything about your situation with us," said Zou Run. "I can recognize good people, and no matter what your circumstances, Master Pu and I give you our word that you belong to us. We will protect you."

"It has to do with our beloved daughter," said Xinru. "She's on the run for murder. And we're on the run as accessories to the murder."

"Murder?"

"She never intentionally murdered anyone. We were framed. She was raped in front of us by a corrupt *yamen* runner. She killed him. You may find this hard to believe, but she did not kill him in anger or revenge. She is innocent, though she killed him."

"What happened? Did she stab him in self-defense while struggling with him?"

The congregants were hanging on Xinru's every word.

"No." Wiping away tears, she went over the events that led up to the killing and explained how it happened.

"Where is she now?"

"We have no idea."

"We must find her," said Yin Yan. "Can you think of where she might have gone?"

"She knows how to survive alone in the mountains and forests. She's in a forest somewhere. She's very smart, and she's alive. We are certain of that. But we can't return to our village, as Xinru and I will be recognized," said Yan Xian.

"We can scout the territory and will find a solution along the way. We have strength in numbers," said Puqing.

"We will find her," said Sai'er. "Let's start preparing. We must set off tomorrow."

Puqing added: "If any of you feel you won't be able to bear the hardship of mountain travel and you need to stay with your family, decide that now, but be prepared for the worst. Throw out your white garments, which will implicate you. Wear ordinary clothes."

7

The Magu goddess

he next day's departure was delayed a day to gather needed provisions. This gave those still wavering more time to decide whether to uproot their families for the perilous journey to an unknown destination. It was not an easy decision. Imagine a family member rushing in to confess their membership in a strange sect whose fanatical and possibly insane leader had announced imminent destruction at the hands of an approaching army of ghosts: a band of ragtag rebels for which neither evidence nor word of mouth was anywhere at hand. Yet however doubtful it sounded, there was a real risk in asking around town for confirmation: your family might be fingered among the culpable if the news turned out to be true.

Few of Taiping's households were well off; most were dirt poor. It was harder for the poor to tear themselves from their domicile than it was for the rich. The rich would face a psychological upheaval in their rude introduction to topsy-turvydom, to life on the road, but they did have their title deeds and as much jewelry and silver *taels* as they could carry. The poor were born survivors, but their equity was bound to the land—

dwelling, farm, animals. For many in the congregation, the initial shock upon the unbelievable news was followed in turn by denial. By the time denial gave way to reality it was too late, for Taiping would soon be overrun by thousands of rebels followed by thousands more militiamen and Imperial troops.

The wise have the mental agility to anticipate and adjust to dire circumstances faster than most. Or at least the devoted do, and it turned out that those who committed themselves to flight were the same eight who were instrumental in rescuing the previous evening from utter fiasco. While a motley group, the five women and three men enjoyed a few advantages. Puqing, Zou Run, and Sai'er, as well as the newly recruited Shaanxi couple, were experienced travelers; they were handy with knives and knew how to secure food. Puqing, Zou Run, Sai'er, and Shen Wei were literate—useful for reading public notices and scrolls on doorposts. Only three pairs of feet were bound. In outrage years earlier at her misogynist indoctrination—she might not have expressed it in quite these terms but clearly felt it—Yin Yan had unbound hers. To be precise, it was only because her ambivalent mother had not fully broken her arches in the first place that her feet could heal once let out. Zou Run's and Sai'er's had been broken and they knew it wasn't worth the effort. Yin Yan was planning on curing He Le of the evil, whom she had taken under her wing like a daughter, on the hope her half-broken feet might still be viable, but the arduous procedure would take several years and would now have to be delayed until they found a new home. At least the owners of the three pairs of bound feet had muscular thighs and could march along with their canes or be carried by the men for spells when exhausted.

As the Buddha teaches, attachment to worldly matters causes suffering. Well, most things of material value could be replaced. Sai'er took a final stoic look at her finely carved rosewood canopy bed and prized porcelain cupping jars which would soon be smashed or burned. Rules were laid down as to what could be brought along and distributed in sacks of equal weight: a cleaver or hunting knife for each and a few tools, spices, and silver *taels*.

Each could have their robe for added warmth at night (to be dyed on the road with tree bark to muddy their incriminating whiteness), along with some winter wear. It was already well into the ninth lunar month. While their Shaanxi destination was only several days away on foot, they had to prepare for the unexpected and the prospect of cold in the coming weeks.

They didn't make it very far before more bad news reared its head. They followed the Back River until it veered east and continued north on foot until they reached the Ren River, which according to plan would take them into the heart of south Shaanxi. They had crossed into Shaanxi by noon on their second day when they met travelers coming from the opposite direction, fleeing a rebel outbreak in Xing'an. Xing'an was further afield, another three days hike downstream from Yan Xian and Lai Xinru's home territory on the Han River, but it meant, as Puqing explained, the rebellions were spreading and would be coalescing. Refugees would likewise be moving in both directions along the very route they were now taking. Both rebels and troops from Sichuan would soon be on their heels to aid their Shaanxi brethren. They could join this treacherous highway or backtrack to the Back River and head east into quieter if still precarious territory. The problem, however, was where would they then be headed?

Puqing had a backup plan, though it would considerably lengthen their journey: the Daoist refuge of Wudang Mountain. He knew the way. There were traversable valleys and inns where they might stay (those few that didn't criminally overcharge), but also mountains and snow, he warned. The fast-bonding party of eight agreed.

As the temperatures dropped in the evenings, they worked out a sleeping system. One person sat up all night on guard duty, armed with Puqing's bow and quiver of split-bamboo arrows smeared with enough aconite resin to kill a horse. The others embraced on their sides in compact formation in their layers of padded jackets, pants, robes, and blankets. Those at either end of the row who were coldest were rotated and could choose whom to sleep between the next night. This group felt no fussiness or shame over the sexes being in tight proximity. It was not simply their penchant for stroking and caressing each other to sleep whenever feeling anxious (relax in turn your ankles, wrists, throat, jaw, and tongue; absorb each other's sleep-inducing Qi, Zou Run taught them). Well aware were they that merely passing the night under the same shelter constituted a crime. But a larger crime not of their own making awaited them at any time. Who might commit it didn't matter. The stark truth was enough. It rearranged priorities and brought clarity, relief, and humor. It freed them up to do as they wish, not because it was forbidden but because the entire moral order was defunct and irrelevant.

They did as they liked, and it became a running joke among the women as to who would next be poking their backside, and whether they would loosen their pants or reach around to relieve the guy manually so that he could fall asleep (while using his garment to wipe their hand off). These amusing bedtime tasks were a reward for the long day. They were carried out with the same ease and dexterity as assembling their makeshift shelters (unless an abandoned farmhouse turned up), catching river fish, building fires to roast their catch, roots, and tubers, and cleaning up after dinner.

They spent the late hours amidst the dying embers of the fire in contemplative silence. Once they lay down at night talking ceased, because they needed to listen, and keep listening, for anomalous, hostile sounds. It kept their minds busy. Over the first few days, they thought about the difficulties of adapting to harsh conditions, having been yanked from the warmth of the hearth to subsistence on the precipice. There was no point in crying or complaining, only in wondering afresh each dawn at the daily gift of life.

They thought about Puqing's teachings on the problem of fear. All fear could be reduced to fear of bodily assault, whether proceeding from attack, accident or disease. In their present circumstances, human violence was the main enemy. They would need to master the urge to panic. Panic got in the way of sizing up a situation. If it was an attack by superior forces, grab your knife (which they all kept by their side), disperse, hide from arrows, and fight back at close quarters. The women were not necessarily at a disadvantage in fighting since their arms were shorter and they could stab faster. Whether an attacker proved lethal or harmless hinged as much on your attitude as on your fighting prowess. He was counting on your panic, and therefore your cooperation, to make things easier for him. He was not counting on your refusal to panic. The only thing to do was to turn this panic round and your knife into a mirror in which he saw his own panic. And always, always, hold your gaze on his. There was no guarantee of the outcome, but mastering your fear would greatly increase the odds of survival.

To shore up these points, they practiced combat moves and rehearsed emergency scenarios. Their first crucial test came only days later when they were set upon by four bandits one morning as they prepared to set off. So quiet and efficient was their daily packing that the bandits themselves were caught off guard. They had hardly nocked their arrows when they realized too late they were better off with daggers. Who came out of nowhere to swing her cleaver into the ringleader's neck but Yin Yan (being the most adept at killing chickens and hogs). All went silent except the blood spraying her as she stood there stunned at how easy it was. Time resumed and Puqing and Shen Wei finished off two more, surprising everyone that a poet could fight (and embarrassing Yan Xian who would need to prove his mettle upon the next robbery). The last bandit managed to get an arrow off but was stabbed by He Le before he could get off a second, who bounced up to him on adrenalin-sprung bound feet and swiveled away in time to escape a direct hit from the arrow, or at least she didn't feel anything.

Only once the bandits had all been dispatched did she notice blood seeping through her jacket. She pulled off her clothes and found an areola pierced through and dangling half severed. Zou Run and Yin Yan leapt to the rescue. They laid her supine, staunched the bleeding with cloth, cleaned the wound with grain alcohol, and made her drink the remaining spirits as Zou Run sutured her areola back in place with mulberry thread and affixed a plaster to her chest. He Le took it like a man, gritting in silent torture, though her tears flowed. *We need to see if the arrows were poisoned!* said Puqing as he examined the bandits' unused arrows. *Check the bandits for any poison flasks.* The arrowheads were clean and dry and evidently untreated, meaning He Le was safe, though her breast was now throbbing with pain.

They dumped the bodies in the river, cleaned up blood-drenched Yin Yan, and got back on the road. The men took turns carrying He Le. Walking helped get the jitters out. They talked about what went through their minds as they killed. Puqing said his awareness expanded such that he was able to time his sword thrust precisely. Yin Yan thought she was performing a part in a play. He Le said she didn't have time to think, much less observe. Shen Wei attributed the calm finesse with which he cut down his victim to his vocation. A true poet is always at work carving word sculptures wherever he may be. Daily business that gets in the way is put on hold. Business that won't wait, such as approaching death, is dealt with ruthlessly so that he can return to his wordcrafting.

This latest disturbance would also provide material for a poem, abetted by Puqing's hemp medicine, to which Shen Wei had taken the keenest liking. They would sprinkle it on the embers and inhale it through a bamboo tube after grilling their dinner. Not all took to it at first. For some it countered the cold, brought on sleep, sharpened alertness, or tugged deliciously at the groin, while for others it only caused confusion or conjured up demons. For Shen Wei, it had the marvelous effect of aligning spontaneous ideas and images in glittering rows. It helped him, for example, rearrange lines from his idol, the Tang Dynasty poet Li He, to fashion a new poem:

Under the moon a beauty weeps, missing her native village,
From the Xiang River at midnight emerges a startled dragon.
His silken garments are stained with the dragon's brains,
Gorgeous girls sit close to him, tossing back jade goblets.

He'd have a whole book's worth of poems by the end of their journey, but he had to keep them to himself for the time being: Puqing and Zou Run hadn't the patience to listen to abstruse language that wasn't part of familiar ritual.

All were invited to divulge their domestic situations and secrets, a vital matter as some had torn themselves from their families and they needed to come clean about their loyalties. Shen Wei's circumstances were simple, he affirmed. He was an only child. His father had abandoned the family when he was little. A failed civil-service examination drunkard took up with his lonely mother and bullied them both daily. She was too much under the man's thumb to stand up for her son, so Shen Wei left home for good and without regrets, finding jobs as schoolteacher and later government office clerk. His mother had been cold to him since he was a child, and the beneficial effect of this was to instill a strong sense of self-reliance. The congregation was the first family he felt at home with.

He Le's situation was more complicated. She was none other than the daughter of the drunkard, who had raped her at the age of fifteen. Rather than do the honorable thing of taking her own life, she took refuge in her uncle's house, a widower, agreed to share his bed in exchange for shelter and sustenance, and blackmailed him into transferring his deed and property to her name—if he didn't want to be accused of her rape at the county *yamen*. Shen Wei admired her pluck and acuity, and they became lovers. He was only five years older than her, but marriage hadn't occurred to either of them. Woman's virginity wasn't an issue, indeed was a matter of supreme indifference to them both. For He Le, there were men enough. As for Shen Wei, he would have counseled her to initiate her *yindao* with a carrot before submitting to the shabby, sham ritual—had she been a virgin.

They lived with Yin Yan and her big family of farmers. Shen Wei had met Yin Yan at a vegetable market. To the civilized, nothing was more degrading than a cultured man hooking up with a vegetable seller in the town market. Shen Wei was, again, unmoved by such prejudices. He understood that nature didn't discriminate and the classes were all endowed with beauty and native wit. She had to be a good fifteen years older than him but he couldn't take his eyes off her. When she leaned forward to grab several cobs of corn for him, he saw her breasts. He asked her where she lived. She smiled but wouldn't answer. He waited for her to leave for the day and followed her. When he caught up with her, she invited him home. He was in for a surprise.

Who's the latest chap to be snagged by the slut today? said one of several men at their big round table, as they sized him up. *Treat the guest with respect and shut your foul mouth*, snapped an older woman Shen Wei assumed to be Yin Yan's mother. Yin Yan carried on as if they repeated the same conversation from script every day. *Thanks to this gentleman I sold the rest of the corn. Is the guest bedroom made up? Nope!* laughed one of the men. *He means*, said another, pulling a baffled Shen Wei down to the table, *after dinner you'll have to shack up with our daughter here.* More guffawing. *I hope you don't mind their vulgar joking. We do have a guest bedroom and it's all ready for you*, said her mother. *I wasn't even expecting dinner, let alone such hospitality as being invited to stay over*, protested Shen Wei, who was persuaded to spend the night.

Over rounds of yellow wine, the meal was succeeded by the raucous finger game (the Chinese version of rock, paper, scissors) when Yin Yan, fearing Shen Wei was growing bored, led him to her bedroom. He was torn. Trailing his fingers through her temple braids and over her chest, he confessed to having a lady friend. She made it easy for him by escorting him to the guest bed. She even invited He Le to come and live with them, once he had explained their circumstances. When He Le arrived, she urged Shen Wei to sleep with Yin Yan to repay her family's generosity and defuse jealous tension. But Yin Yan insisted on setting boundaries, and it wasn't until Puqing's initiation rite that he was able, however briefly, to consummate the act with her.

It was Yin Yan who introduced the couple to Kang Sai'er. Sai'er had been a frequent face at the vegetable market, talking up the comelier sellers for any who might turn out to be a little, for want of a better word, "precocious." Yin Yan soon found herself being feted to dinner at Sai'er's place and dragged into the voracious woman's bed. But Yin Yan's family didn't take to Sai'er when Yin Yan first brought her over, sensing a vague mortal threat. Yin Yan's allegiance now became clear when rebel activities forced the drastic decision to leave. Her incredulous family didn't believe a word of it and gave her up for lost, swallowed up in the Shandong spinster's strange Daoist cult.

Sai'er had known Zou Run and Puqing for years, when her family had resided for a time in Hubei's Xiangyang before their final move out to Sichuan. On the Han River several days journey on foot east of the Wudang mountain range, Xiangyang had long been a hotbed of esoteric Buddhist, Daoist, and White Lotus proselytizing. Sai'er's family wanted nothing to do with the White Lotus, after their horrendous hometown siege in Shandong two decades earlier. Most White Lotus believers were as harmless as Buddhists and Daoists. But as Sai'er explained, they were neither Buddhists nor Daoists. They were confused. They claimed the Maitreya Buddha took orders from Daoism's Eternal Venerable Mother. When they combined two faiths into one, it was because they didn't understand either. Buddhism disciplined the body to purify the spirit, while Daoism purified the body to achieve longevity. The two faiths were incompatible. Sai'er was emphatically a Daoist, not a Buddhist.

As Yin Yan, Shen Wei, and He Le were immune to religion in any form, Sai'er simply got them drunk and out of their clothes. Her Daoism, which required patient instruction, came later. What distinguished what she was doing from garden-variety Daoist, or White Lotus teachings for that matter, was firstly, the equal role given to women in leadership, autonomy, and the bedchamber arts, and secondly, the refusal to amass power and influence through financial coercion (though she wasn't averse to wielding apocalyptic "black wind" rhetoric to scare simpletons into her compass if that was the only way). Instead, she recruited people for their skills and trades, with the end of building a self-sufficient community.

The worst of the proselytizers were those who claimed to be

the very Maitreya himself, returned to earth to exact vengeance on the world and overturn the regime. This only drew the attention of the government. To preempt the inexorable sweeps and crackdowns, these charlatan-led sects armed themselves and escalated the violence. It always ended badly not only for the sects but for everyone. All groups suspected of having any ties to the White Lotus—those involved in any religious activity not confined to state-approved temples—were rounded up and persecuted, along with many innocent neighboring families who hadn't the faintest idea what they had done. That the rebellions were spreading in Hubei, Sichuan, and now Shaanxi could only be described as an unqualified disaster.

Puqing and Zou Run were in wholehearted agreement with Sai'er. They had been friends with her and her family for two decades and shared the same values: embracing the secret Daoist arts as a socially acceptable means of escaping from oppressive tradition—or a hateful family. Before eloping to Hubei's Xiangyang, the couple had been teenage lovers in their hometown of Nanyang in Henan Province, where Puqing cultivated *taijiquan* and other martial arts, and Zou Run, whose family had taught their children to read, scoured the Daoist scriptures at a local temple (where she met Puqing) for advice on bodily rejuvenation for women, as opposed to men. Her parents deemed her the ugliest of the three daughters and hence unmarriageable, and of incorrigible disposition as well, they were quick to add. He'd have an incorrigible disposition too under such circumstances, Puqing told her. He convinced her that her parents were discouraging her from marriage only to make use of her labor in sewing and embroidering the family's clothing. He ferried her away one night while the house was asleep. There were no goodbyes except for a note she left; any foreknowledge and they would have locked her up for good.

As the eight congregants wended their way nearer Wudang Mountain, they were warned by passing refugees to avoid urban areas as much as possible, which had been ravaged the previous spring by White Lotus uprisings. Those that hadn't been abandoned were garrisoned by Imperial troops. The walled city of Fangxian was near at hand. It too had been attacked but succeeded in fending off the rebels. As such, it was comparatively safe and might be a good place to rest and recuperate—if they were allowed in, that is—before their final three-day ascent up the mountain.

They emerged from forests into paths between fields and untended farms. Scattered amidst the weeds and debris, diamond-backed snakes slithered through the rib cages and eye sockets of skulls and skeletons. One abandoned village was encircled by a stockade, and rotting heads hung on pikes before the village gate—rebels or soldiers decapitated for plundering or rape—as a belated warning.

"The landscape is devastated," said Xinru.

"Not everything," said Puqing. "See the smoke rising from that village over there? And another one over there? That smoke is from cooking, not pillage. There's movement and life. I'm guessing only a quarter or at most a third of the towns and villages have been destroyed. Four emperors ago, at the start of the Qing Dynasty, it was much worse. Do you have historical awareness?"

"What is that?" said Shen Wei.

"How was it worse?" said Yan Xian.

"The extreme situation is when tigers start appearing."

"Tigers?"

"Take rebel leader Zhang Xianzhong's destruction of Sichuan during the Shunzhi Emperor's reign, for instance. When he ruled over the capital, Chengdu, he had the citizens' arms cut off—the right arms of males to render them harmless, the left arms of females to create matching pairs of arms. Many bled to death. Many more were massacred outright. He experimented. His soldiers assembled massive piles of noses, ears, feet, women's breasts. When he abandoned the city, tigers entered and feasted on those still alive. This caused the tiger population to explode and inhabit thousands of abandoned homes. Tigers also preyed on those who escaped the city. The violence spread everywhere and most of Sichuan was depopulated, apart from a few survivors cowering in caves and bereft of the power of speech after what they had seen. Historical awareness means that when I trekked back through Sichuan last month, I *saw* not only White Lotus rebels but also Zhang Xianzhong's victims with their missing noses and ears and limbs. They jostled among the people and were every bit as real. And I *saw* the tigers swarming along my path. I still see the tigers. I'm not even sure I could tell a living tiger apart from them."

"You saw their ghosts?"

"No. My awareness of the past is as vivid as reality. So I see them alive, out there. That's historical awareness."

"You have a powerful imagination."

"Today Sichuan has recovered, but the people who live there now are all migrants from the provinces to the east."

"Just like us," said Sai'er.

"So, you see, we don't have it so bad now," said Puqing.

"Was Zhang Xianzhong a White Lotus rebel?" asked Xinru.

"No. He was a bandit who grew powerful and, as they say of those peculiar types obsessed with peeling off their scabs, an entire province was his scab! He was fascinated by mutilation. But most of the rebellions since the fall of the Ming Dynasty have been attempts to restore the Ming. That includes the White Lotus, who hate the Qing. But they're wrong when they speak of the coming Great Cataclysm. The cataclysm already happened: upon the fall of the Ming and the oceans of blood spilled before the Qing gained supremacy."

Yan Xian and Lai Xinru were curious about Xiangyang, the walled city on the other side of the mountains. Puqing shook his head. No, it was a notorious breeding ground for illicit religious activity and under extreme internal surveillance since the spring uprisings. The rebels had burned the unwalled facing city of Fancheng and attempted to capture Xiangyang but floundered trying to cross the Han River under a hail of fire from the city ramparts. In the aftermath the city was turned into a fortress. Even if they approached it from south of the river, the whole area was bristling with government troops. Before the trouble began, people could come and go through Xiangyang's gates. Puqing could still get in after the uprisings but only because the gatekeepers recognized him.

A more immediate problem was being apprehended anywhere without a *luyin*, which none of them had. Puqing explained to Xinru and Yan Xian that traveling without a travel pass, issued by their local *yamen*, was illegal. Relay stations questioned stray refugees, and those with no claim to prior residence were pressed into local militias or arrested as suspected rebels. They wouldn't be allowing vagrants into Fangxian either. They were going to have to purchase counterfeit passes and hope they weren't betrayed by their accents when the gatekeepers questioned them. Let us do the talking, said Zou Run.

As they approached the walled city it wasn't long before Puqing tracked down a black-market *luyin* dealer. They were charging five *taels* per person. After haggling, he bargained them down to thirty *taels* for the lot of them. The Shaanxi couple were still shocked at the price, but Sai'er told them not to worry; that's why they had brought along *taels*. Most of the money, Puqing added, went to bribing the gatekeepers, who knew all about fake passes. But they still had to go through the motions and perform their roles convincingly. Wouldn't it be better to skip the walled city and head straight for Wudang Mountain? the couple asked. No, they needed to make inquiries in town on the situation on the mountain.

The bogus travel passes gave each of them an assumed name and indicated Fangxian as their town of residence. A calligrapher penned quick portraits of each of the travelers on their pass. Mimicking well-creased paper was an art, and the eight passes had already been rendered into varying states of disintegration. Some were coming apart. They practiced fitting the grimy segments together and memorized their new names.

The small city was bounded by a turtle-shell-shaped wall eight *li* in length with four cardinal gates and battlements spaced at equal intervals along the top. Puqing led them to the busy west gate. The chief gatekeeper pulled the group aside to examine their passes and look them up and down. "What color clothing should pregnant women wear?" he barked.

"Red," said Puqing.

"Why?"

"If they're pregnant they don't have menstrual blood to charm the weapons with."

They were let in.

"What was that all about?" said Yin Yan once inside.

"Code for weeding out strangers like us. Luckily I knew the answer. Everyone was discussing last spring's battle when I passed through here on the way to Sichuan. When they were under attack, they wiped down their muskets with the blood of black dogs and stuffed women's bloody period rags into their cannons. Pregnant women had to wear red and stand over the cannons as they were being fired. They believed it enabled their weapons to jinx the enemy."

"Do you believe that?"

"Of course not. But it got us in. The rebels got slaughtered not because of magic but because all they had were homemade guns that shot nails and pebbles."

Puqing cashed a *tael* at a money shop, and they went for a quick bite to eat at a restaurant, ordering bowls of noodles in spicy pork and peanut sauce and sitting at two square tables placed together. Zou Run warned them not to talk as they ate. They were too ravenous to talk anyway and ordered second helpings. Perhaps it would have been better had they conversed, for their silence made other customers curious.

"Looks like you people have been on the road for some time. Where are you from?" one asked.

"Out west," said Zou Run.

"What are you doing in Fangxian?"

"We're on the way to Wudang Mountain."

"You're not coming from rebel activity, are you?"

"We haven't seen you before," said the owner. "How were you let into the city?"

"We're Daoist pilgrims."

"He asked you what you're doing in our city," said the customer.

"And I'm asking you to mind your own business," said Zou Run.

"*Wa!* A *woman* getting fresh with me?" The customer came up and struck Zou Run on the head, knocking her off her stool.

Puqing lifted the man up and slammed him against the wall. "We're taking you to the *yamen*, where you can explain to the magistrate why you enjoy striking women."

"Are you all right, Zou Run?" said Yin Yan, helping her up, while the others had their knives and cleavers out.

"It's just a cut," she said, finding blood on her fingers as she wiped the wound.

"Give us a hot towel to wash her wound," demanded Sai'er.

The proprietor blocked the restaurant entrance to prevent the group from dragging the man off with them. "I'll take care of this. Why don't you all just walk out of here like happy customers and you won't see any more trouble."

Back out on the street, they asked around and were directed to a Daoist temple. Puqing's gentle queries—and a few donated *taels*—persuaded the abbot to allow them temporary lodging. Runners routinely showed up to check lay guests' papers and they were thus advised to make their sojourn short; and the three men and five women would be staying, of course, in segregated sleeping quarters.

"What happened to you?" the abbot asked Zou Run, who had sat down on the floor and was being attended to by He Le.

"I was hit by a violent ruffian in the restaurant we just came from. I'm only a little dizzy and will be fine."

He came up to her. "That's quite a gash. And it's still bleeding. A doctor lives not far from here. He should have a look at you."

"There's no need. I'll be fine."

"You don't have to go see him. We're well acquainted and he'll come here." The abbot moved Zou Run onto a chair and summoned a young priest to fetch the doctor. He Le insisted on accompanying him.

Several more priests had gathered around. Puqing asked them about present circumstances on Wudang Mountain and which temples were providing employment. None of them had traveled there recently and had no idea. Puqing, Shen Wei, and Yan Xian were then shown the men's sleeping quarters, while a nun led the women to theirs.

In the men's dormitory, a guest jumped up from his bed at the sight of Puqing. "Pudu!" he shouted.

"What?"

"Pudu, you've returned!"

"Forgive me, but I have no idea who you're talking about."

"You're not Pudu?"

"No. Who is Pudu?"

"But you *are* Pudu. You've returned from Wudang Mountain. You are he."

"I tell you I am not Pudu and I have no idea who you are talking about. We are on the way to Wudang Mountain now, not coming from it."

The man was at a loss and stared at Puqing. "You are the spitting image of him. The same height, the same narrow face, the same beard, the same clothes. It's uncanny."

"Who is this Pudu that you are so worked up about?"

"Yes, I seem to remember him," said one of the priests. "He did look like you. A lot."

"Do you have the liver disease?" said the guest.

"No."

"Pudu is a Daoist shaman. He had the liver disease and was going to a temple on the mountain where he heard of a healer who could cure him. Some woman healer with a reputation. It was a month or two ago. He never came back. We were concerned he wasn't cured and might have died there, though he didn't appear to be gravely ill when he was here, indeed seemed quite physically active."

"What temple was this? A nunnery? What was the healer's name?"

"He never said. He claimed he had his own large following.

Some sect or other."

"White Lotus?"

"It's very dangerous to speak those words now. You're not White Lotus, are you?"

"Absolutely not. Did he say where he was from?"

"Dangyang, I think."

"Well, he would have been White Lotus, then. You must have heard about the Dangyang uprising. The city was held by rebels for months and was only recently crushed and retaken. He's lucky to have escaped from it alive," said Puqing.

"Again, I'm not sure about the details. But did he ever look like you!"

He Le had returned, and the men came back out to meet the doctor. They saw instead a young woman who was applying a salve to Zou Run's wound. "Dr. Sun sends his apologies but is too busy with other patients to come now. She will be fine," she said.

"And who may you be?" asked Puqing.

"Miaolu. Call me Miaolu. Now, if you don't mind, I'd like to get acquainted with this lovely lady of yours. We'll be back in no time, and I'll have another look at your Mistress here."

"That's an odd name for a woman," said Xinru after the two had left.

Miaolu hooked her elbow through He Le's as they strolled down the street. The doctor's assistant or whatever she was had a clear face and a long braid of hair down her back. And a curious habit of holding her gaze without blinking. But the girl put He Le enough at ease she felt no need to dissemble, and she recounted their group's travails since leaving Sichuan.

"You're smelly," said Miaolu, fixing her big blank eyes on He Le.

"You would be too if you'd been on the road for a month. How did you learn about healing?"

"Don't you want to learn?"

"I'm studying it now. Before we came here. *Aijiu, guasha, baguan*, and so on."

"Is that so? What do you know about medicine?"

"Not much. I do want to learn."

"Did you encounter troubles on the way here?"

"Not too much, no. We had to sleep outside a lot to keep out of the way of populated areas. Although we were attacked once by bandits. I took an arrow through my nipple!"

"I'm so sorry. How is it?"

"It's healing now. Are you from here?"

"How well do you know flowers?" Miaolu said by way of an answer.

"Flowers?"

"How many flowers can you identify and name?"

"The usual—lilies, lotuses, roses, peonies, daisies, chrysanthemums.... Why?"

"Do you like women?"

"Like women? Sure, why not? I am a woman. But I don't want to spend my life in a nunnery if that's what you mean."

"Do you like me?"

"You?" He Le laughed. "Sure, I like you!"

Miaolu seemed satisfied with He Le's responses. They came upon a row of street stalls and stopped at one stand crammed with toys: brightly painted clay figurines, embroidered animals with knotted tassels, rattledrums, shuttlecocks, wooden tops, puzzle rings, *kongming* locks, diabolos, mahjong sets....

"How much are the tangrams?" Miaolu asked the seller.

"Ten cash."

"How about five?"

He shook his head, and they walked away. "All right," he said, calling them back.

Miaolu handed the tangram to He Le.

"You're giving this to me? No, you're too kind. You keep it. And I'm not even familiar with this toy."

Miaolu pushed it into He Le's hand. "You don't know what a tangram is? What a simple girl! Let's stop at that tea pavilion over there and I'll show you how to play it."

"We have different toys back home."

They sat down on stone stools at a round stone table and Miaolu ordered tea. She set the tangram on the table. It consisted of seven flat triangular wooden pieces of different sizes and colors that fit together to form a square. She separated the pieces and said, "You can create any shape or object you want. Make something."

"What should I make?"

"Anything. Use your imagination."

He Le moved the pieces around for a minute or two before hitting upon a shape.

"It's a dog," said Miaolu. "But the head is too big."

"Those are its ears."

"Oh, I see. Tee hee! Let's go, we should see how your Mistress is doing," she said, getting up and paying for the tea just as they were being served.

Back at the temple, Zou Run seemed to have recovered and they were discussing the various routes up the mountain with the priests. They thanked Miaolu for her ministrations as she checked Zou Run again.

"Where did she take you?" Yin Yan asked He Le.

"Down the street. The girl is nice but a little weird and strange," she whispered. "She kept staring at me. And she bought me this toy."

Miaolu seemed reluctant to leave and stood apart from the group, as if waiting for something. They turned to her. "What is it you wish, young lady?" said Puqing.

"Come with me. I have a better option for you all to stay in."

"We're fine here."

"It's better with us. Come and have a look. If you don't like it, you can come back here."

"What is she referring to?" Zou Run asked the abbot.

"I don't know, and I don't want to know," he said, with an unreadable expression. "It's up to you."

"Well, let me go have a look. Do you want to come with me, Zou Run?" said Puqing.

"All of you must come together," Miaolu said. "We're not far away. You can leave your belongings here and fetch them later."

Once out on the street Miaolu said, "You'll have to be interviewed by our Mistress. That's why you must all be present. I can't promise you will be accepted but I reckon it shouldn't be a problem."

Not half a *li* away they came upon an apothecary's shop. Miaolu led them inside and through the back into a reception room with a few chairs lined against the walls. She brought in more chairs and bade them wait. Soon she returned with a pleasant middle-aged woman she introduced as Miaoyin, who pulled up more chairs for her and Miaolu. The two women were dressed in identical blue tunics and pants.

"Tell us about yourselves and why you've come to Fangxian," said Miaoyin.

Puqing went over the highlights of their flight from the rebel outbreaks in Sichuan and their desire to find refuge and service on Wudang Mountain. He introduced each member of the group.

"How acquainted are you with the healing arts?"

Zou Run perked up at this and expounded on their skills with Daoist bodily technologies.

"We can perform demonstrations on you if you have the instruments," added Sai'er.

"You have an eastern accent," said Miaoyin.

"I'm from Shandong."

"How about you?" she asked Yin Yan.

"Sichuan."

"I detect Henan accents in you two," she asked Puqing and Zou Run. "Am I right?"

"That's correct."

"You all seem to be from everywhere. How did you end up together?"

The eight looked at each other, not sure how to answer.

"Don't worry, you are safe here. Miaolu told me you came from the temple and assures me you are trustworthy people. You got in the city with false passes, right? We would never report you for that. But we need to learn more about you before introducing you to the Mistress."

"Oh, so you are not the Mistress?" said Sai'er. "What do you practice here?"

"As you can see, this is a pharmacy. A small pharmacy, an apothecary. We study and administer medicines."

"So does her daughter," Yin Yan said, pointing to Xinru.

"Unfortunately, she isn't with us," said Xinru. "But I'm sure she'd fit in well here, with all her knowledge."

"I seem to detect in you a Shaanxi accent," said Miaolu. "I also—"

At that moment three young women entered. The first one stared and exclaimed, "Mama! Baba!"

8

The apothecary shop

n their little bower near the temple nunnery, they found the privacy they needed to take instruction without distraction when the nuns took their afternoon nap. Qiezi was a strict disciplinarian, making her two devotees collect and identify a veritable materia medica of leaves, flowers, insects and their uses, alone and in combination, to effect cures for which injuries and diseases, above all for women's nether region, about which scandalous ignorance reigned. It wouldn't do simply to show Yuejiang and Jingjing how she kept her jade gate clean and supple by massaging it wet; she made them quiz and examine each other. Replenished with the flower, Qiezi had become very dangerous of late. The exchange of saliva, or the mere kiss of her jade gate, might be lethal. She had no idea how long it would take, how many more hells Yuejiang would have to undergo, before she could tolerate more of the poison. Perhaps she never would because the flower needed to be eaten in childhood.

Jingjing was envious of Yuejiang and demanded to be poisoned. It was torture to keep having her face pushed away whenever Qiezi opened her legs. *I want to get sick!* she pleaded. To compound the torture, the disciples were under orders to love each other, but their jealousy was getting in the way. *If it's too hard to love each other, just pretend to and love will follow by repetition and habit*, insisted Qiezi. Yet progress was rocky, and Qiezi's efforts to make them kiss and exchange their tongues backfired when Jingjing bit Yuejiang's tongue hard enough to draw blood. *How dare you bite her!* yelled Qiezi, who slapped and beat Jingjing and reduced her to sobbing. *Stop it!* said Qiu Lu'er, who had poked her face in the secret grotto. *How did you find us?* said a shocked Qiezi. *Who cares how I found you? Don't let me tell the Mistress what you are doing. This behavior doesn't become you.* The three of them were afraid of Lu'er. It was not so much their being unclothed together (it was no secret Lu'er herself was the bedmate of Mistress Xie, a woman more than twice her age), and in a location an inquisitive male might ferret out, but the loss of composure that would reflect badly on them.

They were lucky to find the leisure to be alone together in any case. As word got out of their pharmaceuticals and customers grew into a steady stream, the girls were kept busy preparing the medicines they foraged for storage and sale. Whatever specimens were not consumed or applied in their raw state had to be sorted and prepared for extraction in a running chain of steps they rotated among and requiring everyone's cooperation. It was this shared labor more than anything else that sped up the healing of Yuejiang and Jingjing's mutual enmity. They also knew it was the only way into Qiezi's heart. In fact, it was the only way they could be alone with Qiezi at all; she was only intimate when the three of them were together and refused to see them alone. They were witness to each other: if one were to get poisoned from reckless contact with her, the other two would know how it happened. This kept the three of them in a delicate balance and restrained them. They must have realized as well that Qiezi made them kiss with abandon since she herself could not. Yet after initially being nauseating for them both, once accustomed to it, this kissing with abandon became halfway pleasurable.

Upon the first watch one evening when sunset blanched the

medicines of their richest hues and the work of the day was done, seven male customers appeared at the entrance to the women's quarters, led by a tall man with a long thin beard. It was evident from the way they carried themselves that they were armed, whether for protection or mischief, with swords hidden under their cloaks.

"I have heard," said the leader, "there is a woman who can heal. A woman with magical powers, a shamaness. May we come in?"

"This is a nunnery," said Qiu Lu'er. "No men are allowed. Go down to the main reception hall and ask for the resident doctor whose patients are male."

"It is essential that I see this woman. I am ill and I have come all the way up the mountain to see her. What can I do to persuade you? I have *taels*."

Lu'er sighed and considered for a moment before escorting them around to the rear patio, where they were told to wait. A quarter of a Chinese hour later (half an hour), Lu'er reappeared with Ren *daozhang*, Mistress Xie, and two male guards borrowed from the temple. "What business do you have?" said the *daozhang*.

"Who is the woman healer we have heard about? I am ill and require the best medical attention. I have money. We come in supplication and are not a danger to you."

"What is the matter with you?" said the Mistress.

"Let me handle this," said Qiezi, squeezing through the two older women. "I am she," she said to the man.

"So young! How can you have acquired all the medical knowledge attributed to you?"

"You're welcome to go down to see the temple's resident doctor who is elderly and more experienced than I am."

"But he does not have your reputation!"

The man, who introduced himself as Pudu, explained his symptoms to Qiezi. Examining his pulse and tongue and pressing and prodding his bared torso, she then disappeared into the nuns' chambers. She came back with several paper packets and told him how to prepare and consume their contents. "You should rest for as long as you take the medicine. Laymen's quarters are available for you and your company if you inquire at the main reception hall," she said.

After the men left, the Mistress was angry with Qiezi for revealing herself to their leader, who could well be expected to find the youthful healer irresistible and would be returning to cause trouble. Qiezi responded that she would rather take responsibility for any trouble herself than bring bad repute on all of them. She claimed she knew what to do and he'd be satisfied.

A week later they were back and bearing food. "Thanks to your miracle healer, the medicine is working and I feel better," said Pudu. "We wish to show our gratitude with a feast. If you would kindly accept our offer, please eat with us."

Tables were set up in the patio for Pudu, his six followers, the *daozhang*, the five women healers, and their two guards. After eating in silence for several minutes, Pudu said, "Young lady, you are famous but also nameless. What is your name?"

"Call me that—Wuming: the Nameless One."

"You are very beautiful. Where are you from?"

"I cannot tell you that."

"How did you learn the healing arts?"

"That is also a private matter."

"So mysterious! What healing spirits do you consult?"

"I don't consult spirits."

"I will get to the heart of the matter. Have you heard the mantra, 'Eternal and Venerable Mother in our original home in the world of true emptiness'?"

"I'm afraid not. What does it mean?" said Qiezi.

"That's a Daoist expression," said Ren *daozhang*. "It refers to Xiwangmu, the Queen Mother of the West, who lives on the mythical Mount Kunlun. She is also known as the Eternal Venerable Mother."

"That is correct. But there is more. I am the leader of a sect that believes in the Eternal Venerable Mother. I have a large following. We seek longevity and immortality through the healing arts. We are awaiting your Wuming to join us."

"You want me to visit your sect? You have more ill people?"

"I want you to join our sect."

"I have no need to join your sect. I am content here."

"I am asking your hand in marriage."

"And I'm afraid I must respectfully refuse. I am a Daoist nun."

"I am aware this is sudden. I will give you time to think about it. We will be back in one week to ask again. If you must refuse, so be it. But before we leave today, we have a custom that we practice in the spirit of generosity, which is that a male host offer his wife to his male guest for the night, and this favor is returned in kind when the host visits the guest."

After a moment of stunned silence, the *daozhang* said, "What does this have to do with us? We have no men among us."

"I am your male guest. I ask that a bed be prepared for me and Wuming."

"We count ourselves generous in spirit, but this of course must be refused. It would be the ruin of any of our girls, who are virgins and not inclined towards men."

"I am acting not out of lewd desire but because it has been decreed by fate. I would not expect every host to comply, but these are not ordinary circumstances. Fate has brought me and Wuming together. If all of you join our sect, you will be safe with us."

"Safe from what?"

"The black wind."

"We are safe enough here," said the Mistress. "We are also under the protection of the temple. That is enough for us, and it should be enough for you."

"I will tell you why you cannot sleep with me," said Qiezi. "I am poisonous and you will die."

Pudu laughed out loud. "I don't know whether to call that a clever or a silly response." He laughed again, as did his six followers. "Or a funny one." He stood up. "And it only enflames me the more. By awarding me the honor of your body, Wuming, you can be queen of thousands of followers. Prepare the bed now so that we may depart and leave you in peace after the ceremony has been performed!"

"My whole life I have been saturated with the deadly golden ocean flower. Any man who sleeps with me dies, and I have killed not a few."

"She tells the truth," said Yuejiang. "I was sickened from accidental contact with her and almost died."

"It is impossible to die in this manner," said Pudu. "And even were it possible, I would welcome such a glorious death. I would wish to die in no other way. But I am invulnerable to the residue of a mere flower. Now put me to the test."

Pudu took a step toward Qiezi, and the guards stood up.

"Damn you!" said Qiezi, losing her temper. "I am tired of killing people! Now you listen to me. Your six followers will have a dead body on their hands. There will be an investigation: a man who today looked hale enough, dead from my medical treatment the next day. I could be charged with your murder. Do you not respect me enough to consider the consequences for *me*?"

"Let me be proof you have this ability!" said Pudu. "I will sign a statement with my blood that you are all absolved of any responsibility for my death, and that my death results from my own self-administered poisoning. My six followers will vouch for you. Now prepare the bed," he commanded.

"All right. Let's do it. But only on condition everyone here is present to witness the act and see with your own eyes that no sorcery or trickery is involved, nor any visible evidence of poison."

The *daozhang* and the Mistress were appalled. "You don't mean to do this?" they said to Qiezi. "It's outrageous and unheard of. How can you consent to your rape? When he and his men leave, what's to prevent them from bragging about their violation of one of our nuns, violated in our presence no less!"

"*Daozhang*," said Jingjing, "what she says is true. He really will die. She told us things in private that she has not divulged to you or the Mistress."

"It is quite impossible," said the Mistress. "No one can die from poison in a woman's *yindao* unless it is put there for the purpose, and in that case she will die too. The datura flower does not have this power."

"Oh, yes it does," said Qiezi. "Pudu, you will feel nothing at first. After a few hours, you will become incapacitated and by this evening or tomorrow at the latest will expire."

"Master," said one of Pudu's men, "Let me have her first, in case she truly is poisonous. Let me be sacrificed so that you may live."

"It is nonsense, I tell you," Pudu retorted. To Qiezi he said, "Let me make my intention plainer. I will now also put down in blood that if I survive, I will carry you down the mountain with me as my wife. But if I die, bury me here, and let my six followers carry you down the mountain as the new leader of our sect!"

In the back entrance to the women's quarters and without the inner chambers was a room set up for honored guests with a canopy bed. The fifteen women and men squeezed into the room and stood around the bed as Qiezi and Pudu dropped their garments. Qiezi lay back on the bed and parted her legs. Not inclined towards men, the women covered their faces with both hands while their distressed eyes wondered through their fingers how this young Daoist healer could bring herself to engage in the act so shamelessly. To flush out my poison so he can die a speedy death, she would have told them, and to ensure the poor devil's final fuck is the best he's ever had, not because he deserves it but because this is how it's done and it must be done right. She even arched her pelvis upward to meet him halfway, "raising her Yin to meet his Yang" as they say, and moaned and yelled as they slapped against each other and her womb expanded and her muscles contracted to milk his jade stalk of its last drop. Her expression, as she withdrew and cleaned herself with a hot towel, was calm, even beatific.

They returned to the patio. Qiezi reminded Pudu that the poison had no antidote. A confident Pudu told her not to worry, he wouldn't need any. But it wasn't long before he grew drowsy, disoriented, and finally delirious. They had to return him to the bed. His followers thought he was asleep and assumed he would be fine in the morning. He was in fact already in a coma and quite dead by morning. Two of his followers were disbelieving and enraged.

"What did you do to him?" they demanded. "We are going to inform the temple authorities that you have used sorcery to bewitch and murder our leader. We would have you understand, if you don't already, that homicidal witchcraft incurs slicing and dismemberment!"

The *daozhang* had prepared for this moment, having anticipated the worst, and bought the two men's silence. "By accepting these *taels*," she said, "you acknowledge that your leader was already deathly ill and beyond cure upon your first arrival here. And have you forgotten already that we have his statement signed in blood absolving us of any responsibility? At all events, if the temple authorities become involved, it is you who will fall under suspicion. You are not from the mountain. You profess to believe in the Eternal Venerable Mother and the so-called black wind, which as you are surely aware makes you rebels and outlaws whom the government has been hunting down throughout this region."

This was enough to convince the two, and they departed with the corpse wrapped in a shroud.

The remaining four prostrated themselves before Qiezi. "We serve you, Mistress," they said. "Let us lead you down the mountain so that you may lead *us*."

"I need not be present among you. I can lead as well from here. I have no wish to leave. Those who need our medicine can send for it. That is all I will do."

"Our followers will demand to know what happened to our leader. They will come here in search of him. Pudu was right that the fates have intervened today momentously. You have no choice. You must come with us."

"This turn of events is unbelievable and most unfortunate. We are not prepared for this," said Mistress Xie.

"Where are they taking your Master's body?" the *daozhang* asked.

"To have him buried in Henan's Nanyang, his hometown, the

only proper place, even if it is against his wish to be buried on the mountain."

"Tell his followers to find him there," said the Mistress.

"No, they are right," said the *daozhang*. "They will come here seeking answers. We cannot escape the problem by hiding in these walls."

"Mantuoluo cannot be expected to leave with them under such sudden circumstances," whispered the Mistress to the *daozhang*. She turned to the four men. "Come back in one week, while we work out a solution."

"A week is too long. The master's body will already have arrived in Nanyang by then and word will have spread. Word may spread even before they reach Nanyang. That opens the door to chaos and exposure to government spies."

"Where do you intend to take her?" said the *daozhang*.

"To the walled city of Fangxian, two days down the mountain on foot at a fast pace, where we have one of our largest and most secure networks."

In compromise the men agreed to return in three days' time. By then the *daozhang* and the Mistress were of one mind on the matter. The only recourse was for the Mistress to collect her girls and join the new sect. Qiezi became the new Mistress, though she decided to keep the name by which she was already known, Mantuoluo. Xie Yinhe was content to manage Qiezi behind the scenes and teach her confidence and the proper comportment and reasoned severity of a leader. They and the men also hit upon the most logical solution as to where to lodge them in Fangxian, and that was to open an apothecary business in a dwelling large enough to accommodate the five women and the four men, who were invited to live with them as equals and protectors.

Fangxian had several pharmacies and apothecaries scattered throughout the city, so when a new one opened it did not call too much attention to itself. New businesses were opening left and right now that the violent upheaval of the past spring had settled down. Yinhe had *taels* enough from their burgeoning medicinal business at the nunnery, but Pudu's organization had far more from sect member contributions. The combined wealth enabled them to purchase a large courtyard dwelling whose street entrance was converted into their shop. The ordinary shop front gave little indication of the size of their operation. That was how they wanted to keep things.

Qiezi, Yuejiang, and Jingjing shared a canopy bed in one room; Yinhe and Lu'er another; and the four senior males shared two more rooms. Another two rooms served as dormitories for more male and female assistants hired for the many labor-intensive tasks. Several more rooms were set aside for guests. Still more rooms were needed for the chopping, grinding, pounding, boiling, steaming, frying, sifting, washing, and drying of medicinal plants and their storage, for the milling of grains, for cooking and eating, and for bathing (the dwelling had its own well). It wasn't long before the crowded compound was stretched to capacity and looked like it had been lived in for a generation. The sect's many other followers resided in their own homes throughout the city and surrounding countryside. It was too risky to hold nighttime gatherings even in politically relaxed times, being of course illegal. Instead, privileged sect members (those who contributed the most money), posing as customers, would assemble at the compound every few weeks for daytime meetings and seances. Meanwhile, Xie's girls rotated their services at local doctors to gain more hands-on knowledge of the healing arts (there were no hospitals to speak of).

One day at the start of the cold season, Qiu Lu'er arrived back from doctor duty with eight exhausted and bedraggled newcomers in tow, more than the usual number of customers at one time. Their poise suggested they were more than mere vagrants looking for free medicine to cure whatever frightful ailments but pilgrims of a sort who had been traveling long and far. They could only guess at their purpose and their connection, if any, to their own sect. Lu'er trusted her instincts they might be useful folks, and Yinhe trusted Lu'er to bring useful folks in. They were gathered in the reception room where Yinhe and Lu'er began to grill them.

Whenever unknown customers or guests were invited in to be interviewed, Yinhe made Qiezi, Yuejiang, and Jingjing hide themselves for the sake of their anonymity and mystique, unless or until informed they could present themselves. Normally the three were too preoccupied with pharmaceutical tasks to notice, if they were even at hand and not out on a foraging mission. But today the uncharacteristic bustling caught their attention. They hovered in the background catching fragments of conversation, while keeping out of view. When Qiezi heard a voice she recognized, she rushed into the room and flew into her parents' arms. The three collapsed in tears. Everyone else stood around speechless. Then they all spoke at the same time.

"Is this your daughter?" Kang Sai'er asked Lai Xinru, as if more confirmation was needed.

"Is this your daughter who is expert in medicines?" said Yin Yan.

"Baobei, how did you get here?" Xinru asked Qiezi.

"How did *you* get here?"

"We were fleeing the rebels in Sichuan," said Yan Xian. "But how did you ever wind up here?"

"Everyone, please, we're as confused as you. This is simply incredible. Can we start from the beginning?" said Miaoyin.

Each side wanted to hear the other side's story first.

When Qiezi recovered herself, she said, "You cannot imagine my tangled journey. It will take me the rest of the day to recount it. First of all, Baba, tell me who these friends of yours are and why you are here in Fangxian."

"Yes," said Miaoyin. "Let me propose that our honored guests be the first to unburden themselves so that we can be better acquainted. As I mentioned, you need not fear divulging anything. I'm confident we have a lot in common, and we may soon be working together. But I'm sure Mantuoluo is eager to hear your story."

"Mantuoluo?" said Yan Xian.

"Baba, it's the name I assumed when I fled our home. I'll explain later over dinner. We shall prepare a banquet. And beds for you all tonight. This is Miaoyue," she said, pointing to one of the two young ladies she had entered with, whose hair was bound in a crescent tiara, befitting the "moon" of her given name. And pointing to the other, "This is Miaojing," who had short hair and quartz crystal earrings, befitting the "crystal" of her given name. Gesturing to the four men who had joined them, "These are Jueyi, Jue'er, Juesan, and Juesi." The men bowed to the guests and sat down on either side of the five female hosts. All were dressed in blue except Qiezi, whose tunic and pants were immaculate white; her hair had grown out to the same length as Miaojing's, and her ear held a purple triple-nested datura flower. Miaoyue and Miaojing sat on her right, Miaoyin and Miaolu on her left.

"So *you* are the Mistress?" Zou Run asked Qiezi.

Xinru and Yan Xian were still too overcome to talk.

Sai'er took over. "I met your lovely parents in Taiping in Sichuan." She proceeded to relate all that had happened from their first encounter at the temple fair up to the present. "We've heard so much about you from your parents, Mantuoluo—shall I call you Mistress or Mantuoluo?—and we have heard what happened to you and why you had to flee. You have nothing to fear from us, I assure you. And I must say, you are even more ravishing than I had imagined."

"She still prefers Mantuoluo, but I told her she will only become a 'Mistress' when she demands to be called as such," said Miaoyin.

"If I may ask, why do you all share the same first character in your names?" said Yin Yan.

"It's the custom among many healers, though we haven't adopted it," said Sai'er.

"Yes, they are our venerable names. They show our commitment to each other," said Miaoyin. "We'd like to address you likewise. Simply add the character *miao* to your given name if you are female, and *jue* if you are male."

Reintroducing themselves afresh to their hosts, Sai'er thus became Miaosai, Xinru became Miaoxin, Zou Run became Miaorun, Yin Yan became Miaoyan, and He Le became Miaole;

Yan Xian became Juexian and Shen Wei became Juewei.

"Puqing already has a venerable name, so he needn't adopt a new one," said Zou Run. "And I'd like to keep my own name as well for now, thank you."

All except the Shaanxi family then left to fetch their belongings from the temple, while their hosts set about preparing the feast. Qiezi lay in her mother's arms, as Xinru stroked her hair.

"Ma, you two need to get cleaned up and in new clothes. We have a bathing room and you can do that now. Your friends can bathe when they're back."

"Where will we sleep tonight? Is it safe here?"

"You and Baba will sleep in my bed with me. I'll put Miaoyue and Miaojing in another room. We have several rooms and will work something out for everyone after we clear some space."

"Are they the two beautiful girls who came in with you? I already can't remember anyone's name."

"I'll explain everything over our meal."

After the eight had bathed, they were given blue outfits. As the two guestrooms contained only a single canopy bed each, the hosts fretted over how to divide up the remaining four female and two male guests, as it was unheard of (more out of acculturation to the nunnery than adherence to traditional proscriptions) for unrelated mixed-sex guests to sleep in the same bedroom, let alone the same bed. Still, Zou Run and Sai'er insisted on sharing one of the beds, with Puqing on a mat on the floor, and likewise Yin Yan and He Le in the other room's bed, with Shen Wei on the floor—an arrangement tolerated for the time being. Miaoyue and Miaojing joined Miaoyin and Miaolu in their room. The hosts scrounged stray tables and pushed them together to accommodate the large dinner party. Xinru and Yan Xian got pride of place on either side of Qiezi. As the guest of honor, Puqing sat across from them. The occasion required that the fare be elaborated beyond the usual with a variety of fishes and meats.

Qiezi recounted her days of hardship in the mountains with Ye Yuejiang (now Miaoyue) on her back and their rendezvous with Gu Jingjing (now Miaojing) and Qiu Lu'er (now Miaolu) at

Wudang Mountain's Purple Cloud Palace. She told of her desperate search for the flower and the threats from the gardener whose datura flowers she stole, fortunately resolved without serious incident. She told of the sharing of her extensive knowledge of plants with Xie Yinhe (now Miaoyin) and the temple's resident nuns, and of their growing reputation as healers and the income it provided. But when she moved on to what happened next, her voice broke. Miaoyin took over and recounted the portentous arrival of Pudu at the nunnery and the events that brought them down the mountain to Fangxian, and the conversion of the present courtyard home into an apothecary business.

"Pudu," said Shen Wei. "I seem to recall that name from somewhere. No, it was today, that man in the Daoist temple dormitory who mistook Puqing for him."

"Well, Puqing?" said Qiezi.

Puqing sighed. "Yes, my estranged twin brother. Pudu."

"What!" gasped everyone apart from Zou Run, Sai'er, and Qiezi herself, who said, "As soon as I saw you, I knew you were his brother. But I wanted it to come straight from your mouth."

"You have an estranged brother?" said Yin Yan. "Why haven't you told us anything about this?"

"I felt no need to divulge the sorry history. Until now, that is."

"You two also knew about this?"

Zou Run and Sai'er nodded.

"Are you pregnant with Pudu's child?" Puqing asked Qiezi.

"No man has ever gotten me pregnant. The poison in me takes care of that. Unless—no, let's get back to the topic at hand, Puqing."

"Let us first finish our feast. And before I relate all, a toast to our fortuitous encounter!"

"*Ganbei!*"

Puqing kept everyone in suspense while he gazed in the distance. The meal had been thrown together in a rush. The female guests helped in the kitchen after suggesting a rather primitive yet sumptuous travelers stew, a soup of everything (chicken, potatoes, cabbages, carrots, onions) tossed in and boiled down to a rich gravy, while chunks of cornmeal dough were pressed around the inner edge of the giant wok and steamed into cakes. "Don't eat such a rich meal too hastily after surviving for so long on scraps," he cautioned his party. "Chew thoroughly."

"Your daughter must be very experienced in the wild," he said to Yan Xian.

Miaoyin asked him, "We are eager to hear as well about your knowledge of bodily rejuvenation, as you were mentioning before Mantuoluo entered."

"You and your new Mistress are the real healing experts and must be more knowledgeable than us. But I wonder if you have seen this medicine," said Puqing, retrieving his leather pouch from beneath his tunic and passing it to Qiezi and Miaoyin.

"What's this?" said Qiezi.

"The leaves and flowers of the hemp plant."

"It's a medicine? I thought the plant was used only for its fiber," said Miaoyin.

"It is the finest medicine, and I'm surprised you don't know of it. Its powers are described in both Shennong's and Li Shizhen's great herbal compendia."

"The silly medicine," grinned He Le.

"Oh, yes, I recall reading that," said Qiezi. "But I don't often encounter hemp plants. What does the medicine do and how do you prepare it? And what do you mean the 'silly medicine'?" she asked He Le.

"It makes me silly and stupid. I can't talk. As soon as I start saying something, I forget what I was saying."

"You still haven't learned how to let it work its magic," said Puqing.

"It does help with pain, though."

"We were set upon by bandits and an arrow pierced her breast," Zou Run explained.

Miaoyin and Qiezi went up to He Le. "Show us."

He Le pulled up her tunic.

"It's healing. But does your plaster contain the three-seven plant?" said Qiezi.

"Of course," said Zou Run.

"Let us show you the powers of the hemp medicine," said Puqing. "Bring a plate of coals from your stove or brazier and set it on the table."

Qiezi and Miaoyin picked out and smelled the dried buds from Puqing's pouch. "Sort of a pine smell," said Qiezi.

"It's an aphrodisiac," said Sai'er. "What with so many exquisite new creatures here, Puqing will certainly be inviting you all to join his *Yellow Book* initiation rite."

"What's that?"

"In due time. All in due time," said Puqing. "Inhaling the fumes of hemp fires the powers of thought. And I need it now to clarify the complicated circumstances we find ourselves in."

"It indeed works," said Shen Wei. "I write poetry with it."

"Does it cloud the awareness and render one helpless?" asked Jueyi.

"If your awareness is easily clouded, it may. If you are easily rendered helpless, it may. For me, it strengthens the awareness. For now, let the Mistress alone try it. Take it into your lungs with this bamboo tube and hold it in, like this," he said as he sprinkled the medicine onto the coals and inhaled the ignited buds.

He handed Qiezi the tube. She inhaled and coughed it out. "It's harsh."

"Try again."

"The smoke has a strong and fresh fragrance, like incense. Like burning moxa but sweeter," said Miaoyin.

"It reminds me of the magic *lingzhi* fungus," said Qiezi after a couple more tokes. She wiped the tube's mouth end off with a cloth dabbed in alcohol and handed it back to Puqing. "Have you tried the golden ocean flower?"

"The datura flower? No. It's poison. I wouldn't want to end up like my brother."

"I don't mean a lethal dose but eating a small amount of the flower. It will give you visions. The *mantuoluo* spirit can teach you many things. I can introduce you to her and be her interpreter."

"I will try it when the time is ripe. We are now in a period of passage and must attend to the journey."

"How long does the hemp medicine take to work? I don't feel anything."

"You may not feel anything at first. You must learn how to summon Magu, the hemp goddess. She can be startling when she makes her first appearance. You might forget where you are. But you will cease to be overwhelmed once you let her embrace you. As you can see, I seem normal after smoking it."

"We want to hear about Pudu," said Miaoyin.

"Right. My brother and I both had fiery temperaments, suitable for captivating and leading people. We were both involved in the White Lotus underground in Xiangyang. The difference between us is that I allowed the hemp goddess into my life, and he did not. He had no interest in the medicine. He boasted to his followers that he himself was their medicine. Magu transformed me and I saw the folly of the sect's teachings. He espoused violence and I did not. He and his followers rushed to Dangyang when the rebels took over the city earlier this year. I and my followers stayed in Xiangyang. He called us cowards for not joining them and said the rebels would be coming for Xiangyang next and everyone within its walls would be killed. *What do you mean everyone will be killed?* I asked him. *You too will be killed,* he said. I was shocked. *Are you threatening to kill me, your own brother? Are you threatening to kill innocent people?* He said, *You are either for us or against us. If you're against us, it's war. We will spare no one within Xiangyang's walls. How can you not understand this?* I said, *You are a fool to think you can take over a city as large and well-guarded as Xiangyang.* He then brandished a sword I hadn't seen before, a brass sword inlaid with jade. *This sword confers the authority to decide matters of life and death. O brother, it will soon be too late! You cannot stop the turning of the* kalpa. *A black tempest thick with the damned will fill the sky and vomit down mountains of bones and fill the ocean with blood!* That was the language he used to frighten people into joining his sect. We parted ways. When the Dangyang rebellion was put down I gave him up for lost." He turned to Pudu's four followers. "What happened? And do you still espouse violence?"

"We escaped with our lives from the Banner troops—Pudu and the six of us. It is too terrible to describe what happened to our families, all lost. After that experience, even Pudu renounced violence. But now is not the time to tell our story, which will occupy another evening," said Jueyi.

"Why are your venerable names numbered one through four? Is that the order of your ranking?"

"Yes. We had been numbered three through six, until Puyi and Pu'er fled with Pudu's corpse down the mountain. We have now changed our venerable names from Pu to Jue, numbered one through four."

"That is all I have to say for the moment about my brother," Puqing continued. "What is past is past. It is more important to consider what is to come. You said they took Pudu's corpse to Nanyang? I suspect they will not stay for long but will be returning, directly or again by way of Wudang Mountain, here to Fangxian, where Pudu last stayed before ascending the mountain. They will not come with friendly intent but instead to track you down, Mantuoluo, whom they will regard as the sect's false pretender. How long have you all been here and how well are you known by Pudu's followers?"

"About one month. We are already known by everyone," said Jueyi. "We have considered this question. We know which followers in Fangxian regard us favorably and accept the Mistress as Pudu's successor. Pudu was never in Fangxian long enough to take root among his followers here. He was regarded by many as elusive."

"But that won't stop Puyi and Pu'er from returning here to claim his mantel and worse: to accuse the new Mistress of practicing witchcraft."

"They can't accuse us of anything without casting suspicion on themselves," said Miaoyin. "And they will have no evidence."

"True, but when accusations start flying around, the authorities prick up their ears and trouble always ensues. But Mantuoluo, are you still not feeling the effects of the medicine?

Because if you are, you may already surmise what I am about to propose."

"I'm not feeling anything. I'm too busy trying to work out everything you are saying. But I think you mean to propose that you become Pudu."

"Exactly."

9

𝒯he inquest

ot arsenic," said the first runner.

"No, not arsenic. Must be aconite," said the coroner, examining the corpse laid out on the table. "You sure they didn't mention what poison was used?"

"We have no idea how he died," said Puyi.

"But you must have had some connection with the people who gave you the corpse."

"As I said, we had no prior contact with them. They were strangers. They could see we were heading for Henan."

"How long did it take for him to die?"

"I told you we don't what happened. We don't know anything about him."

"But you know his hometown."

"That's the only thing they told us. They paid us to bring him here."

"You know his hometown but not his name? You came all the way to Nanyang without knowing where to take him or how to contact his kin, only to dump him at a random funeral home?"

"Right."

The coroner stared at them. "Of course, you know his name. If you truly had nothing to do with this, you would not hesitate to reveal it. The fact you don't want to reveal it can only mean you have something to hide. You must be implicated in his death and don't want his relatives to be involved."

"You should be grateful we brought him here instead of abandoning him in the forest to become carrion," said Pu'er. "Corpses are found everywhere with no identity. It should be a simple matter to take care of this. How much are the caskets? We'll pay for an expensive one. That's all you need to know."

"You're telling *us* that's all we need to know? Casket or no casket, we have an inquest to perform. You can ask the magistrate himself if he thinks it's a simple matter."

"Why would we want to talk to the magistrate?"

This comment seemed to catch the coroner and his runners off guard. They coughed out a laugh and frowned. "It's not a question of whether you want to talk to the magistrate or not," said the first runner. "Or do they have any choice in the matter, Lao Li?"

"Finger press. Pop. *Aiya!* Elbow press. Scream. Ankle frame. Crunch," said the second runner, combining grunts and hand gestures.

"Lao Li is not as skilled at grammar as he is at extracting the truth out of people. He means you can ask the magistrate if he'll let you choose your instrument. I'm not sure he'll agree but you can try. We do have quite a collection. Shall we head over there now? It's not far," said the first, jangling a pair of iron cuffs attached by a chain.

Puyi and Pu'er looked at each other. Pu'er was beading with sweat. "All right. We'll come clean if you'll let us go," he said.

"Please do come clean. But we can't promise we'll let you go," said the coroner.

"We're Daoists, and the man's name is Pudu. He was our superior and that is the only name we knew him by. He had a bad liver and word had gotten round of a medicinal healer in the nun's quarters at Purple Cloud Palace on Wudang Mountain. We went there and located her. We were shocked such a young girl of barely marriageable age could be a healer, yet she indeed treated his affliction. But he was not in his right mind and a week later insisted on going back and seizing her for immoral purposes. We tried to dissuade him but he was adamant. At first, he said he only wanted carry her off as his wife but then demanded to do the act with her right in the nunnery. At this the girl seemed to become possessed and spoke with a different voice. She claimed her body was filled with the poisonous datura flower and he would die if he slept with her. And she demanded that we all be witness to the act! There was no trickery. She could not have stealthily given him poison since she was present the entire time. That's why she made everyone watch, so that she couldn't be accused of administering poison apart from the poison in her body. She warned him of the consequences. And he did die."

"She removed her clothes and had illicit sex with him before your very eyes?" said the coroner.

"She removed her clothes and had illicit sex with him before your very eyes!" echoed the first runner.

"We all witnessed the act, nuns included, crowded around the very bed."

"No one could make up a story this crazy," said the first runner. "They may actually be telling the truth."

"This enchantress, witch or whatever she was wouldn't reveal her name, nor would the nuns. They bribed us with *taels* to take the body away and not speak of the crime. That's the complete truth. We can lead you there to confirm everything we have said. She should still be there, if she hasn't run off somewhere or isn't a fox spirit, that is."

"It's not possible to die from the datura flower unless orally ingested," said the coroner. "Did they offer him anything to eat or drink?"

"No. We brought food for them."

The coroner considered for a moment. "Was she a tribal

woman, a Miao*? Was she immodestly dressed, say in a short, pleated skirt hemmed along the bottom with flower embroidery and no undergarments? Was her belly exposed?"

"The weather was already chilly. They were all in robes."

"Weren't they in purple garments?" said Puyi.

"Taoists don't wear that color," said the first runner.

"Oh, I recall now. She and several other healers lived at the nunnery but were not actual nuns," said Pu'er. "The healers were dressed in purple and yellow, including the girl. I have no idea if they were Miao. What does that have to do with it?"

"Were her feet unbound?" said the coroner.

"Yes, they were, in fact," said Puyi.

"Did she freely engage in illicit sex with your leader or was she raped?"

"She freely engaged in it. And she shouted in pleasure during the act."

"She *shouted* in pleasure during the act?" said the first runner. The coroner and runners were hanging on Puyi's every word.

"We were disgusted."

"Did you notice or feel an unusual amount of heat emanating from her body? Were her eyes red or bloodshot?" said the coroner.

"I don't recall."

"What struck us," said Pu'er, "was her lack of shame and her confidence that our master would be dead by the next morning, as if she was very practiced at killing men in this way."

"What were his symptoms before he died? Any vomiting? Bloody diarrhea?"

"Nothing. He only became sleepy after a few hours and they

---

* The Miao (aka. Hmong) (苗) are an ethnic minority concentrated in Guizhou Province. In the Qing Dynasty "Miao" was a derogatory signifier for any ethnic minority or outcast in China's southwest, comparable to the Western "gypsy." Note that the name bears no relation to the "Miao" (妙) of Miaolu, Miaoyin, etc., designating the female healers' religious affiliation or "venerable" names introduced in the previous two chapters.

returned him to the bed. We couldn't rouse him after that and he died in his sleep."

"Well, this all seems consistent with *gu* poisoning," said the coroner. "But it tends to take effect only over the course of several days. He must have succumbed uncommonly quickly."

"What is *gu* poisoning?" Pu'er asked. "I've heard of it but am not sure what it is."

"It's made of worms and insects, isn't it?" said Puyi.

"Yes, they fill a jar with centipedes, vipers, and toads and let them eat each other. The last creature to survive is ground to a powder and put in the victim's food. But I have heard that a witch need only create the poison and cast a spell, without the victim having to ingest it. Were any paper cutouts of men or dolls in evidence?"

"No."

"In any case, this is the theory we will have to go on for the time being," said the coroner.

"Miao women are sexually bold and notorious for *gu* poisoning," explained the first runner. "This witch sounds like a Miao. We would like to investigate her ourselves. Wouldn't we, Lao Li?"

"Yep," he said, with shining eyes.

"But it's no simple matter to go up the mountain. It's across the border in Hubei and out of our jurisdiction. The trip would need the magistrate's approval and the cooperation of the local authorities in Hubei. And it might all be for nothing if the witch has vanished and the nunnery denies any involvement. Not to mention the journey's dangerous enough as it is, what with all the banditry along the way."

"How about twenty *taels* to spare you the effort?" said Puyi, reaching into his robe.

"Twenty *taels*! Who do you take us for?" exclaimed the coroner.

"That's all we have."

"We'll see about that." The runners proceeded to strip Puyi and Pu'er bare and examine every square inch of their garments.

They also emptied the contents of their sacks. "Now that's more like it," said the first runner, as they scooped up scores of little silver ingots that tinkled onto the floor. "Ah, yes. Twenty, forty, sixty, eighty *taels*. These will do!"

"Wait," said the coroner, who grabbed a *tael* and examined it in the light of the window. "Yes, perfectly formed pine rings on the surface. They're genuine enough."

"Please, sirs, leave us something for our return trip," said Pu'er.

"Where are you heading?"

"Fangxian."

"In Hubei? You can beg for alms in Dengzhou on the way. I hear they're generous to priests," said the first runner with a grin.

"Let's get out of here," Puyi said as he pulled Pu'er by his sleeve out the door before he could protest any further.

"They robbed us! Luckily they didn't examine our daggers."

"Oh, they know about every secret stash, I can assure you," said Puyi. He clicked open the hollowed-out handle of his dagger as if to confirm he still had his emergency *taels*. "I think they were afraid we'd use our daggers on them in a rage if they took the last of our money. Why did you reveal our destination? They could follow us and have us arrested."

"We won't be passing through Dengzhou, remember? It's too dangerous. We're returning the way we came, back up the mountain."

"And why were you so honest about—"

"Hey, where are you going?" said a woman with an unkempt shock of hair who skipped up to them. She was attired in a dirty robe, striped leggings, and sandals.

"Who are you?"

"Are you heading for the gate? Can I go with you?"

"If you're a beggarwoman, go away."

"No, I'm not. Are you heading south? I'm going to Xiangyang and don't want to travel alone. I saw you two leaving the funeral home and thought you must be reliable and respectable men. Are you Daoists?"

"Young lady, look at you," said Puyi. "You're in no shape to travel. We don't have money. Go back to your hovel."

The two men pressed on to the city gate. The girl kept pace with them.

"I'm not as bad as I look. I dress like this so I don't draw evil men's attention. You must be staying in temples. Let me go with you."

"What makes you think we're going to Xiangyang?" said Pu'er.

"What business do you have there?" said Puyi.

"Are you White Lotus?" she said.

"Why? Are you?"

"Which direction are you headed?"

"Wudang Mountain," said Puyi.

"Lady, we can't help you," said Pu'er, tugging at Puyi's sleeve.

"I'm familiar with that route. I can show you temples where you can stay."

"We're not going the usual route but the northern route."

"I know that route too. I can tell you're not from here. Let me guide you."

"What kind of nonsense is this? You said you were going to Xiangyang," said Pu'er.

"I am. But I can delay that.'

"We can't support you. We have no money."

"Let me go with you. Please. You don't have to feed me."

"Are you dangerous? Do you have a weapon?" said Puyi.

"Not at all. See?" She opened her robe, revealing a threadbare patchwork of rags serving as an undergarment.

The two men continued walking as the girl trailed behind. "Make her leave," Pu'er whispered. "Did you see her eyes, staring off in two directions? Something's wrong with her."

"That's not a mental problem. Some people have eyes pointing away like that. Let her come. She's harmless and might even come in handy. And she doesn't have bound feet so she won't slow us down."

"Do you think she's a Miao? Did you notice those underclothes of hers all full of holes?"

"Why a Miao?"

"Unbound feet and immodest dress. And she looks different."

They glanced at her. "Are you a Miao?" they asked.

"What's that?"

"A Miao woman. Or are you a Han?"

"A what?"

"You sure are a simpleton. What's your name?"

"Bi Yaoyao."

"Where are you from?"

"Hunan."

"How did you wind up here?"

"My family fled here when I was little."

"How old are you? Where's your home?"

"Twenty-two. I have no home. My parents passed away years ago."

"You look older than that. How do you live?"

"I run errands. I carry women around town on my back. I'm supposed to run an errand for someone in Xiangyang that pays well but it's dangerous to go there now. Can I be your friend?"

The men sighed. "Just don't cause us any trouble."

"Oh, thank you so much!" she said, grabbing Pu'er by the arm. She stuffed a wheat cake Puyi handed her into her mouth. "Where are you two coming from?" she said.

"Wudang Mountain. We're heading back there now. We heard the western route through Dengzhou is too dangerous. Have you heard anything about that?"

"All the routes are dangerous. That's why I need someone to travel with."

"Were you with the rebels?" Pu'er asked her.

"Whenever I hear of people taking up arms, I avoid them. I hate violence."

After an hour of walking, it was getting dark. They came upon a village with a row of several inns. "Let's call it a day and find something to eat," Puyi said to Pu'er.

"Yeah. I'm exhausted as well. Though I'm so upset about the money we lost I don't have much of an appetite."

"I don't like the look of these inns," said Yaoyao. "Don't you want to stay at a temple? I know of one a few *li* up ahead."

"Keep your advice to yourself. You're safe enough with us," said Pu'er.

One inn advertised free dinners for staying guests, with tables set up inside and out in the front, sheltered by a makeshift canopy. Several customers were eating and the food smelled good. They were told they had to register and affirm their identity before being served.

"Since when do inns require travel passes?" said Pu'er.

"It's the law," said the innkeeper.

"You're the first inn to request them."

"The 'law' is only their excuse for demanding a higher rate if we don't have passes," added Puyi.

"No free meal without a travel pass," reiterated the innkeeper. "Moreover, women must sleep separately so you'll be charged for two rooms."

The price quoted was too high and they started to walk out.

"We do have space in the garret," said the innkeeper, pointing to the ceiling.

"The garret?" they said.

Standing up on his desk, the innkeeper pushed open a disguised trapdoor with a pole and drew down a rope ladder with the pole's hook. Puyi and Pu'er climbed up and looked inside.

"There's not much room to stand up in and no windows, but as you can see, there is enough space to sit up in. You three can have it for the price of one room. And I'll even throw in the free meals. You folks look like garret types anyway. Don't make any noise or there will be big trouble for you if you're caught by any runners doing the rounds. You'll be charged with illicit sex just for being in the same room together."

"How about a bathing basin and a lamp?" said Puyi.

"Twenty cash to borrow a lamp with enough oil to last an hour and thirty cash for each bucket of water. You'll have to heat the water and haul it up yourself. If you spill so much as a drop, that's a thirty cash surcharge."

After a meal of stir-fried garlic shoots and pork intestines, the three got settled in the garret, Puyi lifting the water bucket up to Pu'er perched on the ladder, who handed it to Yaoyao through the trapdoor. They let her wash herself in private before heading up themselves. She stayed put during their turn, huddling away from them in her robe.

"Don't you have any kind of home? Where do you live?" asked Puyi.

Her damp lips angled into view in the light of the lamp. "I share a room with two other women. I don't get along with them."

"Why not?"

She turned to them and bored her eyes into Pu'er as he squatted in the bathing basin. The lamplight somehow flattered and dignified her faulty eyes' strange gaze. "They're always talking about magic and ridiculous stuff and cursing and complaining."

"Don't all women believe in magic?"

"I believe in life. Life is magic enough for me."

"What do they complain about?"

"Petty little things. Like drying my unlucky-day rags with the stains facing outward. I tell them, *Hang up a sheet so you don't have to look at me and I don't have to look at you and you can do whatever you like.* They start yelling at me over that. I say, *Don't you have more important things to complain about? If you don't like my rags, why don't you use that magic of yours to cast a spell on my unlucky days so I don't have them anymore. I'd be more than happy about that. And while you're at it, why don't you use that magic of yours to rid the room of the lice that creep out of your mattresses because you're too lazy to change the straw. You're accusing us of your lice, you wall-eyed cunt?* one of them says and slaps me. I say, *Why don't you just kill me and get it over with!* I hand her a cleaver and tear my shirt open, like this. I say, *Go ahead, cut out my heart so you can eat it! Isn't that what you really want to do? Isn't that what you were born on this earth to do? But you're too cowardly to admit it so you just complain all day.* That shut them up. Oh, no, it looks like I shut you up too. Don't be afraid of me."

In their undergarments and robes the two men slipped under filthy blankets on the remnants of two straw mats, while Yaoyao went back to fiddling with herself by the oil lamp. When the flame went out, she crawled onto the mat next to Puyi, who had pushed Pu'er to the wall to give space for her on his other side. In the darkness Pu'er couldn't tell whether she still had her clothes on, but their rustling was obvious enough. Puyi heaved, and Yaoyao got up to wash herself. Pu'er turned on his side, facing the wall. The steady eye contact she had been giving him, the younger and handsomer of the two, made it plain where her designs lay next. Still, this raw woman terrified him, as if he now had to undergo the same trial Pudu had in the Daoist nunnery. His heart pounding, he pretended to be asleep when he felt her pulling his blanket up, wiggling between them and embracing him. Grabbing his erection, she climbed on top of him.

Soon after dawn the three of them jumped up off their mats with a collective scream. "A rat!"

They opened the trapdoor to let in light. Yaoyao chased the rat into a corner and crushed it with the edge of the water bucket. Dangling the rat through the opening by its tail, she shouted at the innkeeper, "You should be paying *us* to stay here!" She tossed it at the cook and it landed squarely in the bubbling oil of his wok.

"You're paying for the dishes you ruined!" the innkeeper yelled back.

They dressed and gathered their belongings. Yaoyao was the first to descend the ladder.

"Here, let me help you," said the innkeeper. As he eased her off the ladder, he slipped his hands under her robe and let her body slide through his grasp as she lost her foothold, leaving her dangling naked by her arms. "Oops!" he smirked.

The guests at their breakfast sniggered and laughed. When Puyi and Pu'er descended the ladder to rescue Yaoyao, it snapped from their combined weight and they tumbled to the floor.

"And you're also paying for breaking the ladder!" he added.

As Pu'er attended to Yaoyao, Puyi got up and slugged the innkeeper so hard he was knocked out flat on his back. The guests overturned their tables getting out of the way as the cook in turn flung the wok's boiling oil at Puyi, which caught him on the face.

Puyi and Pu'er made for the cook with their daggers.

"Let me take care of this," said Yaoyao, grabbing Pu'er's dagger. While the cook was fending them off, she severed the strings fastening the canvas tarp to the awning's frame, which sheltered part of the kitchen, and the tarp caved onto the cook and the stove.

"Help me out of here!" the cook screamed, struggling under the tarp. It was smoking and catching fire.

People from the adjacent inns had gathered out in front to gawk at the commotion. Puyi and Pu'er waved their daggers at them to warn them away as they walked off. Those inside the inn were too busy trying to snuff out the fire to do anything about the trio. They didn't look back to see if the fire was out of control but headed off down the main road. "Stay calm. Don't walk too fast," said Pu'er.

"Don't touch your face," Yaoyao told Puyi. "We need to find some cold water and hold a soaked rag to it. How does it feel?"

"It's starting to burn."

"Did it get in your eyes?"

"I don't think so. I can see all right."

Yaoyao knew the territory well enough to lead them to a path skirting around and past the village through a series of fields, before rejoining the road to Wudang Mountain.

As they approached the mountain a few days later, they debated whether to visit the nuns at Purple Cloud Palace for medicine to treat Puyi's facial wound, now blistering with pus. Perhaps Wuming, the young shamaness, would still be there, and they might learn more about her and Pudu's poisoning. When they reached the temple, however, they found several male guards stationed at the nunnery entrance and were turned away without explanation. Worried they might be recognized by others at the temple, they headed down the other side of the mountain straight for Fangxian, where they'd have a choice of apothecaries and could reconnect with former contacts in the city.

Upon arriving in Fangxian, they were directed to the nearest pharmacy by a passerby. They asked the shop assistant how they might treat Puyi's wound.

"It looks like it got infected. Hold on, I'll have to go ask," he said.

Shen Wei returned with a woman who examined Puyi's wound.

"Wait a minute," said Pu'er. "Haven't we seen you before?"

"I don't think so."

"Yes, we have. You're the same woman who greeted us at the Purple Cloud Palace nunnery on Wudang Mountain."

Qiu Lu'er looked confused, before evincing a modicum of recognition. "On what occasion were you there?"

"Don't you recognize her, Puyi?"

"I do. We were a group of seven men who sought out your young healer to cure our leader. Don't you remember?"

"And your young healer ended up poisoning him before our very eyes," said Pu'er.

"Oh, yes, I do remember your visit. But I have no idea what you're talking about. We gave you medicine and you left," said Lu'er.

"That was the first time. We came back with gifts of food. We had a feast. How can you not remember this? We acknowledge our leader compelled your mistress to sleep with him in front of us, but he should not have died as a result."

"I haven't a clue as to what you're talking about."

"You cannot evade responsibility by denying it happened," said Puyi.

"Your group visited us once and left, and that was that," she said.

"Why are you here, then? You must have fled the nunnery to escape suspicion."

"We did not belong to the nunnery but were only passing through."

"This is outrageous," said Pu'er. "You pretend none of this happened? I saw you and the other women standing around that canopy bed while your mistress had illicit sex with our leader. How can you not recall this shocking act? Perhaps we can have the magistrate help you remember once he starts to investigate it."

"Go ahead. Go to the *yamen*. You will be laughed out of Fangxian." Lu'er turned to Yaoyao. "Lady, can I help you with something? Or are you with them?"

"Actually, yes." She whispered something to Lu'er, who led her inside.

"Where are you going?" Puyi asked Yaoyao.

She had already slipped through the back door when Puqing emerged in her place. "Do we have a problem here?"

"Pudu!" exclaimed Puyi.

"No!" said Pu'er.

Puqing appeared as startled as they were. "You've come back, Puyi and Pu'er. Why did you leave? How did you find us?"

"Why did we leave? We carried your corpse to Nanyang. That's why we left!"

"My corpse? What are you talking about?"

"You died! How have you come back to haunt us?"

"What's the matter with you? Are you sick in the head?" said Puqing. "You can see me right here, alive and well. You two abandoned us."

"No!" said Pu'er.

With slow deliberation, Puyi shored up his crumbling reality. "We visited the nunnery twice with you. All seven of us. The first time, the shamaness gave you medicine. We rested in the temple for several days. You got better. We returned to the nunnery bearing a feast. You insisted on taking the healer as your wife. Then you insisted on sleeping with her. She warned you not to, as she was poisonous and you would die. You were adamant and she forced all of us to witness her rape. Later that night you passed away in their bed. You would not remember that, of course, but you must remember everything up to that point. Isn't that right, Pu'er?"

No sound came out of Pu'er as he mouthed the word, "No."

"This is unbelievable to me," said Puqing. "You are imagining this. We only visited the nunnery once. After that visit, yes, we rested at the temple. Several days later, we woke up to find you two gone. We had no idea what happened or why you left. Later we were approached by one of the healers from the nunnery to ask if we could accompany them to Fangxian, where they were planning to open this apothecary shop. And we agreed. I can call Pusan, Pusi, Puwu, and Puliu in to confirm this, if you would care to see your brothers again."

"Don't let him fool us, Pu'er. Something's not right here!" Puyi then asked Lu'er, who had returned, "What have you done with her, the woman who is with us?"

"She has a sex disease, and we're keeping her for mercury treatment. Did she catch it from you?"

"You can't keep her here against her will."

"She wishes to stay here."

"Can you call her back? We want to speak with her."

"No!" gasped Pu'er, who turned on his feet and collapsed on the shop floor.

"He fainted!" said Puyi.

Puqing and Shen Wei tried to rouse him and checked his pulse.

"No pulse. Let me get more help," said Lu'er, who rushed out the back.

"It looks to be true heart pain. Or wind strike of the brain?" said Shen Wei.

"Save him!" said Puyi.

They looked up at him. "He's dead."

"What have you done to him? This is the second person you have killed! What kind of sorcery is this?"

"The second person? What do you mean?" said Puqing.

Puyi placed his ear over Pu'er's heart and tried to slap him awake. "First, they killed you, and now they killed Pu'er. Or is it you who killed him, Pudu?"

"You know me well enough, Puyi. Have I ever shown any interest in magic? He seems to have died of fright. You'd better get your bearings lest you die of fright yourself."

Four more men entered through the back of the shop. "What's going on, Pudu?"

"Puyi and Pu'er have returned," said Puqing. "For some

strange reason they are under the delusion that I died and they carried my corpse to Nanyang. They couldn't believe their eyes upon seeing me here. Pu'er has collapsed and died of fright!"

"Puyi! Why have you come back? Why did you leave us?" they said.

Puyi was crying. "You too are all cooperating in this grand deception? Why don't you at least summon the coroner so an inquest can be carried out. Or shall we take the body to the funeral home together?"

"Are you crazy? Informing the coroner?" said Puqing. "The coroner will inform the magistrate and there will be an investigation. They will come here. Even if you keep your mouth shut about your delusion, our medicine will come under suspicion as a cause of his death. Our identity documents will be examined. If deemed to be inauthentic, as you know they are, we will all be implicated, including you! We will be tortured until someone spills our past activities. If that happens, the outcome for all of us will be either a quick execution if we're lucky, or a slow execution if we're not. Don't think you are in a position to accuse us of anything. At the very least, it's our word against yours and you alone may be held responsible for Pu'er's death. Let us take care of his body. We have experience in this and know how to dispose of it."

"You have no right to take his body away!" said Puyi. "He was with me. I am responsible for giving him a proper burial, which you cannot be trusted to do. At least do him the honor of wrapping him in a shroud and providing me with enough *taels* to hire a mule to return him to his native village."

"What's the matter with you? You think they're going to let you out of the city gate without the coroner's approval? You will soon find yourself in the *yamen*. You'd better do the right thing and beat a hasty retreat. We can accompany you to the city gate without the corpse and make sure you get out safely."

As the four men took hold of Pu'er's corpse, Puyi brandished his dagger. "Stand back! I will not allow you to touch his body. Give me the money I need to take care of this matter myself."

"Out of the way!" the men shouted.

Puyi stabbed one of them in the arm and another in the belly before they were able to disarm him and hold him down on the floor. One placed a knee on his neck until his flailing stopped and continued pressing down until he was dead.

"Are you all right, Jue'er? Juesan? Get Miaoyin and Miaolu to attend to their wounds. Also call Zou Run and Yin Yan," Puqing told Jueyi and Juesi.

The corpses were brought in and laid out in the reception room, leaving a trail of bloody footprints. Lu'er and Shen Wei breathlessly related the events they had witnessed in the shop, while Puqing and Zou Run laid the wounded men down on the floor and pulled off their tunics.

Yaoyao rushed up wrapping her robe around herself, her medical inspection by Yinhe and Yin Yan interrupted. She covered her mouth in shock. "Oh, heavens, what happened! What happened to Pu'er and Puyi?"

"How did you get involved with them?" they asked her.

"I met them in Nanyang. I am at a complete loss. They didn't tell me much about their corpse or how he died. Now they too have died! How could this have happened so suddenly? Are you really the same people they were talking about in the shop front?"

"How bad are the wounds?" Yinhe asked Puqing and Zou Run.

"Judging from the blood on the dagger, it didn't penetrate that far into Jue'er's stomach. He's lucky and I think he'll be fine. Most of the blood is from Juesan's arm. We're stopping the bleeding. Prepare the dressing and plasters and heat the black felt for cauterization."

Yaoyao felt something pinching her scalp. She turned and faced a white-robed young woman with a purple flower behind her ear. "Look, a louse," she said, holding it up between her fingers.

"Mistress, we have a good impression of her so far. She speaks well and seems educated. But she's not in good shape," said Yinhe.

"Let's have a look at you." Qiezi opened Yaoyao's robe. "No pants? Undergarments?"

"I lost them."

"How could you bear the cold dressed like this? Burn her robe and find her some fresh clothes."

"We can't dress her till she's been deloused and bathed," said Yin Yan. "She's infested with lice. We need to shave her all over."

"Are you a beggarwoman?" Qiezi asked her.

"No. I'm a guide and errand-runner."

"They don't have much tolerance for stray women in this city," said Yinhe.

"I am not a stray woman."

"But you're all skin and bones," said Qiezi. "Look at your breasts. They're like an old lady's dugs. We need to fatten you up and make you presentable."

"Are you the shamaness?"

"I am Mantuoluo."

"She's the Mistress," said Yinhe.

"So young and beautiful."

"If you leave and try to cause us any trouble," Yinhe continued, "you will be taken for a madwoman and jailed. Also, you are infected with *meidu*, the bayberry disease, which will eat at you and cut your life short. Since it's in the early stage, we're going to try to cure it. It could take a week. It's going to make you sick and you'll feel quite ill before you're better."

"What kind of treatment?"

"Arsenic and cinnabar. Just enough arsenic not to harm you but enough to cure you. And the *tufuling* root to help with the side effects. Do you agree to cooperate fully with us? Do you have family in Nanyang?"

"No."

"Good. You won't be going back to Nanyang. You will stay clean and cured and learn our rites and observe strict obedience, or we will throw you out. Do you agree?"

"I'm grateful for your help and will gladly join you. But this is all a bit too much for me," she said, wiping away tears. "Why did they have to die? They weren't bad men."

"They betrayed us. And now they stabbed two of us in the shop while you were being examined."

"What's your name?" said Qiezi.

"Bi Yaoyao."

"Once you've been initiated, you will adopt the venerable name of Miaoyao. Do you like the name?"

"Miaoyao," said Yaoyao, listening to the sound of it. "What initiation?"

Qiezi led Yaoyao over to Jue'er and Juesan. "I think I'll have you attend on them. You can start by observing how we fix their wounds. Do you have any skills?"

"Apart from sex, that is. Did you sleep with them?" Yin Yan added archly, pointing to the corpses.

"Yes, I slept with them," said Yaoyao.

"For food?"

"No. I am generous with my body. And proud of it."

"Why?"

"Why not? Why is it all right to give alms to monks, but not to give myself to lonely men?"

"Your health," said Yinhe.

"She sounds like Kang Sai'er," quipped Yin Yan.

"Yin Yan, dear, I don't choose my victims lightly. Otherwise, you wouldn't be here," retorted Sai'er.

"And that's why you're quickly acquiring a body no one will want," Yin Yan told Yaoyao. "You must take care of yourself. You can start by not spreading disease. Where are you from?"

"Hunan."

"I thought so. You're from the south. That's where most sex diseases come from, spread by people like you."

"I was only born there. I've been living in Henan for most of my life. What about the person who gave this disease to me? How would I know who it was?"

"That doesn't answer the question."

"So you've never slept with anyone? How did *you* know who you were sleeping with?"

"I'm careful about who I sleep with."

"How do you know you're careful? Do the men you sleep with tell you they have a disease? Do they even know they have a disease?"

"What gives you the idea I sleep with a lot of men? Or do you assume all women are whores because you are?"

"At least I don't sound like one, unlike your coarse country drawl."

"Listen, sassy girl, you need some putting in your place," said Yin Yan as she twisted Yaoyao's breasts.

"Now, now, you two, let's not get out of hand," said Yinhe.

"She's tough. I like her already," said Zou Run.

"I like her too. She may be of use to us," said Puqing.

Qiezi pulled He Le over to Yaoyao. "I'm assigning Miaole to you. But first let's clean you up. We're here to help you. We're healers. And we're all friends."

"Are you White Lotus people?" asked Yaoyao.

"Why? Have you experience with them?" said Zou Run.

"They're shabby and violent people. I got out. But you seem to have some of their better values at least, like accepting women with unbound feet."

"Accepting women at all, not just those with unbound feet. What did they teach you?"

"That we're going to die in a great cataclysm unless we rise up and kill all the Manchus. You don't believe any of that, do you?"

"We are Daoists. That's enough for you to know for now. But how did you ever become mixed up with them?"

"In Nanyang."

"The Primal Chaos faction or the Return to the Origin faction?"

"I'm not sure about that."

"The Three Yangs faction?"

"That sounds familiar. Yes."

"They're not anti-Manchu. They only believe in the end of the world. Everyone's going to die, they believe. Manchus and Han alike," said Zou Run.

"The first sect I was involved with believed that. Then I got passed on to another group. You all can keep a secret?"

"If it was an important secret, you wouldn't be divulging it to us! But who do you think we are, the government?" said Puqing.

"I was assigned to protect a very important man who was in hiding in Nanyang."

"Who?"

"Liu Zhixie," said Yaoyao in a whisper. "Have you heard of him?"

"Liu Zhixie! Of course, we've heard of him. The government has long been on his trail. You were right to leave."

"This is getting interesting," said Zou Run. "Why are you still not involved with them? And what is Liu Zhixie doing in Nanyang? Is he still there?"

"He fled Xiangyang for Nanyang because the government troops pulled out of Nanyang and went to Xiangyang. And Dengzhou. That's why we took the roundabout route through Wudang Mountain to get here. A twenty-year-old acrobat prostitute nun is commanding an army of ten thousand rebels. I heard they are somewhere in the area west of Dengzhou, not all that far from here and could be heading here next. Are you ready to flee if she comes?"

"You sound as crazy as the stories you're making up," said Yin Yan.

"What's her name?" said Zou Run.

"Wang Cong'er."

"The widow of executed rebel leader Qi Lin?"

"Yes, that's her."

Puqing stood up. "Wang Cong'er!"

"Wang Cong'er."

10

The bandits

here did you hear this? From Liu
Zhixie himself?" said Puqing.

Yaoyao nodded.

"How did you get so close to
such an important person?" said
Zou Run.

"I was sent to bring him food. He was hiding in the hollow
wall of a house and only came out of the wall at night."

"It doesn't look like you got much food yourself in return for
your service."

"I only had contact with him last spring. He was later moved
to a different location. I heard he's in Dengzhou now."

"Don't tell me you slept with him too?"

"I don't want to talk about that."

"I can guess what happened."

"What is an 'acrobat prostitute nun'?" asked Lai Xinru.

"Wang Cong'er's family belonged to an itinerant drama
troupe. With her beauty and sword-fighting skills, she was the star
performer. They were known all over western Hubei," said
Puqing.

"She was well known for other reasons, as Puqing can attest," quipped Zou Run.

"You knew her in person?" said Yaoyao.

"Drama troupes are traveling brothels," Zou Run explained to Xinru. "They showcase talented girls with acrobatic skills to wow the men in the audience, who pursue them backstage after the performance. That's the most lucrative side of their business."

"Right, but how could she also have been a nun?"

"I never did anything with her, Zou Run," said Puqing. "You know that. I was friendly with her and Qi Lin and it never went any further. She was so famous no one could afford her anyway. But by then she was committed to Qi, who had joined their troupe and married her. They started using the stage to proselytize for the White Lotus. The main grievance among locals was always landlord exploitation and they knew how to work their audiences. And then Qi got caught in the big dragnet of two years ago. Wang Cong'er went into hiding. She fled to some temple or other and became a Buddhist nun. I lost track of her after that."

"Oh, I see," said Xinru.

"What's the latest about her?" Puqing asked Yaoyao.

"All I know is she came out of hiding and joined rebel leader Yao Zhifu. She must want revenge for Qi Lin's execution and has taken over. They say she's a natural leader and is fierce on horseback."

"Before the crackdown she had to stop performing due to a back injury. So she's back in fighting shape now?"

"The barrel-juggling thing? I heard about that. She must have recovered from it by now."

"What happened?"

"The Zhang Pengliang affair," Zou Run explained. "He was a gangster who colluded with local landlords to injure her when they came to their township to perform. You know the *denggang* act, where they toss a barrel onto the acrobat's feet which she spins and tosses back and forth? Well, unbeknownst to her they secretly filled it with sand and glue, and the force of the barrel on her legs injured her back."

"She killed him," said Yaoyao.

"How?" said Puqing.

"When she came out of hiding last spring that township was the first place they went to. They surrounded the town. They found him and those landlords and their families, dragged them naked to the marketplace and executed them. Wang Cong'er beheaded them herself. They stuck their heads on pikes and called on all the residents to join their ranks. No one refused. Liu Zhixie told me. He was very close to her and Yao Zhifu when he was still in Xiangyang."

"But how do you know she's in the area?"

"Grapevine. The rebels have been moving west since they were forced out of Dengzhou. They're now in the hills around Gucheng and Guanghua."

"That's only a two or three-day march away. We need to have an emergency meeting this evening," announced Puqing.

In the meantime, the invalids needed attending to. That included Yaoyao, who was locked in a room with nothing but a cot and a blanket for sequestering until cured. Yinhe, Lu'er, and He Le looked after her. Calibrated curative doses of arsenic and cinnabar were added to her food. Shaving the hair off her head, armpits and groin, they scraped her body from head to toe with a copper blade and tea-tree oil infused with the *baibu* tuber, effective on lice. While the arsenic and the mercury from the cinnabar went to work on her bayberry malady, they did double duty on the invisible lice-egg colonies infesting her hair follicles, vagina, and other orifices missed by the blade.

Mere healers were they, yet she was in good hands, in better hands than anyone else in Fangxian. They were the city's best-kept secret. Their shabby little apothecary shop, which appeared at first glance to be a fly-by-night operation, kept a low profile: they didn't want to be swamped by the entire city's inhabitants if they found out how good they were. Not only did they source their fresh and potent medicines directly from nature rather than intermediaries, they understood how their medicines worked on the body, and more crucially, they understood the human body.

But they lacked the capacity to handle more than a few select patients at a time. Once word got out in earnest, they would be overwhelmed. They would also be attacked by the pharmacies for poaching their customers, who would not hesitate to use slander or violence in revenge.

Under the regime known as convention and common sense, nobody went to a doctor when they could go to a pharmacy. After the founding of the current dynasty, pharmacists around the country collaboratively worked out the most effective remedies for common ailments. Medicines were standardized, codified, and traded in bulk across the provinces. The pharmacies carried everything. As the official experts in medicines, the pharmacists alone healed and the pharmacists alone were trusted. While doctors purported to understand the body, they could only guess at medicines. The sensible majority avoided them altogether if they could. The only difference between doctors and quacks was that quacks had the gumption to claim their medicines worked. Real doctors knew their place: they would never dare proffer their own medicines but wrote prescriptions to take to the pharmacy. Doctors had it backwards, which is why they counted themselves among the contemptible class, on a par with bonesetters, shamans, prostitutes, acrobats, opera singers, and magicians, and only a degree above runners and nightsoil collectors in social status.

Indeed, doctors had more than a thing or two in common with magicians: pulling tricks on stubborn patients to make them cooperate, above all women, who refused to let the dirty rascals examine their body (apart from midwives there were no female doctors). Contrivance and subterfuge were required to shield the female patient from their lascivious gaze or touch. Instructing family members to hold her down and distract her, for example, the doctor would disappear into another room and with a cord connected to her wrist and passing through an eye bolt, yank her dislocated shoulder back in place. Or he would frighten her into cooperation. In one notorious case (confirming their nasty reputation), a doctor reset a young beauty's frozen hip by fanning open her summer slip and exposing her, causing her to kick him violently in anger—and curing herself at one go. When doctors succeeded in curing a patient, it was ascribed more often to luck than skill or expertise. This is not to say there were no famous doctors, but the public never saw them; they were snatched up by elites, if palace eunuchs didn't get their hands on them first.

Now, our healers had no patience for such claptrap and applied themselves to the body regardless of the patient's sex. Nature didn't harbor moral qualms about "modesty," so why should they? They tended to humans with the same care they tended to plants—complex, moving plants. With their dedication to the body and indifference to reputation, one might wonder why they needed to masquerade as a pharmacy at all and not set up shop as doctors, in truth the more honorable profession. For medicines could not stitch up a gash, palpate the source of a pain, or set a broken bone. Though they were loath to admit it, people relied on doctors. Our healers' dilemma was that drawing too much attention to themselves might turn them into victims of their own success and unleash an upheaval of unknown consequences, as the population turned to them and the pharmacies turned on them. Discreetly they distributed their concoctions to wholesalers to maintain a steady inflow of cash and looked on placidly when anyone happened to walk into their shop front, take one look around and walk right back out. But posing as a quack operation couldn't be sustained forever. In fact, as of late an unnerving number of people in need of medicines and cures seemed to be showing up at the shop.

"We have to be ready to leave Fangxian at a moment's notice," Puqing told the congregation that evening.

"Is Wang Cong'er's army approaching?" they asked.

"No. From what we can gather based on the girl's information, the rebels are not now on the move but are scattered in the hills and digging in for the rest of winter. Government troops are likewise holed up around Xiangyang and Dengzhou and won't be setting out again until spring."

"Why then are we having an emergency meeting if there's no emergency? We're already aware we need to be ready to move if our reputation gets out of hand."

"I'm only reminding everyone not to get too comfortable since our situation remains precarious. We don't know for certain the rebels won't be coming this way. But the real reason for our meeting tonight is the girl."

"The girl?"

"She'll be no danger to us so long as she's locked up in the room. She's cooperating so far. We explained the bayberry disease to her. It goes through several phases and gets progressively worse. She still has the lesion marking the first phase, happily for her since she only recently caught it, in the past month or so. The lesion soon disappears, giving the illusion one is cured. One to two months later, the disease returns as a rash on the body. If she gets the rash, it means our treatment failed. There is nothing more to be done at that point, though the disease progresses slowly over many years, without symptoms, before the final lethal stage kicks in. If she's not cured, we'll be faced with a choice. Keep her here to infect all of us or send her off to infect countless others."

"Even if she's cured, who says we have to sleep with her?" asked Yan Xian.

"You will not be able to resist her."

"She's not very attractive. And even if she was, that doesn't mean I have to sleep with her. I have a beautiful wife."

"The fact you are even raising the possibility means you have your eye on her," retorted Lai Xinru.

"When she gets out of that room, you will see a transformation," said Zou Run. "You will see her bloom into a beauty, a devilish beauty. It's hard to notice that now in her sickly state."

"I agree," said Qiezi. "As soon as I laid eyes on her I could see trouble."

"Who finds a woman with crazy eyes like that attractive?" said Yan Xian.

"You can't see beyond that, Baba? Her skewed eyes are distinctive and alluring," said Qiezi.

"More to the point," said Zou Run, "what you're seeing in

those crazy eyes of hers is another disease: the *sedan baotian*
disease—the lust disease. She's a *dangfu*. A *yinwa*. She will not
discriminate between men and women but will go after each and
every one of us, starting with," here Zou Run turned to Qiezi,
"the paragon."

"Good idea. Problem solved," said Yin Yan, to general
laughter.

"We will protect her from the Mistress, and the Mistress from
her," said Jingjing and Yuejiang.

"She will go after you two to get to the Mistress."

"We have no interest in her."

"She will have an interest in *you*. All three of you. You must
understand the law of passion—and its obverse. Passion is
insatiable. But everyone ultimately loses sexual interest in the
same person, even a goddess like the Mistress. The girl knows this.
She will use language, crafty words. She will gain your confidence
and bind you to her without your realizing it. Before you
understand what she is doing, you will start becoming intrigued
and fascinated by her, driven mad with curiosity, soon to be
enmeshed in her erotic devices. And once caught in her trap, it's
all over. She will fasten onto you like a giant insect and inject
her Yin into you and suck out all your Yang."

"Zou Run is right," said Puqing. "She will not stop until she
has consumed all of us and spat us out. She will then abandon us
and proceed to seek new victims elsewhere."

"I've heard about this disease," said Shen Wei. "Isn't it the *gu*
disease? She's a Miao, isn't she? Unbound in foot, body, and
mind."

"She's not a Miao. That's a silly prejudice. Anyone can be
infected with the *gu* disease. And with the *sedan baotian* disease as
well."

"I thought they were the same thing."

"They are not. The lust disease is first mentioned in the
ancient book, the *Zuo Zhuan*, where it's compared to the *gu* disease
but is not the *gu* disease. Over time a misunderstanding arose, and
people began treating the two as the same. They aren't the same.

Even Zou Run fell for it. We've gotten into many arguments about this. The *gu* disease is lethal. The lust disease is not. You can be afflicted with it for the rest of your life and be perfectly healthy. In *The Plum in the Golden Vase*, it's mistakenly called *selao,* a consumptive disease like the *lao* disease—tuberculosis. Death from sex. Surely you know the novel?"

"Of course."

"It helped spread this idea. But you can't die from too much sex."

"Oh, yes you can," said Zou Run. "Well, women can't die from too much sex. But men can. They waste and wither away once they exhaust their lifelong supply of semen, their essence. We have hundreds of years of testimony from the Daoists on this."

"No, Zou Run. Men can rejuvenate their essence with the right techniques and the help of nubile girls providing their Yin secretions. You can't die from sex but only from a sex disease. But as for the lust disease, there is no cure. Restoring the girl to health will only enable her to resume her predatory activity with a vengeance, especially after she's been locked up for so long. The only recourse, besides getting rid of her, is—"

"Controlling it. As best you can. Gaining the wisdom to control it," said Kang Sai'er.

"Thank you, Sai'er," said Zou Run. "I wanted you to mention it but it's better you mention it yourself. As most of you are aware, Sai'er herself has the *sedan baotian* disease."

"It's easier to control it as you get older and your physical drive starts to fall off. But the desire itself never weakens. I don't overstep any boundaries that would harm our congregation or do anything to turn anyone against me."

"Well, we've been discussing how we can make use of the girl, and we have an idea," said Puqing. "She'll be in the room another three months, by which time if she hasn't gotten the rash, we can safely assume she's cured."

"Will she put up with being quarantined that long?" asked Yinhe.

"She'll be kept busy. We're teaching her some of the healing arts. She already appreciates her new home. By the time we let her out, spring will be approaching. We will then employ her as a spy. She will need to prove herself in this role if she wants to remain with us. We're going to send her off with Jueyi and Juesi on a reconnaissance mission to see what the rebels are doing. They will keep an eye on her as she infiltrates the rebels and gathers information."

"How long will the mission last?" said Yinhe.

"Until they return with the news that the rebels are mobilizing. The rebels won't be staying put forever, if they aren't chased out by government forces first."

"If she sleeps with any of the rebels, might she not become infected anew with the bayberry disease?" asked Yinhe.

"Not only the bayberry disease. That's a chance we'll have to take. Once she's back we'll keep a close eye on her and regularly examine her. I think she'll cooperate. She already realizes she's better off with us than back with the rebels."

A month and a half later, Jue'er and Juesan had fully recuperated from their dagger wounds. Bi Yaoyao had evidently recuperated as well, but another month and a half would be needed to be on the safe side. She was growing restless. Chinese New Year arrived, and the congregation celebrated the Spring Festival with firecrackers in the compound's inner courtyard. The muffled cacophony was audible in Yaoyao's windowless room. They didn't forget about her. Yinhe and Lu'er brought her a bowl of rice dumplings. In tears she begged to be let out to join in the festivities but was declined.

The next day Yinhe and the Mistress conferred with Puqing and Zou Run. They agreed to let Yaoyao out into the courtyard for a few minutes for some fresh air and sunshine, after undergoing her daily examination for any signs of a rash; it was still too cold to stay out longer than that. Soon they accommodated her request to wander around inside as well, chaperoned of course, and get better acquainted with everyone. With her short hair starting to grow back, she looked like the Buddhist nun Qiezi herself had resembled only months earlier.

But with the poison cure completed and her diet restored, Yaoyao's figure had filled out. Her visage radiated vitality, confirming suspicions she was not meant for a nunnery but more ambitious ventures. Nobody got to see her new figure, however, except Yinhe, Lu'er, and He Le. When everyone expected the hussy to brandish her body, she kept herself primly bundled up. This prodded some to ask if she could open her robe for them as they were dying of curiosity to see how hale and hearty she had become. They were politely refused.

When strolling about, Yaoyao likewise showed no amorousness to her wary colleagues, nor even much interest in friendship. This was not out of unfriendliness. Rather, in monastic-like supplication and gratitude, she inquired of their talents. They were flattered by the ease with which she set her personality aside and focused on the skills and techniques they had to impart. She already knew how to spin, weave and embroider, as most urban girls did, but that was about it. In short order she picked up the basics of grinding corn, millet and wheat, wielding the big wok for the daily meals, processing and packaging medicinal plants, and applying medicines on patients accepted for treatment. Before long she graduated to foraging and surviving in the wild, making and firing shortbows (practiced on animals with her arms now strengthened from Qiezi's tree-climbing training), and the martial-arts of hand-to-hand combat.

Her rapid progress persuaded the congregation to send her off on the expedition a few weeks before her quarantine was up. Another reason for her early departure was that she hadn't had any unlucky days in a while. Before she had left Nanyang, her periods had been irregular, attributed to her malnourished state. But she had now had several months to fatten up and her periods weren't returning. This was now attributed, correctly, to pregnancy. It could not have been Puyi, she claimed, whose jade stalk was more akin to a candle once it's been consumed by the flame; he couldn't get it inside her and she had to finish him off by hand that night in the inn garret. It must have been Pu'er. He was the last man she had been with, she insisted, there had been no others for months prior to that. In any case, the battle raging inside her between the arsenic and mercury and the bayberry venom put a successful outcome of the pregnancy in doubt.

Jue'er and Juesan felt healed enough by this time and were eager to join Jueyi and Juesi, arguing for safety in numbers. Four men could better police each other in keeping a seductress with the lust disease in check. Until they returned from the mission, they were to refrain from any illicit contact with her on pain of excommunication. This was easier to do when staying at inns where she was sequestered in a private room; things were tenser when they were thrown together in the dirtier inns or in straw-strewn sheds among animals. Hard conditions wore away propriety, inexorably if not immediately. For what kind of moral imperative upheld chastity among the armed and dangerous? Did their descent into bandit territory—indeed they now disguised themselves as bandits—not change the terms? Did not access to the siren devolve to the leader by virtue of his courage and heavy responsibility? What if *she* was the one to lead the expedition and embark on the most perilous forays, heading straight for mountaintop smoke, the telltale sign of a rebel stockade, for instance?

At the first stockade they approached, they found the path to the stream used by the rebels to collect water. Stealthily they worked their way up to the palisade, looking for gaps in the tight formations of sharpened bamboo stakes. They hadn't been there more than a few minutes when deafening blasts erupted.

"Musket fire! Take cover behind the trees!"

They heard shouts of "Bandits!" coming from the stockade. They also heard shouting from around and behind them. Jueyi and Jue'er got out their longbows, the rest their shortbows, barely nocking them with shaking hands despite countless hours of practice, before they were surrounded.

"Our arrows are poisoned!" Jueyi shouted. "Back off if you don't want to die."

"Surrender! You're outnumbered. You have no chance against us. Who are you? You are not from the stockade."

"Who are *you*? Also bandits? If we fight each other it will only draw the rebels' attention. Let's cooperate!" said Yaoyao.

"A woman!" exclaimed their ringleader. "We've already been discovered. Follow us!"

They descended the mountain with the bandits to their camp. All twelve of them. "Where's *your* camp?" they asked.

"We're further away, to the southwest. What are you doing trying to take on the rebels?"

"We want to join them. What are *you* doing?"

"We're trying to find out where they're going next."

"How would anyone know that? I'd guess Henan. When the weather warms up."

"I'd guess Shaanxi. The rode to Nanyang is blockaded and all but impassable," said another.

The bandits started a fire and prepared their dinner. The Fangxian band offered their own food. They were invited to partake in the meal but had to sit in a designated spot so they could be watched. It was tacitly understood they would be kept captive until Yaoyao did her duty with the bandits, starting with the ringleader. Things happened fast, absolving us of the need to record any shameful details. In the glow of the brazier in the ringleader's tent, Yaoyao began to disrobe. In one motion, she pulled down her pants, pulled out a dagger hidden in them and slit his throat. His severed vocal cords prevented him from screaming. She tipped over the brazier and made sure the fire caught before she stepped out, yelling, "The tent is on fire!"

Quick thinking dispatched several of the distracted bandits with arrows before the five made their escape. They ran all the way down the mountain before catching their breath to speak.

"We knew you would do him in somehow but how did you manage it so quickly?" they asked Yaoyao.

"He wasn't expecting it. You need to stay one step ahead, throw them into confusion. If it doesn't happen quickly, it doesn't happen at all."

"That was brave and risky."

"Don't be fooled by their friendliness. If I hadn't killed him outright, all twelve of them would have raped me in turn. And then we wouldn't have had to worry about my catching any more sex diseases because they would have killed us. You owe your lives to me."

They huddled together for a sleepless night in an abandoned house. In the morning they found a stream to clean off the splotches of violence on Yaoyao's clothing, before heading to a familiar inn, one that allowed them to room together. Yaoyao demanded a noonday feast with lots of well-warmed yellow wine.

"We didn't manage to get any information," one of them said over dinner in the inn. "How can we ascend the mountain again without being discovered by the bandits? We can't go back to Fangxian empty handed."

"How could we ever penetrate that stockade, let alone avoid the bandits?" said another.

"Yesterday I was thinking of giving myself up to the rebels and then escaping from the stockade after talking to people," said Yaoyao. "But I can now see that once inside that fortress, there would be no way out until they left the mountain, and even then I might not be able to escape. But I have an idea. Why put ourselves in such extreme danger when we have a better chance of gathering intelligence in Nanyang, where I'm already in the grapevine?"

"What will the congregation think if we're spending all our time lolling around Nanyang?"

"We don't have to tell them! Use your brains. Our job is to gather intelligence. We need to get it the best way we can, however we get it."

"You said you knew some rebels in Nanyang. What do they want? Where do you think they'll be heading next?"

"It depends on whether they're on the chase or being chased. They've long set their sights on south Henan somewhere for a homeland. I can also see them fleeing to Shaanxi. As it's a different province, the government would have to decide which troops to dispatch and that would buy the rebels time. I honestly have no idea, though. But we are better off in Nanyang than here."

"Where can we stay in Nanyang?"

"I know of a place."

"How can we get there safely with the route swarming with government troops?"

"I know the area. I know back roads." Yaoyao leaned forward. "It's not safe to talk here. Let's bring the wine up to our room where we can relax. Then we're going to bed, if I don't pass out first. My three months are almost up. You're all going to give my body a final examination." She pointed her finger at them when their eyes widened. "Straighten out your priorities. The only thing that matters is that we make it through each day alive, not what we do together."

Yaoyao requested four bathing basins be brought up. They pacified the incredulous innkeeper with a sufficient tip, and she slipped upstairs while the men ferried up buckets of steaming water.

She planted herself in a basin, brazenly facing the four of them as she scraped and dissolved the previous-day's encrusted blood off her belly, pubis, and thighs with the dagger, in no hurry to let the men have their turn. "Look, the water's already red. As I suspected, I need another basin to get clean. Go on, bandits, get cleaned up! Don't mind me. We'll dump this water out the window after dark. You four can share the other two basins. But first come and examine my body."

"We can't see any signs of a rash," they said. "I think you've recovered."

The men bathed and put their clothes back on. Yaoyao then drew a curtain over the paper window to darken the room but for the glow of an oil lamp. All helped themselves to more wine. Yaoyao pushed the room's four cots together to form a large bed. She got into bed naked with a cup of wine and covered herself in several blankets. "This is how I sleep."

"Aren't you worried about lice?" one said.

"You can't prevent lice. Just live with it and get rid of them later."

The men sat around the room's square table talking to Yaoyao across the room. They acted very much as a unit. Yaoyao still didn't know anything about them. "Why are there no children in the congregation?" she asked, suspiciously. "With so many beautiful women and handsome men, I would expect the place to be crawling with children."

"We were two groups who only lately came together. Not much goes on between us at night."

"Why not? I thought you were all the freer sort of Daoists. Are those women truly the *zhenjie lienü* sort? So pure and chaste? I don't believe it."

"Well, not quite," they said after an embarrassed silence. "They're simply not inclined towards men."

"Ah, I see. So they're 'mirror polishers,' are they?"

They nodded. Yaoyao noticed that Jueyi had rested his hand on Jue'er's. "Oh, don't tell me you're also—'short-sleevers'?"

They smiled.

"All of you?"

They smiled.

She held out her thimble cup. Jueyi got up to refill it and they toasted.

"The strapping lad, Juewei, is not," he said. "He's with Miaole, one of the girls assigned to you. And she's not. The other two assigned to you, Miaoyin and Miaolu, are together."

"The older one and the younger one with the braid?"

"Yes. The older couple, Juexian and Miaoxin, are not. They're the Mistress's parents."

"Her parents?"

"Miaoyan, the woman who argued with you, is also not. She's very close to Miaosai. We don't know what goes on between them. Miaosai is a bit crazy—like you," said Jueyi, covering his mouth with a giggle.

"She too is a mirror polisher?"

"She's equally at home 'on land and in water.' She kept going after us until she gave up."

"I can't keep all these names straight. The leader, Puqing? And Zou Run?"

"They are not. They're together."

"And the Mistress?"

"She's also amphibious. But you'd better stay away from her."

"Why?"

"She's toxic and you'll die."

"What? Oh, so she *is* the same person Puyi and Pu'er said killed your leader at the Wudangshan nunnery by sleeping with him?"

"Yes, that was Pudu, the estranged twin brother of Puqing. We were with them. We were Pusan, Pusi, Puwu, and Puliu before our names were changed."

"What was all that deceptive stuff about in the apothecary shop? What happened between you?"

"Those two were not like us, if you know what I mean. Things came to a head in the shop."

"Pudu looked the same as Puqing?"

"Exactly the same. Identical twins. We filled in Puqing and the congregation all about his brother's recent travels with us, culminating in the Wudangshan nunnery affair, so that we were well prepared for the two when they inevitably arrived. We even fixed his hair and clothes just like his brother's and playacted Puyi and Pu'er and their manner of speaking."

"They didn't know Pudu had a twin brother?"

"No. He didn't want his authority to be challenged so he kept that a secret."

Jue'er got up to refill Yaoyao's cup.

"I see. You confounded them. Turned their world upside down. Who is the leader now? Puqing or the Mistress?"

"The Mistress. But Puqing, Zou Run, and Miaoyin are the operational leaders. They have all the experience. The Mistress is a master of medicines, though. Her knowledge is extraordinary. Everyone holds her in awe."

"You worship her?"

"You could say that."

"But no one can touch her."

"Right."

"Oh, I understand now. You're not mere healers. You're a *yinsi*—an obscene temple!" laughed Yaoyao. "You'd better be careful. The authorities are always cracking down on *yinsi* and arresting everyone."

She held out her cup for more wine.

"The *yinsi* are not just about, as they say, 'men and women mixing at night and dispersing before dawn.' The term applies to any unauthorized temple, whatever goes on inside."

"I'm aware of that. The rebels are all keeping *yinsi*. I could never put up with them. The chanting of stupid mantras and the strict vegetarianism. Are you vegetarians?"

"Mostly, yes. But not so strict. We celebrate with meat and fish on special occasions."

"I don't understand why they must be so strict about it when there's enough food to go around."

"We agree. Most White Lotus people are both Buddhists and Daoists. We're Daoists, not Buddhists, remember. But how did you become involved with them?"

"That's a long story. I'll talk about that another time. I'm tired now. This wine is honey on the tongue. But it's doing me in."

"And how is it a city girl like yourself doesn't have bound feet?" asked Juesi. "That's practically unheard of. I don't mean I think you should have bound feet. I'm only curious."

Yaoyao was already asleep.

They piled into the bed after her and fell fast asleep themselves. Now, as the dreamworld is disconnected in time and place from the real world, we will use this excuse to jump forward a week, after they had arrived in Nanyang and ensconced themselves in Yaoyao's old room. It's not clear how she rid herself of her former roommates but get rid of them she did. The four gentlemen split the two empty beds between them. The straw mattresses were replaced, and the five of them daily checked each other's heads for lice. With the men safely tucked away in her obscure lair, Yaoyao scurried about town asking questions.

"I'm getting contradictory information. What's clear so far is that Wang Cong'er's rebels are on the move. They have left the Gucheng area," she said.

"They left the stockade we visited?"

"There were a number of stockades. But they're all joining up and seem to be heading southeast. Now why would they be heading southeast? To Xiaogan? An uprising there last summer was brutally crushed. The Hubei capital is only a little further beyond that."

"Wuchang? How could they ever take Wuchang?"

"That's why they got slaughtered in Xiaogan. The government can't afford to lose Wuchang."

A few weeks after that Yaoyao arrived with more enigmatic news. "The latest is that they cut eastward through the Tongbai mountains. That can only mean one thing. They are not going to Xiaogan or Wuchang. They are circling north through Henan. They're coming our way!"

"How would they be able to take Nanyang? The forces stationed around Dengzhou would rush here to confront them."

"We're not sure if they're aiming for Nanyang itself or the general area. I suspect they're terrorizing everything in their path and picking up new recruits. By the time they make it here, they may be swelled in numbers, a big army on the move."

"How long will it take them to get here?"

"Soon enough."

"What shall we do?"

"Wait things out and see what happens, or head back to Fangxian. If we wait it out, we may be trapped here. Or the whole circling business may be a diversionary tactic and they'll be heading straight south for Xiangyang again, in another attempt to take the city. Or Dengzhou—and Fangxian itself, if fighting spreads westward."

They decided to wait, and another week later Yaoyao came back with yet more surprising news. "They bypassed us. They circled northward around us and are moving straight west into Shaanxi! Who knows where they are headed now."

"So they are moving well away from us and we're out of

danger?"

"I have no idea. Perhaps this is a good time to return to Fangxian. They might better understand what's happening. Aren't some of the congregation from Shaanxi?"

"The Mistress and her family are. And several of the girls. But how would they know anything if they're not there in person?"

They gave it one more week. Yaoyao then came back with the news that there had been a major battle in the Wuguan Pass over the Henan border in Shaanxi. The rebels won and had doubled the size of their army, perhaps tripled or quadrupled it. But they had stopped moving and it wasn't clear what was happening. They might be recruiting existing sectarians in the impoverished region, where the poor and dispossessed had grievances.

The five headed back to Fangxian. When they arrived at the apothecary shop, they found it abandoned.

11

The executioner

n Yunxian city on the Han River in northwest Hubei Province, four men with pack mules popped their heads in a riverside inn and asked, "Any vacant rooms?"

"At the moment only two. One more is in use and should be free later," said the innkeeper.

"It'll be ready shortly," said a pair of lotus toes mincing down the upper-floor steps into the main room. The maid wore an uncharacteristic outfit, a cropped cyan cotton jacket over tight rose-colored silk slacks. She disappeared into the kitchen.

"Put your mules in the stable in back," said the innkeeper. "There's water and feed. And keep them apart from the horses."

The men came in and rapped the table. "Wine and snacks. Two jugs will be enough." They looked around and saw one table occupied by a man and another by a man and a woman. The woman sported pink silk slacks, embroidered lotus shoes, and the same cropped cyan jacket as the maid. She got up to fetch a plate of beancakes and sliced tofu for the guests as the innkeeper heated the wine. Both women had penciled-in eyebrows and made continuous eye contact with the guests.

The newcomers scanned the meal and room fees. "Is the maid service extra or included in the room?"

"Extra. You negotiate that with the maid."

"How many maids do you have?"

"On hand today only two, Miss Pink here and Miss Rose whom you saw just now."

Miss Rose emerged from the kitchen.

"And *she* is?" the guest asked, pointing to a third female dressed in a plain blue smock who followed Miss Rose into the room. A cook poked his head through the kitchen door.

"My wife," said the innkeeper.

All eyes were on the next person to descend from the upper floor: a man buttoning up his tunic, a runner. He pulled the innkeeper aside but was audible to all. "If you want to stay out of trouble, you need to take down that 'Personal Maid Service' sign you have out front. A lot of people pass through here and we want to keep the rumor mill under control. You don't need to get rid of the maids, only the sign."

"No problem."

"In fact, I'd like to try Miss Pink out next time. See if her service is up to par with Miss Rose's."

"How about if I change the sign to just 'Personal Service'?"

"Well, all right. Oh," he added as an afterthought, "and does your wife provide personal service?"

"She's only a simpleminded rural woman with ungainly feet. I don't think you'd like her." The innkeeper patted his wife's protruding belly.

"I'll be the judge of that," said the runner, giving the innkeeper's goatee a playful twist before leaving.

"Of course, that's *why* he wants to try her out," chuckled one of the newly arrived quartet as soon as the runner was out the door. "It's an obsession with some men."

"Not for me," said another. "Flat-footed women all have flat asses. That's the only reason for foot-binding, if you ask me. Lifts that ass up on a platter and ready to eat. Like these two stunners of yours. Come over here," he said to the maids. "Turn around now, girls, and let's have a look."

The maids lined up their backsides in front of the guest, and he squeezed both pairs of buttocks.

"No touching!" said Miss Rose, slapping the man's hand.

"Both delectable. Hard to choose. Hers is bigger, but yours is shapelier."

"Treat the maids with a little respect," said the third newcomer. "So how many guests do you have now? We haven't seen this inn before."

The innkeeper pointed to the man sitting at the solitary table. "And him?"

"I'm the stable hand," said the man sitting across from Miss Pink.

"We'd prefer you stay in the big four-bed room in case we have new guests," said the innkeeper. "And you'll save money. The other rooms are two-bed rooms."

"Both maids can service the same room?"

"If you don't mind the lack of privacy."

"Is the service by the hour or day?"

"By the hour. Overnight stays are negotiated with the maids, if there are no new guests by the second watch, that is, when we shutter the inn."

"That runner won't come back to cause any trouble, will he?" they asked.

"No. He wouldn't even be doing the rounds at all except that there's a high-cash bounty out for a group of travelers the authorities are looking for," said the innkeeper.

"Oh, who?"

"We heard it's some sorceress who kills men by sleeping with them and then sets fire to their dwelling."

"*Wasa!* You're joking," the men exclaimed, intrigued. "A fox spirit?"

"No, seems to be a real woman. With a train of female followers. Word is she's a Miao and her flashing red eyes give her away. And her unbound feet. Where do you folks hail from anyway?"

"Shaanxi, Xing'an. We're traders in pharmaceuticals. Heading to Wudang Mountain."

"Come to think of it, there was that group we passed in Baihe, right over the border in Shaanxi," said the third.

"Ah, yes," said the first. "At that inn we were staying at. A big group, a good fifteen of them or so. Mostly women, young women, beautiful women. You never saw so many beautiful women in one place. We wondered if they were some kind of singing or acrobatic troupe. And a handful of men, all squeezed into three rooms. You think one of them was the sorceress?"

"I seem to recall at least one or two of them had unbound feet," said the second.

"I was so entranced by their looks I didn't notice their feet," said the fourth.

"Were they in Miao outfits?" said the innkeeper.

"What are Miao outfits?"

"In fact, I don't know. The Miao are mostly down in Guizhou Province, aren't they? But by the time you got back to Shaanxi they'd be long gone, if they're on the run, anyway. And they're already out of Hubei's jurisdiction. Any idea where they were heading?"

"No. Must be further into Shaanxi. But we hear the rebels are amassing there as well."

"Yes, we're aware of that. Do you remember the name and location of the inn where they were staying? We can pass that information on to the runner. If they're caught and we get a reward, we'll split it with you," said the innkeeper.

"How much is the reward?"

"No idea. But if you write down your names we can make a pact. Shall we kill a chicken and drink its blood together?"

"No need. We'll stop here again on the way back from Wudang Mountain and see if there's any more news," said the first. "I'm doubtful they'll be caught by this point. It's been a week or two since we saw them. Oh, and Baihe is on the south side of the river, so you'll have to cross over."

The innkeeper took down their names and the inn's location.

The four guests checked into the big room and hired dual-maid service for the night. They arose at dawn for an early start on the road. The maids went down first to prepare their breakfast. The guests ate and left.

"How much did you squeeze out of them?" asked the innkeeper.

"A *tael* a piece."

"Good work. Here's another thirty-five *taels*. Can you run this inn? We're heading to Shaanxi to try to find the fugitive woman."

"All four of you?"

"Yes, all of us."

"How can we ever run this place ourselves?"

"Just run it. You know the basics. Whatever money you earn is yours. We'll be back at some point, with or without the fugitive. We just can't say when."

"*You're* going with them too?" they asked the solitary guest.

"Strength in numbers," he said.

"When the runner comes back, and he will come back," the innkeeper told Miss Pink, "you'd better give him a free romp like Miss Rose here did. Tell him we're looking for the sorceress. But don't tell him where we're going. We don't want other people sharing in the bounty. You only heard we went to Shaanxi. We'll share the bounty reward with you if we're lucky."

The stable hand, the cook, and the solitary guest strung their sacks on three horses; the innkeeper hauled himself and his wife up on a fourth. She now sported a pair of lotus shoes whose tips poked out of her pant cuffs.

In two days they reached Baihe and found the inn in question, whose innkeeper confirmed the strange train of women had stayed there. He had gathered from their queries they were headed straight west toward Ziyang—another several days on horseback. "You'll have to cross back over to the north side of the river to reach Ziyang," he told them. "Be careful. There are rumors the rebels are also headed that way."

Once up in their room, the five bounty hunters could finally let down their guard. "None of us has been to Shaanxi before but more clues will accumulate as we're closer to the source," said Jueyi. "Yaoyao, I'm not sure we can pull off the bogus inn scheme again."

"It's not a bogus inn. It's a real inn, even if we only had it open for a few days," she said as she pulled off her fake lotus shoes and the rest of her clothes and squatted in the basin to douse herself in steaming water. "If we ever manage to return, they may be doing great business and not even want us back. There's no need for more inn setups. We'll find them."

"That thing inside of you is growing," said Juesi. "How many more months?"

Yaoyao held her belly in her hands. "About two? I'm worried all those poisons and toxins I had in me could cause an early delivery or a stillbirth." She handed him the sponge. As he scrubbed her back, she arched up her buttocks, "By the way, is my ass flat?"

They were on the road again in the morning. In a few days they reached the Han River in the vicinity of Ziyang. Locals told them to keep hugging the river, where it would continue to narrow and be easier to cross. Locals also said if they had any wits about them, they would turn right around and flee as fast as they could, as they themselves were doing: both rebels and Banner troops were in the area.

"What's that noise up ahead?" said Yaoyao a short while later, gazing down the river.

"What noise?"

"Can't you hear it?"

"I do hear something. People shouting."

They continued on the path along the south bank.

"There they are!" said Juesi.

"They're crossing over from the north bank. Who are they? Rebels?"

"They're all kinds of people. Look, they're being ferried across on boats and rafts. Women and children and old people. Hundreds of them. They're rebels."

"How do you know they're rebels? They might be people

escaping the rebels."

"Should we tether the horses and get a closer view on foot?"

"Get out the bows and arrows. We don't know who they are."

"What's that popping sound?"

"Gunshots! Someone's firing at them. They're firing at the people crossing the river! You can hear their screaming. Oh, look, some of the rafts are capsizing!"

"The guns are coming from the other side. Must be troops shooting at the rebels. We'll never make it across—"

"Down with your bows, now! Who are you?"

The five found themselves surrounded by a band of angry armed men.

"Eternal and Venerable Mother in our original home in the world of true emptiness!" they shouted in unison as they dropped their bows. "We have been looking for you. We wish to join you!"

The rebels drove the five further along the river until they reached the point of the river crossing. "Down from your horses! Prove to us you are with us. Go and rescue those who are struggling in the water! Bring your bows and use them against the enemy. Move, quick!"

"I can't swim!" said Yaoyao.

"Jump on my back and shoot for me," said Jue'er. "The water is only waist high. I think we can manage."

"You three go help the people on that boat which is sinking," Jueyi and Juesi shouted. "We'll head over to the flank to distract them."

The river was not two hundred *bu* wide and Jueyi and Juesi were almost across by the time the other three reached the floundering boat. It had been hit with a musket or gingal shot and was taking in water, and its panicking occupants were trying to stabilize it as the boatman dragged it through the current by its rope. Juesan hiked one of the women onto his back and helped pull the boat, while Yaoyao shot arrows at the soldiers, to little effect. They were more than halfway to the near side of the river and beyond a shortbow's effective range but were still vulnerable to the gingals firing across in both directions. Only by sheer chance was she able to fell any of the soldiers. Or at least she thought she saw some falling. They tipped the boat upward to get the breach above the water and this also served as a shield, if a poor one. She was already soaked from the water splashing onto her in the chaos. Gunshots continued to blast around them and another tore through the boat, spraying someone's blood in Yaoyao's eyes. There was indeed commotion on the other side, provoked by a flurry of arrows from Jueyi and Juesi at close range. The guns were now turned on the latter, providing breathing space for the rest to make it across. Yaoyao didn't remember anything after that.

She came to in a tent in the rebel camp. People were rushing about attending to the screaming, the groaning, the silent. It was not quite a field hospital—no such thing properly existed—but a makeshift space for anyone with medical knowledge to show their worth. Yaoyao felt someone blowing in her ear. "Oh, the Mistress! How did you get here?"

"Long story. Tell you later," said Qiezi.

"Is my baby all right?" She felt her belly.

"You'll be fine, dear. You got knocked out when the boat flipped over."

"Did we make it across the river?"

"We are many *li* away from the river now."

Jue'er and Juesan came up to her.

"Where are Jueyi and Juesi?"

They stared at their feet. "They were very brave. Thanks both to their efforts and ours, we got promoted."

Tears streamed down Yaoyao's face. "Promoted to what?"

"To the rank above cannon fodder. We need to get back to work. We've also all been promoted for our healing skills."

Yaoyao looked around at the many injured lying on bamboo mats. She recognized the faces of those attending to them. Miaolu came up and checked the bandage on her forehead. Then she conked back out.

When she again awoke, the room was quieter. "You're all here!" she exclaimed.

"That's the good thing about being healers. You're needed. So they let us stay together," said Miaoyin.

"Did many die crossing the river?"

"Most of those you see here will survive."

Jue'er and Juesan had filled them in on how the five managed to find them and everything leading up to that, how they found the apothecary shop in Fangxian abandoned, how they (and likewise the rest of the congregation before them) were tipped off by their friendly contact Dr. Sun that the *yamen* were hunting a young and beautiful witch with unbound feet wanted for murder and rumored to be hiding among local Daoists; how they fled the city as soon as they found horses for sale, smuggling Yaoyao out in a sack; how they headed north to the Han River on a hunch the congregation were headed there too; how they rented a vacant property and set up their own intelligence-gathering inn, hiring prostitutes to pose as maids, instead of suspiciously inquiring at random inns; and how they learned the congregation was headed into Shaanxi and well away from the rebels. "The only problem is, we learned the rebels crossed right into Shaanxi from Henan. We were going to warn you about them if we had caught up with you earlier."

"Yes, we found that out when they intercepted us in Xunyang a couple weeks ago," said Puqing. "They had tricked the government into thinking they were returning to Hubei where troops were lying in wait for them, but they kept on circling around northward and westward into Shaanxi."

"Why Shaanxi?"

"To stay one step ahead of the government, buy time, and recruit more rebels. And they—we—were well ahead of the government. We could have taken Xing'an—it was protected by only a few hundred troops—but we arrived in the evening when the river was at high tide and couldn't be crossed. We reached Ziyang a week ahead of the government. The river was easier to cross there but it still took five days to get everyone across, all thirty thousand of us. There were so many of us that we had to cross at different points along the river; you saw only the first crossing point. The government had ordered all boats over to the south bank to prevent us from using them. We were still able to wade across and commandeer the boats and build rafts. We were just getting the last of us across when you arrived yesterday, at the same time the government caught up with us and starting shooting! It was sheer chaos. They didn't dare cross the river themselves though since they would have been sitting ducks."

"Where are we headed now? South again?"

"Sichuan. To join up with our counterparts there."

"How do you know all this?"

"When the rebels apprehended us in Xunyang, they had no idea who we were and could have killed us. I identified myself as a friend of Wang Cong'er and she was summoned and recognized me. That's why we're in good circumstances now. You'll soon meet her and co-commander Yao Zhifu."

By the time Yaoyao had come to, they were close to the Sichuan border and headed to familiar territory: Taiping, where they planned to assist beleaguered rebels holed up in the surrounding mountains. As quite a few of the congregants were already well acquainted with the Shaanxi-Sichuan border region, they gained further points as advisors to Commanders Wang and Yao.

Juesan returned to an earlier question. "How did the Hubei authorities ever determine the Mistress to be a murder suspect?"

"Word must have gotten out about what happened at the Wudang Mountain nunnery. But they seem to have only the vaguest notion of her identity. What's weird is she's also suspected of killing people by setting fires," said Zou Run.

"That could be me," said Yaoyao.

"What?" they exclaimed.

"When I left Nanyang with Puyi and Pu'er, we stayed at a horrible inn that was cheating us. The innkeeper tore off my clothes and exposed me to everyone in the inn. Puyi and Pu'er got in a fight with him and the cook, who tossed boiling oil on Puyi. That's what caused the wound on his face. As we were fighting our way out of the inn, I severed the tarp over the kitchen stove and it caught fire. We fled fast. No idea what happened after that. We were only trying to escape. I didn't intend anyone to die. Did people die?"

"So it's the Henan authorities that must have informed the Hubei authorities about you," said Qiezi. "It seems they're confusing you with me and think we're the same person. That's good because it means they know nothing more about us. I hope they don't start communicating with the Shaanxi authorities about me."

"And they think you're a Miao woman."

A day later the rebels set up camp over the border in Sichuan. All were set to work, including the healers, felling bamboo stalks to build a temporary fortification. Yaoyao had mostly recuperated but was excused due to her pregnancy. Qiezi surprised everyone by slicing through a whole bamboo grove without getting tired, whereas the others had to rest between each few swings of the machete. And she was only using a cleaver. Soon another woman had come to stare at her, a beautiful young woman with unbound feet and dressed in white silk and a red turban and cape, surrounded by female escorts. Puqing pulled Qiezi over to the woman. "Wang Cong'er," he whispered.

Qiezi bowed to her. "I've heard so much about you, Commander Wang."

"How can you fell so many bamboos without getting tired?" Wang asked her.

"I climb trees."

Wang felt Qiezi's arms. "Come with me."

She was brought to Wang's tent. The males were ordered out, while the escorts stripped Qiezi and subjected her to a good deal of poking and prodding.

"Only acrobats have muscles like this," said Wang.

"I grew up in the mountains."

"You're from Shaanxi? You're the daughter of the parents who advised us on the trails there?"

"Yes."

"One of Puqing's healers? What's your name again?"

"Everyone calls me Mantuoluo."

"Get dressed, Mantuoluo."

Back in the bamboo grove, a long culm as thick as a warrior's neck was laid on the ground. Commander Wang handed Qiezi a broadsword and told her to work her way along the stalk, slicing each section on the node with a single stroke. Although the joints were harder to hit through cleanly and some were severed at a diagonal or missed altogether, her every stroke counted.

"Sorry for the sloppiness. This sword is heavier than I'm used to," said Qiezi.

"You'll improve with practice. The more technique you have, the less strength you need. Now again, *exactly* on the joint." She made Qiezi run through several more culms until every node was precisely sliced through.

"Look, she's not even out of breath," remarked Wang, who whispered something to an escort. "And you have the strongest arms I've ever seen in a woman who's not an acrobat. You have stronger arms than some of our best men. And your legs are strong too. Can you climb that bamboo over there?" Wang pointed to a particularly majestic specimen.

Qiezi was halfway up and back down in seconds.

"Do you want to be promoted, Mantuoluo?"

"What do you mean?"

The escort had brought back a man who was thrust down on his knees before Qiezi. His eyes darted around in terror and confusion as they bent him forward and exposed his neck by pulling his hair forward and his arms backward. With a soot-dabbed finger Wang drew a line between the vertebrae on his neck and nodded to Qiezi. The first blow didn't cut through all the way, to Qiezi's horror. She quickly finished him off.

"He was already unconscious and wouldn't have noticed," said Wang. "But you'll need to strike more firmly. Keep the blade absolutely straight."

"Why was he executed?" Qiezi asked.

"Don't worry about that. I'll talk to you again tomorrow, Mantuoluo."

The next day they were at it again harvesting bamboo. To hone her accuracy, Qiezi was commanded to produce hundreds more culm segments. Yaoyao's job was to collect the segments for turning into cups, utensils, and other implements.

Qiezi and Yaoyao stole a lot of glances at each other as they worked. They were the odd ones out. All the others—Puqing and Zou Run, Kang Sai'er and Yin Yan, Shen Wei and He Le, Yan Xian and Lai Xinru, Xie Yinhe and Qiu Lu'er (aka. Miaoyin and Miaolu), Ye Yuejiang and Gu Jingjing (Miaoyue and Miaojing), and of course Jue'er and Juesan, had long been or by now become bedmates. There was less borrowing and lending of partners as before, not so much out of hidebound habit than the comfort of familiar embrace in times of uncertainty. Time had brought Yuejiang and Jingjing closer together; the secrets each had once shared only with Qiezi and not with each other were now shared with each other and not with Qiezi. Qiezi still had her parents but she was lonely. She needed a more challenging companion to be passionate about.

In the afternoon Qiezi was called away for another visit with Wang Cong'er. When she returned later in the evening, she plucked Yaoyao out of the medical tent by the hand. "I want to show you something."

They found a nearby grove. Qiezi laid a blanket down and handed Yaoyao a freshly fashioned bamboo cup brimming with a milky substance. "I got this rice wine for us. It's still warm. Don't tell the others or they'll want some too. I've just been through a real trial."

Yaoyao put her arm around Qiezi. "What happened? You're drunk."

Qiezi laid her head on Yaoyao's chest. "I just killed fifty men."

"*Shangdi!*"

"I was forced to. They were traitors."

"What traitors? Who were they?"

"That day on the river when you were rescuing people trying to get across, a bunch of rebels saw that the troops were in confusion on the other side when they were attacked by Jueyi and

Juesi's arrows. They decided to make a break for it and switch sides. They dashed into the water pretending to go help the stricken but then kept going, and they were heard shouting to the troops that they wanted to surrender. But the troops didn't believe them and started shooting at them. They hurried back and pretended as if nothing happened, but Wang and Yao were informed. They didn't do anything about it at first since they wanted to restore order and get back on the road. Today they were rounded up and executed. I was the executioner."

"Why did they choose you?"

"I'm not sure. Perhaps because I could do it quickly without getting tired."

"How long did it take you?"

"A *ke*."

Yaoyao sat up. "You executed fifty men in only one *ke*!"

"I was rushing to finish them off before I threw up, but I still threw up before I was even halfway through. And then I kept going somehow. One neck after the other. I have no idea how I managed it. They were all lined up in a row and held down blindfolded with their hands tied behind their back. So I didn't have to see their faces. I just went up to each one in turn."

"Like you were doing today with the bamboo stalks? Oh, my dear, what a wretched thing they put you through. You had to do it, though. Otherwise, they might have executed *you* for refusing. That would have broken us."

"I would have got back earlier, but Wang Cong'er kept me afterwards to dine with them. I couldn't eat anything. So I had some of the wine."

"Will you be promoted for this?"

"They didn't say. We'll see."

"You should be. But I'll be miserable if they take you away from us."

"That's why I pulled you over here. In case I can't see you tomorrow. We can sleep here tonight. It's warm enough out now. I already told Miaoyin to leave us alone. I'm so happy to be with you." She grabbed Yaoyao's hand and placed it under her shirt.

They caressed each other's breasts. "I want to kiss you, but you know I can't."

Yaoyao dug her tongue into Qiezi's ear. "You can kiss me this way."

"Even that might be dangerous. But I can do this." She reached between Yaoyao's legs and worked her fingers inside her. "You like it?"

"You're making me crazy. Let me have a look at yours." Yaoyao pushed Qiezi back and parted her legs. Her mouth hovered over the exposed jade gate. She curled her lips inward and with dry mouth pulled apart the engorged labia by tugging at the dark tangle of hair. "You have a strong smell, heady, intense, like fresh soil dug up from the ground."

"That's the flower in me. You can't."

"Yes, I can. Watch. Move over here, off the blanket." Yaoyao arched Qiezi's hips upward and spread her legs back. "Hold your legs up behind the knees with your arms and open up your jade gate with your fingers."

Yaoyao proceeded to pour the rice wine into Qiezi's groin until her cavity filled up and flowed over. She drank from it, spit it out and said, "The wine should help dilute the poison. Anyway, I have your taste. Now, you try the same with me."

"We have to stop this. You're going to be sick. Really. You could die."

"Oh, I would die for you for anything." Yaoyao tried to force her mouth on Qiezi's but was deflected.

"We can go further next time."

In the morning, Yaoyao failed to be roused. Qiezi carried her back to the tent and lay her down. She told the others Yaoyao was still unrecovered from her injury and was only resting. But they knew better. Qiezi spent the day with her arm around Yaoyao on her cot.

"Look," said Jingjing, strolling up hand in hand with Yuejiang, "she's in love."

"Mistress, is she as bad as I was?" asked Yuejiang.

"No worse than you were. It helps that I've been short of the flower and less deadly."

Later her mother came up. "Baobei, what's going on? Did you do something to her?"

"She'll come through, but it may take another day or two. If she awakes and speaks strange words or starts screaming, help me hold her down. She'll fall back asleep."

The next day, Qiezi was again summoned to Wang Cong'er's tent. She was asked if she could ride a horse.

"A little. We could never afford a horse when I was young. But I was taught by a few people here and there. I've ridden donkeys and mules too. They're more common in the mountains, you know."

"We're going to teach you."

The rigorous training, personally supervised by Wang, lasted for a whole day and involved firing arrows, wielding a broadsword, wielding two broadswords, and fighting on horseback. Qiezi's endurance enabled her to go for hours at a time.

Once again she was called into Wang's tent and stripped. "Did I do something wrong, Commander Wang?"

"You're making good progress, Mantuoluo. But you'll need at least another week of practice, combat practice against experienced cavalry with bamboo swords and armored padding. I'll hand you off to others for that."

Wang Cong'er removed her own tunic, armored vest and pants and handed them to Qiezi, who looked at the garments and said, "You want to make me one of your escorts?"

"Not exactly."

Qiezi donned the immaculate white silk uniform, while Wang slipped on another set worn by one of her team. "You're tighter than me around the bust so we'll have to find you a larger tunic."

"Commander Wang, I am unworthy to wear your uniform."

"We all wear the same, as you can see. Except that I have a red turban and cape, and theirs are white. We'll get you your turban and cape later."

The next day, Wang Cong'er, her tent, her female escorts, her cavalry, and most of the rebels were nowhere to be seen.

"What happened to them?" Qiezi asked Puqing, who had gone to investigate.

"It seems Wang and Yao had urgent business in Sichuan. Before dawn they were packed up and gone, taking most of the camp with them. They left us a contingent of a thousand rebels and an equal number of noncombatants."

"What are we supposed to do now?"

"We really don't know."

The male escorts soon returned. "Here is Commander Wang's gift to you, her red turban and cape." To the healers they announced, "You must all pack up and be ready to leave tomorrow at dawn. Bear the infirm with you; you are responsible for them."

In the morning, more escorts arrived, unfamiliar faces this time. Mounted on their horses, the congregation followed them to a distant section of the camp, the only place left with human activity, where the remaining rebels and followers were also ready to depart, indeed had been waiting for her, awaiting her command. Qiezi had sat a still insensate Yaoyao before her on her horse, holding her steady with one arm and the rein with the other, as if this would hasten reviving her. The escorts persuaded her to take Yaoyao off the horse, at least for the duration of her speech.

"Address your army, Commander Wang," one of the escorts told Qiezi.

"What?"

Kneeling before her, the escorts repeated together, "Address your army, Commander Wang!"

"I don't understand. I am not Commander Wang."

"You are Commander Wang."

"Is this some kind of performance? Nobody prepared me for this. Puqing, what's going on?"

"They seem to think you are Wang Cong'er."

Qiezi pleaded with the escorts. "I have no idea what this is about. You want me to pretend I am Wang Cong'er? Why?"

"Pretend?" they said, nonplussed. "You *are* Wang Cong'er."

"Where are we headed?"

"Shaanxi. Back to Ziyang. You have to tell them where we are going and give them some encouragement."

"Why don't you introduce me first?"

"That doesn't show leadership. You must address them now."

Qiezi turned to the expectant rebels. "*Dajia*, today we march to Ziyang to hunt down the remnants of the Manchu devils. *Jiayou!*"

"Love live Commander Wang, *Wansui! Wansui! Wanwansui!*" the army shouted in unison.

That seemed to satisfy the crowd and activity recommenced. The escorts led the way. Qiezi followed on horseback, together with Jue'er and Juesan on their horses, and Puqing and Shen Wei on Jueyi and Juesi's horses.

"Did I sound ridiculous?" Qiezi asked Puqing.

"It's not important what you said. You had to say something to motivate them."

"I'm shocked by all of this."

"We are too."

"How in the world can I playact this nonsense?"

"Just go along with it."

"Do they actually think I'm Wang Cong'er?"

"It could be. If they've never had a close look at her. Given the thousands of rebels in the camp, it's possible."

Zou Run chimed in. "These escorts know what's going on and they know you're not Wang Cong'er. They're under orders to treat you as such. But you cannot playact as long as you playact. Don't pretend to be her. You must *become* her. From this point on, you *are* Wang Cong'er."

"Zou Run's right. You have no choice. That's the only way we'll all make it through this," said Puqing.

"Why is this happening? And why in the world are we heading back to Ziyang?" said Qiezi.

"The only explanation I can think of is it's a diversionary tactic to draw government forces away from here and back to Shaanxi—when the rumors reach them about us."

"Why didn't she tell me about this earlier?"

"They didn't want us to know we were being abandoned."

"How can this ragtag detachment of ours fight against the government's tens of thousands of troops?" said Qiezi.

"We've been demoted back to cannon fodder for the benefit of the larger cause, I guess."

"So they made us dispensable, when we're the best healers around?"

"Thankfully so. We'll need us."

12

The ring of fire

When the vanguard's path down the mountain had leveled and widened somewhat, the escorts pulled up alongside Qiezi.

"Commander Wang," one said, "you need protection in the event of an attack. We will ride with you. Also, you endanger yourself by carrying this pregnant woman. Cavalry cannot be weighed down with such a burden. You must place her in a sick cart."

"Is she even alive?" said a fellow escort.

"I will carry her until she is well. If the enemy is sighted, I'll hand her to another's protection," responded Qiezi.

"The enemy can attack without warning," said the second.

"Listen to us," said the first. "We are experienced fighters. In the event of an attack, you will both be thrown from the horse if you are not ready at the reins. You must not bear her. We would have you understand that when we are on the trail of the enemy, or they on ours, we cover up to seventy, eighty *li* per day. Those who are too sick, too old, or too young to keep up with the march must be abandoned. That includes women who are not fighters, above all pregnant women."

"Why bother with her? What possible use can she be to you?" said the second. "Isn't she the blank-faced idiot we were warned about? The mad woman with the stupid stare? Look at her head lolling over your shoulder with her drooling mouth." He gave Yaoyao's face a contemptuous slap with the back of his hand.

"Don't you dare violate her!" said Qiezi. "Are you in command of this army?"

"Carrying a corpse around does not befit a leader. You must act like a leader!"

"The woman is not mad and she is not stupid," intervened Puqing. "She is a shamaness. She is under the spell of a potion that enables her to commune with the gods and advise us on strategy. Commander Wang placed her on horseback to revive her the more quickly."

"Sheer nonsense!" said the first escort. "We are doomed in going along with this charade. Can't you see the strange looks from our troops and hear their grumbling? You are subjecting us to ridicule at the very moment your leadership is called for!"

"Here, we'll help you get rid of the tramp," said the second, who pulled Yaoyao off Qiezi's horse before Qiezi and Puqing could grab her. She fell onto her back.

"Don't you touch her!" shouted Qiezi, enraged. With a clean stroke of her broadsword she sliced off the second escort's head.

The decapitation stunned everyone, including Qiezi. She looked at her sword and back up again. She was about to strike the chief escort himself when two other escorts took advantage of the confusion to lurch at Puqing and behind him, Zou Run. But before the chief escort's own sword could cut down a distracted Qiezi, his horse reared up in clamorous convulsion, throwing him and collapsing onto him. Other horses panicked and took off in different directions. Those who still had their riders were almost out of sight before they were brought under control.

The chaos abated moments later to reveal, at the center of the primal scene, Puqing and Zou Run cut down, the chief escort still mouthing words as he hung by his hair in Qiezi's fist, severed from his body, and a fully recovered Yaoyao pointing a bloody dagger—she had disemboweled his horse just in time. It was she who broke the silence. "Are you with us or with them?" she yelled at the remaining five escorts who found themselves surrounded. They dismounted their horses and kowtowed to Qiezi.

"We obey you, Commander!" they shouted in unison. One of them was looking at his comrades as he kowtowed rather than at Qiezi.

"Stand up!" Yaoyao told them. "All except *you*. Hold him down," she told Jue'er and Juesan, who had also dismounted and were standing at the ready. "Commander Wang!" she called out to Qiezi, who was still staring in a daze at the chief escort's head dangling in her hand. It had stopped talking. "Mistress!"

Qiezi snapped out of it, dropped the head and proceeded to behead the tardy escort.

"We can't go anywhere now with this chaos," she whispered to Yaoyao. "We have to clean up."

"Announce to everyone we're delayed." She turned to Jue'er and Juesan. "How are they all organized? Into squads? Brigades?"

"We have no idea. By the looks of them, they don't have much fighting experience. Their spears and cudgels are nothing but farming tools. They're only poor peasants and townsmen who've been rounded up along the way and pressed into service. The rebel army all left with Wang Cong'er."

"We'll have to organize them somehow. Use the *baojia* system. For now, keep the combatants separate from the noncombatants, or they'll all run away with their families."

The corpses were buried and a tent erected as a command center. In the tent, Qiezi, Yaoyao, and Yin Yan attended to Kang Sai'er, distraught at the loss of her close friends. Qiezi stroked Sai'er's hair, fragrant with fear, her ashen cheeks shivering with tears. "We will set this aright, dear."

"How did you awaken so suddenly from your deathly slumber?" Yin Yan asked Yaoyao.

"I was already coming to when the Mistress sat me on her

horse this morning. I was groggy and confused and trying to make sense of what people were saying, but I heard everything. I pretended to be unconscious to collect my strength."

"Were you hurt from your fall off the horse?" said Qiezi.

"No."

"Where did you find the dagger?"

"I grabbed it from the escort's belt and plunged it right into the horse. That was easy. But I needed all my strength to open its belly. I got splattered with its guts. What are we to do with these ruined clothes? Mistress, your white silk uniform is drenched in blood. How can we replace it?"

"Let's get you two undressed and cleaned up. We'll wash them as best we can. I'll find water and soap," said Yin Yan, who dashed out of the tent.

Sai'er pulled herself together and insisted she'd be fine. A short while later Yin Yan returned with two wholesome females bearing buckets of water. The rest of the congregation also filed into the tent.

"I asked among the women for any who wanted to be promoted and grabbed the first two who weren't diseased, emaciated or slow of speech. And robust enough that their clothes should fit you," Yin Yan said to Qiezi and Yaoyao. She asked the new recruits their names.

"Yu Xiahong," said one.

"Gong Jia," said the other.

"Did you see what happened at the front earlier?"

"No. We only heard there was trouble."

"This is Commander Wang, and this is Deputy Commander Bi. They almost sacrificed their lives today. Their uniforms testify to their heroism, soiled with the blood of the traitors. Let them have your clothes and get to work cleaning theirs. We'll find something for you to wear later," said Yin Yan.

The girls stood mouths agape.

"We can do without the childish modesty. Come on now, *tuo!*"

When they had stripped, the mortified maids were put to work outside the back of the tent.

With Qiezi and Yaoyao now appareled and presentable, the congregation huddled together. Qiezi was upset. "It's outrageous what we've been put through the past few days. And we're all supposed to be on the same side!"

"Where are we even heading?" said Xie Yinhe. "We can't march around in circles. There seems to be enough food and water to go around for now, but there are so many sick people out there. Oh, heavens. Women are giving birth right now. Others are dying."

"In other words," said Juesan, "we weren't simply abandoned in the path of the enemy. They dumped the feeblest of the lot on us so they could move faster."

As the congregation debated what to do and where to go, Qiezi stared straight ahead. "One of those two girls had a Shaanxi accent similar to mine," she said. She went out to talk to them and brought back Gong Jia. She was clad in a mere strip of cloth slung between her legs, fringed with pubic hair and attached in front and back to a string around her waist. She had to cross her arms over her breasts.

"Find some garments for them or they'll be wearing yours!" Qiezi snapped at Yuejiang and Jingjing. She introduced Gong Jia to the congregants. "She's from Hanzhong. Are you from the mountains? How well do you know the territory?"

"Don't go to Hanzhong. Government troops always pass through there since it's the main mountain trail for transporting silver from Xi'an, and it's very well guarded. Rebels are all over the place there as well fighting the troops."

"How do you know all this?"

"Everyone knows it. Everyone knows about the plank trail to Xi'an. Actually, I'm not from Hanzhong but Hanwangcheng, farther downstream."

"That's where you were captured? That's where you crossed over the river with the rebels?"

"Yes."

"Do you know any mountain trails on the way to Ziyang?"

"I heard of Ziyang but I've never gone that far."

"Our home villages may be only a couple days away from each other on foot."

Qiezi returned the girl to her task. The congregation conferred and they jumped to work.

"Wait," said Qiezi. "Call Miaoyue and Miaojing back. I have a better idea of how to clothe those girls."

It was decided that the two thousand hapless ones needed more rigorous hierarchization for their own good. Jue'er and Juesan organized the so-called combatants, males young and old, and with Miaoyin and Miaole at the helm, likewise the congregants' females and young children of both sexes. The roughly one thousand men and one thousand women were each divided into ten groups of one hundred and further into ten teams of ten, with a designated elder leader drawn from a different team. The team leaders then reported to the group leaders on the fitness and food supply of their teams. The seriously infirm—excluding the hopeless—were made note of and the hoarding of food ferreted out and redistributed. The leaders also recommended those of able body who had smithing, carpentry, tailoring, and cooking skills.

In the meantime, those with fighting, riding, and medical skills were summoned to the tent. They were lined up at some distance from the tent's entrance and called to the tent twenty at a time, ten males and ten females. Inside, the first of the groups faced the congregation, which counted two new members, Gong and Yu, now attired.

Qiezi stood up. "I am Commander Wang. Are you willing to become escorts and healers?"

"Yes, Commander," they shouted in unison.

"Are you ready to demonstrate your obedience and loyalty?"

"Yes, Commander."

"Strip. All of you. Everything off! Including undergarments. Now!"

After a shocked interval of silence, they began to shed their attire. Two males and one female, whether from fright or defiance, stood without moving.

"Did you not hear what I said? Strip!"

The three remained paralyzed.

"All right, off with them."

Dragged out the back entrance of the tent, they were forcibly stripped and beheaded.

"You can all get dressed," Qiezi continued. "If you perform your roles well, you'll be rewarded with better food rations and mixed-sex sleeping quarters. Assemble outside the back of the tent and await more instructions. And take note of the consequences of disobedience!"

Those gathering in the field behind the tent after passing their initiation were obliged to witness the somber proceedings dealt out to those who had failed. They were soon at work cleaning up. Being shorn of its clothing was violation enough, and each trunk was carefully joined with its respective head in the burial pit. The corpses' clothes were washed and dried for others' use or converted into cloths and rags.

Now with set purpose, Qiezi's—or rather Wang Cong'er's—army, having rested for the night, resumed their march early next morning. The strong bore the weak. Scouts were sent out to scan the territory for any signs of government troops. They made rapid progress back through Shaanxi in a beeline for Commander Wang's native mountain where they would build their fort.

Approaching the mountain several days later, they discovered the surrounding villages to be abandoned, despoiled or burnt down; the Yan family's adopted village lay further off in the direction of the walled town and would have to wait for another excursion. They had anticipated this. It meant the local population—those who hadn't perished in the tumult—would have been forced up into mountain stockades for protection. This indeed turned out to be the case. The mountain's highest village happened to be Lai Xinru's natal village (Yan Xian had come to live with them after marriage rather than the usual reverse). They now found it surrounded by a stockade.

Qiezi called Gong Jia over. "That's why I was asking you about your territory. In case we're unable to enter the stockade and need to find another mountain. But that's only as a last resort, since we plan to enter it."

"Who's in the stockade and who's guarding it? Some sort of brigands or rebels?"

In taking an active interest in her surroundings, Gong Jia had more pluck than Qiezi and Yaoyao had guessed. They began to take an active interest in her. Zou Run's tunic and pants, bloodstains scrubbed out and newly patched up, fit her handsomely. In her mid-twenties, the initiate's primeval eyes, fierce cheekbones, and broad grin stretched one's conception of beauty until one grasped it. It was no accident she was attractive; Yin Yan had picked her out of the crowd (that looks were held to be an outward expression of strength and intelligence was not controversial).

"Rebel stockades are different," said Yaoyao. "They're hastily constructed and typically perched on the rocky summit of a mountain with steep cliffs. They're smaller but more impenetrable."

"Yet more vulnerable to the banner troops' flaming catapults and fire arrows, because of all the wood and canvas concentrated in one place," added Juesan. "This stockade wraps around existing habitation and as you can see includes a bit of terraced farmland. So they can feed their own."

"It's our old village," said Xinru.

Now dressed in humble peasant wear, Qiezi, her parents, and a train of male escorts armed with bows and arrows approached the stockade gate and announced, "We are an army of refugees captured by the White Lotus bandits. We escaped from their clutch. We wish to join you for our protection. We are stocked with food and medicine and will share it with you. Let us in!"

The gate vibrated with human presence behind it, but they were answered with silence.

"If you don't let us in, we will attack you and force our way in. We know you can see us. We are many and we are armed!"

A bit later, big sacks of rice were tossed over the gate. "Go away!" yelled voices from within.

"They think we're rebels and we're here to invade them for food," said Jue'er.

They tossed the rice back over the gate.

"We do not lack food! We do not have a hostile intent. We are from this territory. You can hear this from our accents," shouted Lai Xinru and Yan Xian.

This opened the gate. As soon as the gatekeepers saw how many people there were, they tried to slam it shut but were prevented by the surge of refugees. Once inside, the refugees faced a human wall of hostility and were pushed into a field within the stockade to set up camp. This better served their purpose. They got to work building tents and forging weapons.

When the congregation ventured into the village to barter goods, the Yan family did not recognize anyone they met. Nor were the militiamen in charge of the stockade forthcoming with information. From private conversations they pieced together what had happened. Due to none other than the Yan family scandal and guilt by association for the unsolved homicide of the runner Qing Da, the original inhabitants had been made responsible for apprehending the family and when nothing turned up were accordingly punished by banishment.

It was a good thing Yan Xian and Lai Xinru had not revealed their names or made it known they were old villagers, or they might have been seized. It looked indeed as if no one recognized them. As the refugees were well organized and disciplined and provided medicines, a delicate truce was held for several weeks. But word soon spread that this was no ordinary mob of refugees but a disciplined band of religious crusaders with a strange sorceress at their head. The stockade leaders were thus motivated to disprove suspicions they weren't rebels after all, if their leader would deign to present herself to them in a more humble and worldly fashion. Qiezi was invited to dine *alone* with the very head of the stockade himself in his own house. Now, such a proposal would have been unthinkable for any member of the female sex. But this was no boastful escapade of a lascivious strongman but a political and existential matter of some importance to the state.

The congregation themselves knew it was only a matter of time before it came to this. Qiezi and Yaoyao had proactively worked out what they wanted to do even before they arrived on the mountain. They informed the leaders that the invitation must be rejected because it was patently a trap. Another negotiator might have added that they were also armed and numbered at least as many as the stockade's own population. But instead of forcing a tense showdown, they invited the leader to dine with Qiezi in a pavilion set up in their camp and open on all sides to witnesses. The leader could bring his own contingent of armed guards to defend the pavilion, but they themselves would be facing an equal number of the commandress's protectors. And the pavilion would be equipped with a bed: if he was indecent enough to propose sleeping with her, let him prove his mettle by doing it in plain view! The leader considered the counterproposal so surprising and singular and arousing that he agreed.

The ceremony site decided upon, the stockade was informed, to their great amusement, that their armed guards would be surrounded not by weapons but rather a ring of makeshift canopy beds with an audience of the choicest girls posing on the beds—the canopies serving to shroud the beds, Qiezi's as well, under opaque hempen mosquito nets when pulled closed. They didn't object to this and even agreed to shroud the pavilion itself with their own luxurious sheer silken gauze for maximum visibility.

Yaoyao suggested to Qiezi a last-minute change. "We should build the beds with pinewood and only the canopies with bamboo. Both burn fast but pine ignites faster."

The canopy occupants were selected from among the new recruits. After a day everything was in place and the participants rehearsed in their roles. At the appointed time the next day, the stockade's guards arrived with their leader in tow. Its population clamored behind and surged around half of the enclosure of canopy beds. Qiezi's army closed the other half of the circle. She was led to the banquet table where her opponent sat in greedy expectation, the only two partaking in the feast. Her flaming-red satin shift, which he had gifted to her, danced upon her as she sat down. As a woman does who is ready to forgo her dignity, she took her time at her meal.

The meal seemed as if it would never end—until all turned to the stockade gate where a commotion was heard. The stockade leader was summoned: an armed contingent from the county seat—the walled town—were amassed out front. Qiezi and the congregants followed. When they arrived at the gate, they were told the Yan family's presence in the stockade had been discovered. They had orders from the magistrate to hand over the family, including the daughter Yan Zhengzai who was wanted for murder, or else the stockade leaders and elders would all be charged as accessories to the crime.

The leader turned to Qiezi and demanded that she produce the fugitive family, unaware he was standing right before them. Yaoyao called Qiezi over to a chink in the wall near the gate. She and her parents peered through. "Do you recognize any of them?" asked Yaoyao.

"Oh, yes, one of them we clearly do—the same *yamen* officer the magistrate had slap us last year, and he'll remember us," said Yan Xian. "The rest of them seem to be hired guards rather than the *yamen*'s own runners."

"Do you think he'll still recognize you?" Xinru asked her daughter.

"Maybe not. He hardly glanced at me when he pulled you two in to be slapped," said Qiezi.

Yaoyao whispered something to Qiezi and her parents, who responded with knowing nods.

Qiezi then brought her parents and Yaoyao up to the stockade leader and announced, "This is the Yan family and their daughter."

The gate was opened and the three were pushed out. The guard received Yan Xian and Lai Xinru uneventfully but glanced oddly at Yaoyao—whose face was cast downward in feigned abjection—before seeming satisfied the family was intact. The contingent departed after clamping leg irons on the trio and plonking them in a cart. Qiezi said to the leader, "Shall we get back to business?"

They were not yet down the mountain on the bumpy path when the three captives looked back and saw a column of smoke rising above the stockade.

In the *yamen* courtroom, Yaoyao knelt before the magistrate, her gaze fixed on the stone floor. Yan Xian and Lai Xinru knelt behind her.

"Do you confirm that you are Yan Zhengzai, daughter of Yan Xian and Yan Shi, née Lai?" began the magistrate.

"Yes."

"On the fifth day of the seventh month of Jiaqing 1, your neighbor Rui Mian, with whom your family had an acrimonious relationship, was murdered by Li Er, one of two brothers unrelated to your family and living unregistered in your household. They were apprehended to this *yamen* the next day, along with you and your family, and other witnesses. Your parents were cleared as accessories to the crime but were slapped as a warning against harboring strangers. Only a day later, on the seventh, our runner Qing Da, assigned to this case, succumbed to poisoning upon returning to the *yamen* after visiting your village. By the time he was discovered, he was already unresponsive and was thus unable to give an account of what had happened. The autopsy revealed apparent poisoning by an unknown toxic agent. An investigation was opened the next day and your village again visited. Several witnesses confirmed seeing Qing Da entering and leaving your home and only your home. But you and your family had fled. A search party was sent out and failed to find you. Your premises turned up no traces of harmful agents such as arsenic or aconite; nor had local pharmacies been visited by anyone in your family. However, you, Yan Zhengzai, already had a reputation among the village for extensive knowledge of plants and herbs, which would include natural poisons. And your family would have had reason to do away with Qing Da if he had discovered evidence of further collusion or crimes on you or your parents' part. To expedite these proceedings, therefore, would you care to confess your poisoning of Qing Da and reveal the toxic agent you employed?"

"Qing Da raped me," said Yaoyao.

"What kind of an answer is that? If that was all that happened, you could have filed a rape charge against him. We would have taken that very seriously. Did you parents witness the rape?"

"Yes."

"How was Qing Da able to force you, with three of you present? How was he able to force you at all? The autopsy revealed no physical marks of attack on his body, which might be evidence of struggle had you tried to fight back. That suggests you must have willingly given yourself to him for some type of gain. And a misunderstanding must have arisen motivating you to poison him and flee. Something else must be going on. We are waiting for you to divulge it!"

Yaoyao was silent.

"Yan Xian and Yan Shi—would you like to explain?"

They were silent.

"Your daughter is quite pregnant. By Qing law and the Emperor's grace, pregnant women are exempt from the instruments of torture, but you two are not. I am giving you now a little more time to consider your fates and the opportunity to confess the truth before we draw it out of you!"

They remained silent.

"Now, Yan Zhengzai, you are not betrothed and yet are pregnant. It cannot be Qing Da who impregnated you because it has been a full year since the events of last summer. Who got you pregnant? Were you raped again? Or perhaps you allowed or invited a man to sleep with you? Your pregnancy can only have arisen from illicit sex, which is illegal and carries a serious charge."

More silence.

"Not only have you engaged in illicit sex, we have further evidence that you style yourself a shamaness who performs sexual intercourse in public as part of a perverted Daoist rite and sacrifices her victims by poisoning them. I can't express to you how serious an allegation this is. Being convicted of premeditated homicide involving witchcraft results in execution by slow slicing. If that wasn't bad enough, you have been implicated as well in operating a *yinsi*, an obscene temple, under the guise of a pharmacy in the Hubei city of Fangxian, where you and your cabal of so-called healers recruited unwitting customers to perform your shameful rites upon. Being the ringleader of a cult also results in execution by slow slicing."

"I know nothing about any of this," said Yaoyao.

"On top of that, you are a suspect in a trail of unsolved murders along the Han River between Ziyang and Xing'an last summer, and another murder in a nunnery near the Hubei border by a young nun who fits your description and went by the name of Mantuoluo. These murders followed eastward in an arc that culminated in Wudang Mountain and Fangxian city. After that the investigators came to a dead end. Can you add anything that would help us solve these murders and bring us up to date on the whereabouts of the perpetrators? If you were to come clean and provide us with the names of your accomplices, I might consider how to mitigate the charges to a lesser punishment before the case is sent to higher levels, after which it will be out of my hands."

"Look, your lord, she's making a mess on the floor," said the magistrate's secretary. A pool of liquid was spreading underneath Yaoyao.

"Ah, what's this? Are you so petrified with fear that you can't hold your bladder? Is this your way of confessing your guilt?" said the magistrate.

Yaoyao turned to Xinru and said something.

"Your lord," Xinru exclaimed, "she's not urinating. She's breaking water. She's about to give birth! Would you kindly pause these proceedings and let me attend to her. We will return after the birth."

"*Shangdi!* Move them into the next room. Summon a midwife and some maids and clean up this mess," the magistrate told the guards. To the crowd assembled in the back of the courtroom (which was open to the public) he shouted, "Is there a midwife among you?"

"We need buckets of hot water and towels," said Xinru.

"You stay here," he said to Yan Xian as Yaoyao and Xinru

were escorted out of the courtroom. "Let us resume. Would you like to explain, Yan Xian, how you came up with the idea of giving your daughter the bizarre and blasphemous name of the great sage Kongzi's mother, Zhengzai, just because you happen to share the same surname? What were you thinking? That any son your daughter might bear would be as wise? Has any Chinese family over the past two thousand years ever entertained such a vain and preposterous notion?"

"It was a noble-sounding name for a girl, so we chose it," said Yan Xian.

"Were you aware that this was Kongzi's mother's name?"

"Maybe not."

"Well, I will refresh your memory." The magistrate turned to his secretary. "Would you read out the passage on Kongzi's biography in Sima Qian's *Records of the Grand Historian?*"

The secretary had his finger on the book and spoke, adding explanatory comments. "The temple priestess Yan Zhengzai of the 'Yan clan copulated publicly in the wilds with a man of the He clan,' who died soon after. She 'gave birth on a sacrificial mound,' and by astonishing coincidence the baby was 'born with a mound on its head.' He was variously named Kongqiu, meaning 'mound,' and Zhongni, referring to the sacred hillock upon which he was born. Yan Zhengzai raised the boy herself. The name Kongzi was later adopted as a title of respect after he had grown up and became famous as a teacher and sage."

"Does your daughter really presume," the magistrate continued, "to style her son after Kongzi and herself after his mother? Does she copulate publicly in order to hoodwink naïve acolytes into believing your lineage goes back to the very same Yan clan? And all due to the vanity of your daughter's name?"

"We *are* of the Yan clan," said Yan Xian.

A newborn's cry was heard in the next room. At the same moment, a guard from outside rushed into the courtroom. "Your lord, an army of rebels is entering the city gates. The gatekeepers are overwhelmed. They are spilling into the city. The crowds are shouting, 'Long live Wang Cong'er!'"

"That's impossible," the magistrate said.

"We heard Wang Cong'er's army has reentered Hubei after being chased out of Sichuan and were driving north. But they cannot have arrived in Shaanxi so soon," said his secretary.

"There are thousands of them!" said the guard.

An attendant popped out of the neighboring room to announce, "Your lord, the accused has given birth to a boy!"

Lai Xinru squeezed past the attendant bearing Yaoyao in her arms, who was too weak to walk on her own, and placed her down on the floor. Yaoyao sat up before the magistrate, cradling the baby inside her robe.

"Let me get right to the point, Yan Zhengzai," he said in a rage. "Are you aware that your parents blessed you with a most sacrilegious given name, styled after the mother of Kongzi? And that you seem to have gone along with this charade and by sheer luck have just now given birth to a bastard boy? I presume you would never intend or pretend to name the boy after Kongzi himself."

Yaoyao opened her robe to reveal the baby. She fixed her disturbing eyes upon the magistrate for the first time and said, "No, I am not *pretending* he is Kongzi. He *is* Kongzi."

"No!"

The secretary stepped up to Yaoyao to examine the baby. "Your lord," he said, "the baby's crown is deformed and failed to join properly. Look, it has a pronounced mound!"

The baby stared at the magistrate while suckling at her mother's breast.

"No!"

Another guard rushed into the courtroom. "Your lord, they are setting the city on fire! The bandits have spread out inside the entire perimeter of the city wall and are setting fires. We are surrounded by fire. We need more men to stop it, but the Green Standard troops that were stationed outside the city are nowhere to be seen!"

"No!"

The crowd parted, making way for a new arrival in the

courtroom, a woman dressed in white silk and red turban and cape followed by a train of armed escorts.

"Wang Cong'er!" said the crowd in hushed voices.

The magistrate had his hands around his neck and seemed to be choking.

Without so much as a word, Qiezi gathered Yaoyao in her arms and calmly made her way with her parents out of the courtroom.

"Wait. I recognize that woman," said one of the attendants, pointing to Qiezi. "*That* is the daughter of the accused parents, not the accused girl. I'm sure of it. We have been deceived!"

"You think we don't know our own daughter?" Lai Xinru shouted back.

No one heeded the attendant: they were too busy trying to revive the magistrate. Qiezi and her train were already outside the *yamen* gate and mounting their horses. Hot ashes were swirling in the air. The crowd continued to chant, "Wang Cong'er *wansui*! Wang Cong'er *wansui*!" As Qiezi and her train made their way to the city gate, the crowd followed: thousands of fresh new recruits. An even larger crowd awaited them outside the gate—Qiezi's army redoubled in size from their mountain stronghold. But not all the city's residents joined Qiezi's army. The screams of many thousands more could be made out in the chaos and smoky haze, already trapped by the fires, which would soon be merging into a general conflagration.

The army passed through her village on the river, now abandoned, and stopped at their former house. Qiezi got off her horse and told her parents to inspect the house and her escorts to wait for her. She grabbed Gong Jia and disappeared with her down the path to the river. Rummaging inside the bushes at the river's edge, Qiezi pointed to a patch of white flowers and plucked several. "Do you know this flower?"

"No," said Gong Jia.

"It's the golden ocean flower."

"Why 'golden'? It's white."

"There are yellow varieties too. That's why it's called 'golden.'

And purple varieties. And it came from across the ocean. It's also known as the *mantuoluo* flower. People call me by the name Mantuoluo."

"Why is the flower so special? Why are you named after it?"

"We'll talk about that later. Do you have this flower on your mountain?"

"I'm not sure."

"Will you help me look for it when we get there?"

"Of course. Why?"

"I need it. Help me carry them back with us. We can plant them as well."

They gathered up the flowers and seed capsules and put them in their pockets. "It's all right if they get folded together and a little crushed."

"I'll take good care of them."

"Wait. One more thing. Sit down here on the old rock while I do something," said Qiezi.

She stuck a datura flower in her mouth and slipped her pants off her hips in a squat. Twisting the petals into a point with her lips, she pulled the glistening tube out of her mouth and inserted it into her vagina.

"Mistress, what are you doing?"

"Don't you ever try this. You'll die. I do it to live. Here, you can do *this*."

Qiezi set a datura flower in Gong Jia's ear and stood back to have a better look. "I'm tired of being beautiful. Now it's your turn."

ACKNOWLEDGEMENTS & HISTORICAL NOTE

Heartfelt thanks to Professor Feng Yihan, Professor Hill Gates, Wang Chen, and Gao Mingzhe, for help with the historical research.

The English translation of the Sima Qian quotations (epigraph and chapter 12) is the author's own, based on the original Chinese and scholarship by L. M. Jensen (1995). A bibliography of historical sources used for this novel can be accessed at:

https://ishamcook.com/2025/08/10/the-tao-of-poison/

Also by Isham Cook

It is the Shanghai of courtesans and concubines, danger and decadence, updated to 2020. American expat author Isham Cook has disappeared. His last known history is chronicled by an exotic woman who seems right out of 1930s Shanghai herself, Marguerite, a mustachioed Afghan-American who weaves Persian rugs and deals in psychedelics. As she tells it, Isham's story all began with Luna, a beguiling but troubled Chinese woman who happens to have a mustache too. Also vying for Isham's affection is the charismatic Kitty, who conspires to entrap him in a cyberweb of obsession and betrayal.

Fans of Cook's fiction will recognize in this psychological thriller set in modern China his signature world of startling plot turns and his unsettling yet compelling landscape of ideas.

"Readers who enjoy quirky, erotic mysteries will savor this tale of love, sex, mystery and revenge."—**BookLife Reviews by Publishers Weekly**

An "erotic thriller" with "an ambitious, Faulknerian structure."—**Kirkus Reviews**